KIFARU

TIERNEY JAMES

Owasso, OK

ISBN-13: 978-1-965460-08-5

DEDICATION

This book is dedicated to my dear friend who likes cowboys, camping, books and art.

Melanie Cox Smith

ACKNOWLEDGMENTS

Every book has a group of people who help bring the story to life. In this case, I'll have to say they helped polish a diamond in the rough. Many thanks to the following people:

Wizards of Publishing: Kate you are a wonder. You continue to make me a better writer and encourage me to see things another way.

Paperback-Press: Sharon, thank you for your hard work and hand holding when I need it. You are a gem. No pun intended! Well maybe a little.

My street team: So many of you offer to read my books ahead of publication, offering insight to areas where I have slipped up or left out a key component to a character's dilemma. You always help get the word out, never expecting anything in return. I love you.

Sweet & Spicy Designs: Jaycee always surprises me in creating book covers. When I have no idea which direction to go, she always manages to help me find my way. Thank you for your patience and beautiful art.

The Three Musketeers: Willy Robbins, Shirley McCann and Melanie Smith, I owe so much to you creative people for believing in me along this author road filled with potholes and incomplete stories. It takes people like you to give me the confidence to continue and the courage to finish the journey each time I start a new book.

Sleuths' Ink Mystery Writers: I would never have continued writing if it weren't for all of you. Bless you and the support you give to all new writers.

PROLOGUE

Botswana, Africa Thirty-Seven Years Ago

The rains refused to come for yet another day to the parched land of the Okavango. The end of winter often reflected a temperamental attitude toward reviving the edges of the Kalahari. The pools that refreshed elephants, marabou storks, and wildebeests shrank to puddles, forcing many species to gather there on a daily basis, ignoring the competition in order to survive yet another cruel trick of Mother Nature.

The only upside of the situation was it provided tourists on safari the advantage of seeing so many species, up close and personal, from their camouflaged Land Rovers. Besides the yip of zebra and trumpet sounds of wary elephants, the wind rustling across brittle grasses created the kind of National Geographic moment they paid good money to experience. The click of cameras mingling with the soft purr of an engine moving across the earth, back toward camp, lulled guests into a satisfied reverie.

The sun painted a postcard sunset as it dipped into the Okavango Delta. Native workers from a nearby village built fires under kettles of water, so returning tourists could shower away the dust kicked up by animals and vehicles. A campfire blazed under the grand community shelter of thatch and timber. Lanterns glowed in the fading light of day to establish an ambience of romance. Linens placed on an eight-foot, rough-hewn table added yet another layer of sparkle to a desperate land thirsty for the life-giving rain promised by hundreds of years of monotonous predictability.

Refreshed and hungry from his daily adventure, Dr. Girard meandered toward the open-air dining room. John, now dressed in khaki-colored clothes, holding a tray of fluted glasses filled with tepid champagne, greeted him by name. The young man had been their guide for three days, sharing the folklore of various birds and plants. His infectious, wide smile drew compliments on his endeavors to entertain them each day. The easy way he mingled with them added to the overall experience promised by the brochures of exotic travel. But the man tended to be more interested in his budding friendship with Dr. Girard than the others. They shared long talks when poling through the Okavango on one of the boats called mokoros.

A member of the Tswana tribe, John bore the smooth, cocoa-colored skin and features of his people. Dr. Girard smiled when the tall, broad-shouldered man told him he knew the tourists compared him to California movie stars. He hadn't seen many movies, but had met a number of the actors who came for adventure. Dr. Girard agreed with him that many of them were self-centered and egotistical braggarts who cared nothing for the environment or the turmoil brewing in the capitol, Gaborone. Yet John ignored the attempt at flattery, and confessed the guests knew nothing of movie stars or geo-political conflict. They were innocent of such things. Dr. Girard agreed with him.

Laughter floated into the darkness along with the tinkling of silverware against china, and glasses lifted in toasts as stars emerged to form the Southern Cross. Roasted pork simmered with pearl onions and creamy potatoes surrounded by sliced red tomatoes satisfied appetites until the bread pudding arrived with more champagne.

"Join us, John!" one Australian invited as he pointed with his glass to an empty chair. "Tell us more stories."

The guide glanced to the white camp director. Dr. Girard noticed the director frown at such an invitation and gave a small head shake. "I think I will clear these dishes and call it a night. My wife is expecting a baby any day. I hate to leave her too long." John offered a wide, almost mischievous smile.

"A baby! How marvelous," a middle-aged Englishwoman said as she pushed her gray-streaked hair away from her face. "Do you have names picked out, John?"

"Yes. But, after meeting all of you, I think perhaps, I should add a few more to the list."

Laughter burst forth, adding another layer of relaxation to the group. Dr. Girard couldn't help but wonder about how well John was treated when tourists weren't around. Congratulations were offered and in return, he promised to keep them informed of any good news concerning his family. The conversation continued as he slipped away.

Dr. Girard leaned back in his chair and listened to the conversation.

"John is full of such wonderful stories and information, Clive. Was he educated at a university?" The Australian slipped a beefy arm to the back of his wife's chair.

Clive drained his glass and stood to hunt for another bottle. "Yes. His father and grandfather came from the village nearby and rose through the ranks of government in the early days. They were instrumental in the creation of our democracy. Their hard work pulled in the surrounding tribes. It was a tough go at first, but, today, we are a stable country. John was given the opportunity for an education in engineering. After graduation, he decided to come home and marry his childhood sweetheart."

"I've heard the Autonomy Party is trying to change things. What is it all about?" interjected Dr. Girard.

"Yes, it's all rubbish, of course. They feel the minority of whites who occupy the Workers Party have too much control over the minerals industry and don't pay enough taxes, which would shore up schools and medical services in rural areas like here." The guests nodded as if they understood. "Can you imagine getting a doctor to come here? Or teachers?"

"I'm a doctor, and I'd gladly donate my time to help these people several weeks of the year. I'm sure mission groups from countries like the United States would love serving time in such a stable country." Dr. Girard covered his glass when the director tried to refill it.

"Do-gooders come and go, but they mostly do more damage than good."

"How so?" The doctor took another nibble of his bread pudding.

"They put ideas into the heads of these people. The natives begin to think they can have a better life. Next thing you know, they are poaching the black rhino to have enough money to send their kids away to school or buy a satellite system to watch CNN. Then they will want highways to drain the Okavango. The tourists bring in lots of money that filters to the villages. These people need to work, not dream about impossible things unavailable in this part of the world for another fifty years."

"What of the diamond mines?" The English lady held her hand up to let the light bounce off her diamond. "Surely, there are jobs there."

"The current government shut some of them down when it surfaced the diamonds were being used to sponsor rebels in neighboring countries who wanted to take down their governments. So, for now, this is not an option. There is trouble in Gaborone. The military has threatened to take over if the elections aren't held soon to elect a more moderate leader, who will stimulate the economy with foreign investments and exploratory mining. Some even want a dam along the Okavango to generate more electricity for a growing population."

"And all of this wild land?" Dr. Girard leaned forward, thinking of John and his village.

"Would be underwater. The animals displaced or drowned. Tourism dried up. Villagers homeless and moved to urban areas where they'd be exposed to drugs and other criminal endeavors. This hope generates conflict. We don't need any more nonsense. John came here to escape the discord. He was expected to go into politics or mining. He chose to help his village and family here. Good man, although I suspect he is into something else at times. I keep an eye on him."

The conversation drifted into less controversial topics as a breeze from the Okavango River swept across the camp and fruit bats made their puppy-like bark from high in the trees. The fire pit glowed with dying embers as the group separated with huge flashlights in hand to guide them back to their tents. They were reminded of an early wake-up call as they said good night to rest for another adventure at morning's first light.

With the rising sun, two Tswana girls, not more than twenty, made the rounds with trays for the campers. Pots of hot tea and small plates of biscuits were placed on a folding chair outside each tent. The girls offered a warm greeting in hopes of stirring them awake. Dr. Girard was already dressed and ready as the sun rose above the horizon. He watched the blue waters of the Okavango turn to blades of wavy silver. When a troop of baboons wandered through camp, the sound of the rapid click of his camera hurried them along.

As the last of the campers entered the dining area, Clive rushed in to speak to the group.

"I'm so sorry to tell you this."

"What is it, Clive?" The Australian couple stepped forward as if they wanted to comfort him.

"Three of our workers were attacked by a Cape buffalo this morning on their way to camp."

"Oh Lord, not John!" fussed the English lady as she laid her hand on her heart.

"Thankfully, no."

A sigh of relief went up among the group.

"Two managed to climb trees, but the third man was gored severely. I must ask you to be cautious of your picture taking. Animals sense when something has gone wrong. Your morning activities must be postponed for a short time."

Dr. Girard placed a hand on Clive's shoulder. "Take me to him. Maybe I can help."

"I hope so. I've put a call in on my radio. A seaplane will be here within the hour. Come. He's on the outskirts of camp."

"How did he get there?" Both men jogged toward a shack where several men stood nervously, speaking in whispers.

"Other workers came along with pistols they used to scare the animals away in cases like this. Usually they travel together, but these three set out early and got caught off guard." He opened the door wider to let the doctor pass through. "I'm going to check on the plane. Tell these men if you need anything that isn't already here. Thank you, Doctor. Mose is a trusted worker. I wouldn't wish this on anyone."

The doctor stared at the unconscious man covered in blood and knew, even before he drew closer, the seaplane would do him no good. The wounds were deep and all in the wrong places to survive. Dr. Girard decided he would go with the man to offer what comfort he could. A few of the men asked him questions, and he made a conscious effort to sound encouraging but vague.

"He is my father," one man confessed. "I have no money to save him."

The doctor frowned and took the wounded man's wrist for a pulse. "I will see he gets what he needs."

Heads bobbed with thankfulness as they spoke in a language the doctor couldn't understand.

The sound of a plane circling reached their ears as he ran outside to search the sky. He blocked the glare of the morning sun with a hand over his eyes. The buzz of an engine drawing closer finally helped him pinpoint the white plane descending to the calm waters of the snake-shaped Okavango River. A flock of birds near the water's edge flew up and away, adding squawking to the revved-up sound of the plane.

At a popping sound, the group of men turned their heads toward the noise They cried out as they pointed toward the bush separating the village and the safari camp, some eight hundred meters away where a plume of smoke rose. They ran toward the village when the doctor cried out.

"What is going on? Stop. I need help carrying this man to the plane."

The son stopped, tears flowing down his cheeks. "I must go. Thank you for what you tried to do." Then he joined the others scurrying through the bush like impalas in fear of a lion stalking them.

The doctor ran inside and recognized the death stare of a man long gone to meet his chosen maker. He wanted to whisper a prayer, but the rapid popping noise drew him back outside where the sound of a plane touching water drew his attention for mere seconds. He heard other disturbing noises: screams from the camp where he'd left his newfound friends. More rapid popping, he admitted, must be automatic gunfire.

A movement caught his attention coming from the bush. It was a tall man carrying a bundle. Blood gushed from a head wound as he stumbled forward.

"Doctor!" It was John, their guide. "Doctor, help me."

"John, what on earth is going on? You're hurt." He reached to touch his head, but John jerked away. He smelled of smoke, feces, and fear.

"The government men are coming for me, for my village. They are killing everyone. You must escape." Dr. Girard followed John's gaze to where a man disembarked from the plane to the dock. John shoved the bundle into the doctor's arms. "Take my son, Doctor, and give him a life I cannot."

Before he could protest, more shots buzzed overhead, and both of them ducked.

"Please, Doctor." John ran back toward the danger as the doctor stared at the child squirming in his arms. The guide circled back, pressing an object into the hand of Dr. Girard who cradled his son. "This is for my son, his legacy, his promise, good doctor. I am trusting you with the future of my village and country." He bent to kiss the top of the baby's head and whispered, "You are the Kifaru."

Another voice reached the doctor. Clive, the camp director, staggered out into the open, a dark spot spreading across his chest, and reached toward him before falling facedown into the ground covered in the droppings left by elephants. Without another thought, he whirled around to see the pilot wave him forward in wide desperate motions before hustling back onboard. By the time the doctor reached the door, the propeller already spun.

The seaplane moved forward even as he slammed the door shut. The mewing of the newborn child brought an anxiousness to his heart, yet he couldn't resist looking down at the Okavango River, the camp, and the bush crawling with men carrying guns. They surrounded one man, who he believed might be John. The muzzle flash of several weapons dropped the man to his back. When the soldiers ran away, the doctor thought he saw the body raise his hand up toward them, but the plane banked away, leaving the slaughter for the evening news.

For the rest of his life, the doctor would wonder if there was more he could have done. He would also ponder why he had been spared by the wings of an angel pilot rescuing him and a baby boy at the exact time when they needed help.

He buckled the seat belt and pulled the child to his chest. "Your father gave you to me for safekeeping. I will find out why."

The child did not fuss or demand to be fed. It was as if he knew this was not a time to protest what could not be changed. The two stared at each other until the plane reached safety. The two had forged a love by then, and life for the doctor would never be the same.

CHAPTER ONE

Present Day – Lake Tahoe, California

Tessa sighed as she waited in the hardware store parking lot for the seat belts of her three children to click. The California blue skies of ten minutes earlier were now clotted with ominous waves of black clouds indicating a weather change. The smell of fresh snow layered with the crunching sound of tire chains pushed through the open windows of her dated SUV. It reminded her of Gatlinburg, Tennessee, where she'd learned to ski in college. The soft murmur of her daughter's singing brought a smile to lips she'd covered with peach-flavored lip balm. After she closed the windows and pulled out into traffic, she focused on her middle child in the rearview mirror.

"Sit still, Daniel. It's distracting. The roads are still a little slick here."

Then her oldest boy, sitting up front with her, twisted around to stare back at something. Before she could repeat the instructions for him, Sean Patrick bent toward her.

"I think we're being followed, Mom."

"Mommy, the man in the store asked me my name, but I didn't tell him," Heather chirped as she connected with her mom in the rearview mirror. "He smelled funny."

Tessa's radar went up when she glanced at her side mirror then adjusted the front one. "Some people work hard and don't always smell good at the end of a day, sweetheart."

"He smelled like weed, Mom. Probably—" Sean Patrick flipped down the sun visor and ran his finger across the surface to remove some dust.

"Wait! How do you know what weed smells like?" Tessa snapped a little too loud.

"She would've told him her name if I hadn't dragged her away," Daniel interjected as he tried to twist his body to find a good way to check on the mysterious car. "Sean Patrick's right. The car is following us, Mom."

"Heather, sweetie, we've told you a million times, don't talk to strangers unless Daddy or I are with you. Don't be so friendly."

"At least I didn't take the candy, Mommy." Her voice indicated her pride in resisting temptation.

"Proud of you, baby girl." Tessa breezed through a yellow light as it flashed to red. The brown sedan followed. "Now about the weed smell… How do you…"

Sean Patrick peered around again to check. "Slow down, Mom. See if he gets irritated."

The fleeting question of how her son got so savvy on evasive tactics slipped in and out of her mind as she refocused on putting some distance between them. One man. No. Two, for sure. Taking her foot off the gas, she slowed, letting the mystery vehicle close the gap.

"He's coming up behind us, Mom. Crap, he's on our tail." Sean Patrick dug through the console. "Where's your phone? I'm calling 911."

The stoplight ahead turned red as she rolled up.

In her sweetest voice, Tessa tried to prepare her children. "Mom is going to do something a little crazy, kids. Ready?"

Only Heather let out a cheer of support. "Ready!"

Tessa stomped on the gas. Barreling through the intersection, she swerved to avoid hitting a soft-drink truck. Her car slid enough to propel her away from the truck so she could right the vehicle. A horn blast was only slightly louder than the screams of her boys warning her to watch out. She was glancing in the rearview mirror to see what happened to the brown sedan when the crunch of metal on metal and squealing tires mixed with a horn blast from the truck. The boys cheered when their pursuer slammed into a truck, sending soft drinks tumbling into other oncoming vehicles which formed pretzel patterns in the lightly powdered street.

"Whoa! Mom, that was cool," Daniel praised, drumming on the back of Sean Patrick's seat with his feet. Her oldest stared at her with a cross between fear and admiration.

Something kicked into her psyche, fueling an overpowering urge to fight or maybe survive. However, the dominant gut reaction was the "momma bear" syndrome. While she let the kids cheer, her eyes caught the emergence of the brown sedan around the front of the crashed truck.

Life had thrown her a few curves the last couple of years. The family she protected thought she taught at the Sacramento University of Science and Technology. In reality, she put her geography skills to good use as an agent for Enigma, a secret government agency handling the president's dirty work. Living a double life grew more complicated by the week. Even though her husband remained clueless regarding what her job consisted of at the university, it didn't make her feel less guilty about all the cloak-and-dagger existence Enigma expected of her.

Secrecy continued to be the mantra of some of the most dangerous people she'd ever known. Resistance became ineffective against an organization where money, guts, and patriotism ruled the day. So, she'd bowed to their will, reluctantly at first then fallen victim to the adrenaline rush. On those occasions, she had the full power of Captain Hunter's team to protect her from her bumbling mishaps and attempts at bravery.

Today appeared not to be one of the times the captain would come riding in on a white horse to save her.

Who were those men? Why were they after her? What past event had finally caught up with her?

"Mom, who were those guys?" Daniel's voice held the quiet of shock.

"Yeah," continued Sean. "Shouldn't we call the police?" He picked up her cell phone from the floor where it had landed when she'd sped through the red light. "Mom?"

Once again, she fiddled with the mirror. "Sure. Dial 911."

He jabbed at the numbers once then again. "Nothing is

happening."

The sedan's driver sped up, not shy about letting their presence be known this time. "Try again, Sean," she spoke through gritted teeth. "They're back."

The kids sat still now, and Tessa wondered if they were afraid. They were kids. The ugly world of terrorism hadn't touched them directly, unless you counted the time a crazed gunman grabbed their father at the White House. Of course, thanks to some quick-thinking agents and the bravery of her protector, Captain Hunter, the children never witnessed the horror. Then, there was the time she went missing in Afghanistan. Once again, Captain Hunter had dragged her kicking and screaming out of harm's way. Why did she keep thinking about him? He wasn't here. She needed to take care of this herself. And her children.

"No signal, Mom." Sean held the phone where she could see it. "What do we do?"

"These mountains cut us off. No problem."

Sean glanced at the side mirror. "We're out of town. Can't we go back? Won't we be safer there? Mom? Are you listening to me?"

Tessa gripped the steering wheel. Even if they made it to the interstate, between Truckee and Grass Valley lay fifty-six miles of twisting mountain roads. Flakes of fluffy snow lit on their windshield as she pondered her son's suggestion.

"Yes, Sean, I'm listening." Was it too soon to panic?

"Mommy, I have to go pee." Heather's chirpy voice pulled her back to reality.

"Didn't you go when we stopped at the hamburger place?"

"Couldn't go. I need to go now."

A huff of exasperation escaped from her boys, along with a disgruntled "girls" comment.

"I need you to hold it."

"Can't. Mommy, Daniel poked me."

"Stop it, Daniel. Be good to your sister. She's little."

"Am not!" Heather fumed. "Why does everyone treat me like a baby?"

"If you can't hold it, you're a baby, Heather," Sean scolded.

Tessa didn't comment. Words of reprimand went a lot further with her daughter, coming from her oldest than from her.

The brown sedan disappeared after leaving town. She hoped this meant whoever they were lost interest in them. Maybe the police stopped them, or they had sustained more damage than they first thought. Either way, she sighed with relief and reached over to stroke Sean's dark hair.

"I think we're good." She slowed the car, not trusting roads quickly being covered with a fresh blanket of snow. If all went well, they'd be home within an hour. "We'll get on the highway and head back. Everyone have a good time skiing today?"

The kids talked at the same time, distracting her with their enthusiasm and ability to put the last fifteen minutes behind them. She loved how they had taken to skiing with such little effort. Even Heather at five years old could make Tessa's hair stand on end with her fearlessness. Robert, Tessa's husband, had never embraced the sport and didn't often come with them to Tahoe to practice. Since the kids had a couple of days off from school, and Robert would be in San Francisco on business, they'd decided to take this trip.

The stop at the hardware store had seemed like a good idea at the time. Maybe the guy in the store and the brown sedan were a coincidence. The habit of paranoid observation plagued her. Understandable, considering the things she'd done and the evil people she'd ticked off in the last two years.

"Being a bit paranoid will keep you alive," Dr. Wu warned. He'd become her therapist and close friend after Afghanistan, another thing her husband knew nothing about. Those words floated up to her consciousness more times than she liked to admit.

"Mommy, I really gotta go," Heather whined.

"I think there's a gas station before we get on the highway. Can you hold it until then?"

"Yessssss," she said with painful drama.

"That's my girl."

"There it is, Mom." Daniel strained against his seat belt to point over the front seat toward their destination.

Pulling into the gas station, Tessa spotted a state transportation sign. It flashed a warning the interstate was closed in both directions because of several accidents involving eighteen-wheelers. "Great," she moaned, releasing Heather from her car seat. The boys had already escaped their confinement and headed toward the mini-mart. "Guess I'd better fill up while we're here. Shouldn't be on these roads without a full tank in this weather."

The wind bent the tops of trees caked with old snow. It dropped in clumps like huge snowballs tumbling from the sky. Normally, she would have mentioned this to her kids, and their laughter might sound like music in such a quiet place. Today, it felt like another element to be concerned with. She called the boys back.

"Take your sister to the restroom and wait outside. I'm going to put gas in the car." She used her credit card only to see it denied. Flipping it over, she saw some of the numbers had been worn down, so she dug in her purse for another one and repeated the process with success. "When Heather comes out, you guys get a bunch of snacks in case we have car trouble. Okay?"

Sean Patrick and Daniel nodded obediently then each took one of Heather's hands and led her inside while she slipped and slid. Her giggles at the boys' mischief caused Tessa to smile in spite of a rising concern for their situation. No phone, a declined credit card, three kids, a mysterious sedan that appeared to have been following her, and unexpected snow, added to a nagging feeling something wasn't right.

"Mommy, can I have a candy bar?" Heather asked when Tessa entered the convenience store.

"I said no, Mom." Daniel raised his chin and scowled down at his little sister. "I thought you'd want stuff with nutritional value."

"You're such a brownnoser." Sean Patrick grabbed the candy bar and tossed it into the basket his brother carried. "If we have to rough it, the sugar will be good for her."

Heather stuck her tongue out at the younger brother, and he retaliated by giving her a shove.

"Enough, guys. We'll save the candy bar for an emergency only. When we get home, it goes in the freezer. Let me see what you have. Granola bars, nuts, beef jerky, peanut butter crackers, fruit. Great. How about some water bottles? Sean, get us a couple of six-packs."

"Do we have a first aid kit?" Daniel walked with Tessa to the cashier.

"Yes. But I think we're out of Band-Aids and antibiotic cream. Oh, and duct tape."

He shoved the basket at her. "On it," he enthused as he headed down another aisle.

"Mommy, how did you get so good at being ready for emergencies?" her daughter asked then slipped an arm around her waist.

"Yeah, Mom." Sean Patrick lifted two six-packs of water onto the counter. "You ever work for the CIA?"

Daniel joined them with his items. "CIA?"

"Actually, it is a lot more complicated." Tessa handed over her credit card.

"Are you getting ready to tell us a creative story again, Mommy?" Heather inquired.

Sean Patrick elbowed his brother. "Code for she's about to tell a lie."

Tessa chuckled as she handed each child a bag to carry. Her smile faded as her eyes fell on a brown sedan with a dented fender pulling into the gas station behind her SUV.

CHAPTER TWO

"**S**ean Patrick, did you put the phone back in the console?"

"Um, yeah," he said following her line of sight.

She faced the cashier who caused her to wonder if his former job was as defensive tackle for the San Francisco 49ers. "Do you have a phone I can use?"

He frowned down at her then shook his bald head. "Sorry, lady. The incoming storm seems to be messing with the cell towers. Switched carriers for landlines. The telephone company apparently didn't finish the job because they haven't worked in two days. I figure their guys will be here tomorrow since it'll start the work week, unless the storm snows us in again. So much for global warming."

Two men dressed in pale camouflage-styled jackets emerged from their car. Both wore white stocking caps rolled up as if to hide the fact they could be pulled down to form a ski mask. Their bodies resembled the lean military type.

Heather slipped her hand into Tessa's. "The one with the beard was the one in the store, Mommy."

Both boys agreed with her.

The men scanned the parking area outside the convenience store section of the gas station. Their focus told her they already knew where she and the children probably were. Checking for others meant they didn't want to be interrupted.

She pivoted toward to the cashier. "Those men out there have been following us. They tried to kidnap my daughter." Tessa gave her best impression of a distraught mother. "I think my ex put them up to this." Thankfully, she'd slipped her gloves on, which hid her wedding band.

Heather parted her lips as Sean slipped his hand over her mouth to prevent her from giving away Tessa's lie. How he knew so much would be addressed some other time. Even beneath his hand, she protested.

The cashier with skin the color of mocha coffee, pushed out his bottom lip and shifted his gaze out the window then spoke in a deep voice. "Go out the back. I'll keep them here as long as I can. You'd best get back to Truckee. This storm will be a doozy by dark."

"Thank you!" she said hustling the children toward the back of the store. "God bless you!" She added a fearful whimper for a special effect. When they opened the back door, her demeanor did a one-eighty. "Okay, kids. I need you to slip out to the car when I give you the sign. Be quick about it. No dillydally. No complaints. Nothing. Clear?"

They nodded like bobblehead dolls with wide eyes.

"Buckle up, hunker down the best you can. Throw your supplies on the floor. I'll be right behind you. I have to do something to slow them down."

"But, Mom…." Sean Patrick whispered in a panic.

"We'll be fine. You have your Boy Scout knife with you?"

"You told me not to be carrying it," he fumed.

Tessa held out her hand like a snapped whip. "Give it to me."

Sean Patrick dug in his pants pocket and handed it over. "Am I in trouble?"

Tessa smirked. "Absolutely." She winked. "Thanks. But we're going to have to talk about this rebel side of you. Knives and weed?"

"At least I didn't try to hack the bank account for Dad's law firm," he said as he focused narrowed eyes on his younger brother who opened his mouth in shock.

"Oh. My. Gosh." Tessa rolled her eyes. She peeked around the corner of the building and watched the two strangers enter the store. "Okay! Scoot. I'm right behind you."

Daniel grabbed his sister's hand and pulled her after him, catching her when her little feet slipped. Sean Patrick reached the car first and opened the doors on the passenger side, facing away from the store. All the kids scampered in without complaint then shut the doors securely.

Bending down next to the brown sedan, Tessa jammed the knife into the driver's side tires before moving to the gas tank, which she tried to open with trembling fingers. She stopped, took a deep breath, and this time managed to get it open. She'd grabbed a liter of some generic brand soft drink when they slipped out the back. Next, she poured the entire bottle into the fuel tank.

Her children could brag their mom broke the law by running a red light, resulting in an accident, told lies to gain a stranger's help, and vandalized a car. Hopefully, they'd never know the entire repertoire of crimes she'd committed while working at her day job with Enigma.

"Mom, the guy at the counter is still talking to those men," Sean Patrick whispered, while she connected her seat belt, as if someone besides her might be trying to eavesdrop.

"Did you steal soda, Mom?" Daniel murmured.

Tessa pulled out onto the road and cast a quick glance back at him. His arms were crossed across his chest, which meant he planned to use the theft as a get-out-of-jail-free card for hacking another person after she'd already covered for him the last time. The kid was a technology and manipulating genius.

"Yes, Daniel. I plan to go back and pay him when this is resolved. I had to do what was best for you guys. Hacking your daddy's work didn't help anyone."

"Probably what those guys said when they money laundered those secret accounts."

Tessa wanted to slam on the brakes, drag her son out by the collar, and poke her finger to his nose as she yelled, "What the hell are you talking about?" Instead, she took slow deep breaths, careful to keep an eye on the rearview mirror for trouble. "Sweetie, I don't understand. When you say money laundering, are you talking about dirty clothes, or something else?"

Both boys burst out laughing, leading their sister to join in like she understood the joke.

"Oh, Mom. We watch NCIS. We know what money laundering means." Daniel sounded pretty sure of himself.

The snow piled up, and her windshield wipers squeaked as they batted the flakes away without much success. How long since they'd been changed? The back window fogged up so she couldn't see if they were being followed. The side mirrors weren't much better.

"We'll talk about this later, Daniel. For now, I need you kids to keep the fog off your windows so I can see. Will you do that for me?"

She took deep, calming breaths. Maybe these guys weren't following her because of something she'd done but because her son had been poking his nose into other people's business: risky business, illegal business.

When she swiped at the windshield with her gloved hand, the cold moisture touched her skin immediately. Was this the pair with a hole in it? She continued to obsess over silly things during stressful times. She decided to examine this behavior when things settled down just like other times. But she never followed through. Other things always got in the way—like having Captain Hunter in her face about needing to get her act together or Dr. Wu guiding her to get in touch with her true feelings about the captain.

She'd love to have the captain swoop in, like he so often did, and make sure her family remained safe. Even though his expectations could be punishing, they couldn't compare to what lay in wait for the person who tried to hurt her. Sometimes she wondered if the back and forth between them hid a deeper, more passionate desire to be one with each other. He remained a gentleman, or at least most of the time. Periodically, he flirted or insinuated various outcomes of their friendship, but nothing ever came of it. He didn't take advantage of married women or Enigma agents. When she wasn't doing Enigma business, their friendship blossomed into something precious, held close to her heart.

The rest of the Enigma team didn't understand their relationship, and truthfully, there were times she didn't, either. She'd lost track of the times he'd saved her life, pulled her from the fire, and given her another chance to live. But this time, at least for the moment, Captain Chase Hunter didn't even know she was in trouble.

Then she remembered the button.

"Sean, reach inside the glove box and feel around the top for a button."

"Got it."

"Push it three times as fast as you can then one long push as you count to seven."

"Done." He closed the box again. "What did I do?"

Before she could answer, a voice came out of the speaker.

"Hello, Mrs. Scott. How can I help you?" At the sound of a female voice with a Southern accent, the children gasped.

"I'm in a little trouble." She gave a description of the sedan, the two men, and the gas station they'd left as well as the overall problem.

"I have your location, Mrs. Scott. Are you alone?"

"My children are with me. We have some supplies, ski equipment, a full tank of gas. Weather conditions are deteriorating. Interstate closed. Headed back to Truckee."

"Do you know these men, Mrs. Scott?"

"No. They had a military demeanor, so I'm not sure if they're carrying any weapons. It was hard to tell with their extra clothing." She remembered the license plate number and relayed the information.

"Stand by, Mrs. Scott."

"Mom, who the heck is she?" Sean Patrick rubbed at the windshield then the side window before directing a suspicious stare at his mother. "And how did she call us?"

"Umm—it's kind of an upgrade of OnStar."

"Volvos don't have OnStar. That's a General Motors feature," Daniel said with a seriousness too mature for a ten-year-old.

Tessa leaned forward then squinted. The road was getting more difficult to see. "You know me, Daniel. I'm not very good with techy stuff." Too late to correct her mistake.

"In Europe, Volvos have a similar service, and it's free."

"There you go. Guess I got a European model."

"Not this rust bucket. Too old. And, in this country, you have to use a smart phone and their fancy app, which I think needs a little work. I sent them some suggestions."

Sean Patrick switched his attention from his brother to Tessa. "Yeah. What he said."

"Mrs. Scott?" came the Southern voice. "Are you still there?"

"Yes. What do you have for me?"

"While we evaluate this situation further, we are sending you to a safe house less than a mile from your current location. We are also sending—help." The word help sounded as if it were code for something else.

"Thank you."

"Are you currently being followed?"

"Not yet. I did a little intervention back at the station."

"Excellent. On the off chance they've commandeered another vehicle, you may not have much time. I see you're almost to the exit. Watch for a mailbox shaped like the head of a moose and turn right."

Sean Patrick pointed as she saw it and twisted the wheel too fast, causing the car to fishtail. She overcorrected catching the back bumper. The kids let out a yell to add to the chaos.

"Are you all right, Mrs. Scott?"

She powered through the bump, tightening her grip on the wheel. "Yes. What's next?"

"Take the next left, and in one hundred feet, go right. Continue on the road and you'll come upon an A-frame house. Park your car in the basement garage in the back." As she pulled inside, the voice returned. "Good job. Help is on the way. Stay put until we finish our assessment. Will there be anything else, Mrs. Scott?"

Seat belts released, and the children gathered up supplies.

Sean Patrick put on his wise-ass voice. "How about switching on some lights? It's pitch dark in here."

Two overhead lights snapped on immediately. "Are we good?" the voice continued.

Sean Patrick blinked as he surveyed the area outside the car. "Yeah. We're good. Thanks."

"You're welcome, Sean Patrick." Then the voice signed off.

"How did she know me?" he asked as they closed car doors and headed up the steps. "Mom, what is going on? Shouldn't we call Dad?"

"I miss Daddy," Heather whimpered. She'd been quiet during their escape, as if she'd understood the seriousness of their situation required concentration. "I'm scared."

"I'm hungry," Daniel said pushing inside and flipping on a

light. "Whoa, get a peek at this place. Pretty nice."

The kids dropped snack bags on the kitchen counters then went straight to the refrigerator to check out the contents. There weren't any.

Tessa squatted down by her daughter and helped her remove her hat and coat. "It's okay, sweetie. We're safe here." The adjoining living room featured expansive windows and a stone fireplace in the middle of the farthest wall with French doors on either side of it. Darkness was falling and snow piled up on the deck.

"Let's pull all the shades." She found the switch for the gas fireplace and flipped it on. "This should warm things up. No more lights. Let's pretend we're camping and don't have electricity."

"I wanted to watch Battle Bots tonight." Daniel frowned and flopped down in a beanbag chair.

"Toughen up, soldier," Sean Patrick barked like a four-star general, which he claimed he would be someday after going to West Point and saving the world.

"I hate it when you pretend to be some weird general," Daniel moaned. "It's ridiculous. Sounds stupid."

"The only thing stupid is your complaining about not getting to see some nerdy robot show."

"Enough, boys. Be good to each other. Come help me get some snacks together, and we'll eat in front of the fire."

"Like a picnic!" Heather clapped her hands and skipped to the kitchen.

Sitting before the fire, their spirits lifted. They talked about their skiing. Tessa bragged on their improved abilities before each retold a funny story about their attempts down more difficult slopes. They especially enjoyed telling Tessa how she reminded them of a cartoon character when she rolled down the slope in a lopsided cartwheel. When their laughter quieted, the roar of a snowmobile cut through the night. Tessa motioned for the kids to get behind the couch as she watched the doorknob turn.

CHAPTER THREE

The woman dressed in a black sequined dress moved like a panther down the long hall of rooms located on the tenth floor of the Paradise Bay Hotel near the waterfront in San Francisco. She walked with the grace and confidence that comes with having others both admire and fear you for most your life. Tonight, she was a redhead with a bob haircut framing her face like a fine painting. The hazel-green eyes, known to paralyze a man with his own desire, shifted from side to side as if expecting hidden danger. The dress hugged her tall frame like a glove and hid the muscles enabling her to punch a man hard enough to induce a heart attack. Only an index finger twitched as it rested against the small clutch where she kept her weapon.

The soft ding, followed by the swoosh of the elevator opening, slowed the woman down. Another woman rounding the corner made eye contact then nodded a cool greeting as her gaze slid over the competition's body. This new player appeared more businesslike than threatening, more careless than observant. One hand pushed shoulder-length blonde hair behind an ear as she glanced from a note she held to the room numbers.

"Excuse me," the panther woman said in an Italian accent. "Is it still raining outside? I'm afraid I left my rain jacket in"—she glanced back down the hall—"a friend's room. I don't really want to go back and disturb him." The panther woman smiled with the coyness of a fox eyeing a henhouse.

"No. And the temperature is still around thirteen degrees Celsius." An eyebrow arched as the new arrival paused in front of a door and compared the number with her note. "You should be fine."

Besides the foreign propensity of using Celsius to measure temperature, the woman spoke with a slight South African accent. "Thank you. Have a nice evening."

The woman turned her head slightly as if to acknowledge the gratitude. The panther woman moved away as the door squeaked open and a man's voice invited her in, followed by a nervous chuckle.

The panther woman stopped two rooms away. "Yeah. Didn't go to her own room. She's not alone." She backed up against the wall and stared straight ahead for a few seconds before reaching into her clutch to remove a thin ski mask and a small pistol. In these situations, she preferred a slimmer, easier-to-conceal weapon. The trigger was an easy pull with less recoil than some of her other toys. She also didn't want to waste time reloading, so this little Colt made sense tonight.

The exit to the stairs opened. Three men dressed head to toe in black, with only their eyes and mouths showing through their ski masks, joined her. The bigger man set down a dark backpack. She unzipped it then pulled out a pair of black sweatpants and a hoodie that she quickly slipped on over her elegant gown. Tennis shoes replaced her stilettos.

"We've got twenty minutes," he said, snatching up the backpack and tossing it to the shorter man who bobbled it.

"Careful," he moaned as he cradled it.

He was ignored as the third man entered each elevator and short-circuited the control panel.

"This way," she said checking her weapon. "She carried her briefcase."

"Did she seem nervous, Sam?" He leaned in to speak close to her ear.

"No, Chase. She seemed annoyed I dressed better than her. Which, of course, I had."

The two other men came up beside them and pulled out their

weapons.

One smelled of cigarette smoke and spoke with an Eastern European accent. "Let's do this. I have some Valentine's shopping to do."

"Since when do you shop, Zoric?" Vernon, the third man, sounded surprised. "Am I on your list?"

The man called Zoric shifted dead eyes to the young tech genius who took a step sideways as they moved toward room 1115. "No."

When Captain Chase Hunter jerked his head around to silence them, a ding at the far end of the hall split the silence. Another elevator opened.

Vernon pulled a key from the backpack, inserted it in his already-open tablet then waved it across the lock on the room across from 1115. It clicked open to an empty room that had been secured along with several others on both sides of the hall. They entered the room and let the door close on its own.

The captain stared out the peephole and waited. In seconds, a waiter in a white jacket pushed a cart in front of 1115. "Appears our target intends to do a little celebrating on some poor schmuck's dime."

Given the nod to proceed, Zoric slipped out and wrapped his arm around the waiter's neck. Even though the man was taller than Zoric, he struggled to free himself, gasping to breathe. He lost traction as Zoric pulled him backward. By the time he'd gotten him inside the room, the unsuspecting man had lost consciousness and fallen to the floor.

"I was going to ask if anyone brought restraints, but I see you thought of everything." The corner of the captain's mouth lifted in a smirk.

Sam drew handcuffs from her purse and kneeled down to secure the waiter as Zoric flipped him over with his boot. "I'm always prepared for a good time." She stood then leveled a gaze of interest toward her boss. "If you know what I mean."

He stared at her for a few seconds as if evaluating the suggestion. "No one could ever accuse you of being subtle. Someday you're going to make some guy very happy."

This time she couldn't resist trying to send a dazzling smile to match the unexpected compliment from the one man who eluded her charms. "I stand ready when you are."

~~~

The idea lost momentum as the four slipped out into the hall.

Vernon tapped on the door of 1115. "Room service."

He stepped back when a woman with her blouse unbuttoned to her waist flung the door open and called to someone over her shoulder in a laughing tone. "Room service. Just in time…" She faced the large man pointing a gun in her face.

"Not a word"—he pressed the silencer to her forehead—"or I'll put a neat little hole on this side and will resemble the Grand Canyon when it comes out the other side. Understand?"

Although fear leaped to her eyes, she didn't cry, whimper, or beg him to take her money if the intruder wouldn't hurt her. Holding up ten fingers, Sam let Chase know time was running out then secured the woman's hands behind her back with zip ties she'd carried in the pockets of her hoodie after removing them from the backpack earlier. Vernon applied a piece of adhesive to her mouth then searched for the woman's computer. Everyone knew their job and tended to it quickly.

Sam led the woman to a chair across the room from the bathroom. When she shoved the target down, the chair scooted, and the woman glared dangerously at her. Her open blouse revealed a black lace bra that pushed up small breasts appearing bountiful.

Chase raised his chin at both Zoric and Vernon as he pulled the cart inside the room and sampled the chocolate-covered strawberries.

~~~

"I'm sorry, Reeva," came a male voice from the bathroom. "I couldn't hear you. I had the shower on."

In his haste, he didn't notice the three men lined up on either side of the bathroom door as a man walked out rubbing a towel across his head, torso naked above a pair of suit pants. He took several more steps into the room toward an open suitcase atop a luggage rack.

"Sorry, Reeva, about this." When his eyes fell on Reeva in the chair, a stranger standing next to her with a gun pointed at her temple, a confused expression took over his face. "What. Is. Going. On?" The words came out slow, as if tangled in thick molasses. The gulp in his throat sounded cartoon-like.

The room occupant spun around only to face a man much bigger than himself, pointing a gun at his chest.

The four intruders froze and exchanged glances with one another.

"I think you've made a mistake," he said, raising his hands. "I've got some money in my wallet. Three hundred dollars. It's yours. Then leave us alone."

The person standing next to Reeva crept closer to the other three and stared long and hard at him then over at the woman in the chair. Directing her attention back to him, he noticed a flare of anger in squinting eyes when the intruder landed a fist upside his head, knocking him on the bed. He moaned in pain as he stole a glance at his attacker.

The tallest of the intruders pushed the man with the gun back. "What is your name?" He spoke with a South African accent, like Reeva's that, until a few seconds ago, he'd found charming.

"Robert Scott. Please. You have us mixed up with someone else."

The man grabbed him up by his hair and threw him against the wall where a shorter man who smelled of cigarettes held him in place by wrapping his hands around his throat.

"Robert. Scott," the big man repeated with a growl. "Is this your wife?" He pointed to Reeva.

"No. I'm. I'm not married." The four exchanged glances with the one who'd struck him. The tall man—likely the leader—paced in an agitated fashion. The one with his fingers on his neck tightened his grip. Another of the intruders rifled through his suitcase. He stopped at Reeva's briefcase, sighing nonstop and shaking his head like a paranoid schizophrenic off his meds.

But the big guy frightened him the most, dark eyes staring at him, lips puckered up and in, several times. "You want to try your answer again? The ring on your finger says different."

"Yes. Okay. I'm married. Not to her. We met tonight."

"Where's the wife?"

What an odd question. "Skiing with my kids, at Tahoe."

"Convenient." The broad-shouldered man stepped inches from his face.

"It's not what you think," Robert insisted.

The person who'd hit him rushed toward him, a guttural growl emitting from a delicate mouth. The big man stopped the attacker by throwing out his arm then shoved the body aside like a pesky gnat. "We'll take care of him later. Do your job."

Fingers snapped, drawing the leader's attention. The silent one held up Reeva's computer, inserted a flash drive, and started copying files. Reeva jumped up only to be shoved back down by the same person who'd hit him. She squirmed and tried to stand again.

He noted the half-open blouse and wondered if these thugs had taken advantage of her. "Reeva, calm down. Everything will be okay."

She rolled her eyes and tried to talk in spite of the adhesive. From the way her eyes squinted and her nose flared, it didn't seem to Robert she cared about being cooperative until his attacker pushed their faces in so close their noses touched. Whatever the whispered words were, Reeva stopped her efforts to get free.

The wiry guy with a smoky smell dragged him over to Reeva then shoved him to the floor in front of her. To keep from toppling over, he placed his hands on her knees as someone clicked several pictures with a cell phone. Could this get any worse?

The computer guy snapped Reeva's laptop shut then connected it to one he'd pulled out of a backpack. Robert was amazed how effortlessly the man balanced both computers. Then, like a choreographed dance, the group moved toward the door, grabbing Robert as they went.

"Don't worry, Reeva!" he called as her captor dragged her to the bed to toss her facedown. He figured she'd be fine, but he was concerned about being taken from the room. Why? "No. Stop. Let me go. I have a family."

The big man swung the door open and peered left and right. "Should've thought about that before getting mixed up with her, you worthless piece of crap." They moved into the hall. "Keep your mouth shut, and we'll release you once we're out of here." He touched Robert's chest with the tip of his silencer, smirking. "What were you thinking?"

"I can explain."
"I bet you can."

CHAPTER FOUR

The elevator dinged at the far end of the hall as Vernon reconnected the circuits of one of the panels, securing their ability to go straight to the underground parking lot. Chase shoved Robert to the back of the car so hard, he bounced off and into Sam who gave him an elbow to the gut. With a grunt of pain, he huddled into a corner and breathed like he'd run a couple of miles. Captain Hunter didn't have time to worry about Robert. Whoever got off at the other end of the hall might be coming for Reeva or to assist in whatever she planned for Robert. There was the matter of the waiter, too. Had he been missed?

The elevator doors opened with a quiet hum as a van advertising Sheply's Cleaners stopped in front of them. Zoric pulled the side doors open and manhandled Robert like a sack of dirty laundry into the space filled with miscellaneous boxes and dry-cleaning bags. Wedding gowns hung on racks in the far back. He, too, scrambled inside and struggled to adjust himself to peer into the front seat where a man stared back at him through a mask resembling President Nixon.

"Are you freakin' kidding me?" Carter Johnson asked when Chase climbed into the passenger side.

Chase stole a peek at Zoric, who slipped a black sleeping mask over Robert's eyes. Sam secured his hands behind his back with a zip tie.

Chase continued in the South African accent. "What was I supposed to do? Leave him?"

"Yes!" Carter circled through the underground parking toward an exit. "Then your problems would be solved."

His friend referred to Tessa Scott, who'd managed to get under his skin. The two of them had played a cat-and-mouse game with their feelings for a couple of years until she was coerced into service with Enigma, a secret government agency sanctioned by President Austin. She continued to be both a pain in his neck and an ache in his black heart. He couldn't live with her, and he didn't want to try and live without her, either. The problem flaring up between them remained she was married to this jerk he'd kidnapped.

"You said you'd let me go if I was quiet," Robert's voice trembled, and he moved his face away to avoid the piece of adhesive being applied to his mouth.

"I say a lot of things." Chase removed his uncomfortable mask as Carter did the same.

The others in the back lay down and pulled a black tarp over them. They stopped at the exit stand to pay. No words passed between them as Carter stuck out his ticket then his money after being told the amount. The van eased out into traffic without further incident, headed toward Orinda, a seventeen-mile drive, a half hour, but due to a traffic accident, took almost an hour.

Robert settled down while the others sat like statues. Carter found a country music station on the radio, but Chase clicked it off soon afterward. He needed to think, and country music wouldn't help his predicament. His buddy behind the wheel didn't try to engage him. Silence kept their unwilling passenger from remembering their voices. Since he'd been the only one to speak so far besides Carter losing it for a couple of seconds, Robert probably would be lucky to remember his own name by the time they let him go.

All of his team carried a special fondness for the bumbling housewife, their newest Enigma agent. The transformation from a scared rabbit to a valued team member, who carried her own weight during times of need, earned Tessa a great deal of respect.

The only person he kept tabs on concerning Tessa was

Samantha Cordova, or Sam as they called her. The two women were oil and water, yin and yang, good and evil. The list could go on for eternity. Leaving the two of them alone for very long gave him nightmares. Sam could easily kill Tessa and make it appear an accident. On the other hand, his little Grass Valley housewife knew exactly which of Sam's buttons to push to stroke her out. Thinking about the innocent expression on her face when she accomplished such moments created a warm feeling inside him.

Then, tonight, when Sam saw Tessa's husband standing half-naked with another woman in his room, something came unhinged in her he'd never seen before. He'd often suspected the two women had a love-hate relationship but didn't care to get involved in the way they coped with each other, as long as it didn't get in the way of a mission. But thinking about their relationship faded to what really concerned him. Why was Robert Scott entertaining a woman like Reeva Kaplan, a known South African money launderer for conflict diamonds, in his room at this hour of the night? Some said she also could be hired as a problem solver: meaning, for the right price, she'd kill.

The van rolled down an alley then up to a steel door highlighted by a flickering bulb over the doorframe. Once he found out why Robert hooked up with this woman, he'd be willing to drop his worthless body off the Bay Bridge. Such a solution pleased him more than he imagined possible.

~~~

Tessa watched the knob twist in slow motion. She grabbed the iron fireplace poker, used for decorative purposes since she only needed to flip a switch to get a blaze going then moved to the side of the door, which creaked open. The dim light appeared to bounce around the room with the sudden rush of cold air ahead of the body coming into the house.

At first, she thought a giant white yeti had entered then realized the padded snowsuit only created a larger image. His profile, although barely visible, revealed a black man with chubby cheeks and a wide nose.

"Hello?" His voice sounded like a deep base drum until Tessa, who stood to the side, reared back with the poker and slammed it
~~~

into his back. With a grunt, he sucked in pinkish lips over teeth as white as his suit. "Damn," he moaned.

Tessa who stared at him in disbelief. How could he still be standing?

When she drew back the poker for a second time, he threw out a beefy arm reminding her of the Michelin Man. He jerked the iron from her hand, and stared at her as his brow pinched in confusion. She bolted toward a small fire extinguisher fastened to the wall. When she touched the cold red metal, a giant hand clamped on her shoulder then spun her around so fast, she wobbled on unsteady feet. She realized too late her boys were sneaking up behind the intruder whose nostrils flared and a sour frown deepened the creases around his bulbous eyes.

"No!" she warned.

Sean Patrick leapt high enough to wrap his arm around the man's neck then hammered his head. Daniel retrieved a decorative piece of birch log next to the fireplace and slammed it into the back of the man's legs. For a couple of seconds, his eyes bulged then he reached back, freed himself of Sean, and held him at bay with one hand while grabbing Daniel with the other.

Both boys swung their fists, and Heather let loose a shrill scream. The man released the boys and covered his ears.

"Mrs. Scott, please quiet your daughter. I'm here to help you. Weren't you notified?"

She rushed to Heather, kneeled and gathered her in her arms. "Boys, stop it immediately."

"But, Mom…"

"Now, Sean Patrick."

Both boys backed toward their mother and placed a hand on her shoulder.

The Yeti pushed back his white hood then unzipped his puffy snowsuit. "Hey, I remember you. You're the guy from the convenience store where we got gas. You helped us get away," Sean Patrick said incredulously.

"Are you sure?" he asked in a baritone voice. "I got one of those common faces."

Sean Patrick and Daniel exchanged glances and offered timid smiles.

"Yeah. Pretty sure." Sean Patrick stroked his sister's hair. "You do kind of look like my sister's ballet teacher."

The Yeti's deep laugh shook his entire body.

Tessa stood and rubbed her hands down the side of her jeans. "I apologize, Mr.—"

"Handsome C. Jones," he said, taking a moment to survey the room before dropping a dangerous glare on her.

"Is your name really Handsome?" Heather asked in a soft voice, batting her eyes nervously.

He nodded his bald head and stepped toward the little girl, who scurried behind her big brothers. "Yep. My momma said I was an ugly baby and figured I'd be a big boy, so she named me Handsome. Everywhere I go, people say, 'Hi, Handsome,' and this makes me feel good about myself."

Tessa took a deep breath. "Thank you, Mr. Jones."

"Handsome. Call me Handsome. Having a pretty woman call me by my name makes getting out in this horrible weather worth it. I should be at home eating the great northern beans I put in the Crock-Pot this morning, and a hunk of cornbread."

"We got peanut butter and granola bars. Mom stole some soda from your store, but I don't know if we have any left." Heather peeked around Sean Patrick.

Handsome shifted his eyes to Tessa.

"I intended to come back and pay. I poured it in the gas tank of those men."

"What kind of mother teaches her kids it's okay to steal?" He stuck out his hand. "Two dollars."

"It was on sale for a dollar fifty!" she protested as she hurried to get her purse. As she dug for the money, her fingers touched the cell phone her son had shoved inside before leaving the car. She lifted it to see there was a missed message from Captain Chase Hunter. Even seeing his name quickened her pulse. Probably a wisecrack about her skiing while he saved the world from a new threat. She wasn't in the mood tonight for verbal combat. Dropping it back inside, she gathered up enough change to give to Handsome.

"There. Happy?"

"I was happy when I thought I was going home to eat beans. Now I'm stuck with you four." He counted the change and nodded. "Okay, it's all there."

"Kids, finish your dinner." Tessa motioned to their seats in front of the fire. "Mr. Jones and I—"

"Handsome. Call me Handsome."

"Yes. Handsome and I are going to have a little chat in the kitchen. I'm going to make him a snack."

The kids crashed on the floor and returned to eating and jabbering about their ski trip. Tessa closed the kitchen door and faced their guest. "What is going on, Handsome?" She laid a paper napkin on the counter.

The big man smiled ear to ear. "I sure do like you calling me that."

He sounded pleasant enough, but she wasn't about to let her guard down. "Why you? Who do you work for, and how did you find us?"

"What is going on is one of your kids hacked into a sensitive data base where a great deal of money laundering is done by some really bad people." He grabbed an apple and chomped on it, juice rolling down his chin. He dabbed at it with the napkin. "As to me, I'm all you got. Taking a break from Enigma. House-sitting for my brother-in-law and managing his station while they go to Florida. Florida!" He rolled his large bulging eyes. "And here I am in ten feet of snow. Our little Southern belle in the sky told me how to get here."

"Taking a break from Enigma? You can do that?" Wasn't it kind of like the Mafia? You never were allowed to leave. "Sign me up."

Handsome shoved the apple core into the garbage disposal and flicked a switch on then off again when the sound changed. "Humph." He eyed her. "Never seen you before but heard plenty."

"I'm pretty sure I'd remember if we met—you being so handsome and all."

This time he pursed his lips, but the edges quirked up. "I'm taking you to my place."

"No. I don't even know you," Tessa refused quietly. "How do I know you're Enigma? Do you have some ID?"

"No. Do you?" he mocked. "The only time we carry ID is when we're impersonating law enforcement. You know, like the time Captain Hunter and some Serbian vampire pretended to be Highway Patrol to get you away from authorities in Auburn." He towered over her, her eyes lifting toward his condescending expression. "You and some old guy who lived next door. You sure stirred up a hornet's nest."

Tessa put her hands on her hips. "Who told you?"

"Do you really want to stand here and chitchat about old times with Enigma, or do you want me to get you to a safe place until we can get you back home? And if your kid has any computer equipment, tablets, phones, or video games, they are off-limits until this is resolved."

"I'm going to call in to see if you're legit."

"And I'm thinking we got about an hour before those creeps at the gas station pick up our trail. They aren't amateurs."

"Why didn't you neutralize them back there?" A likely crack in his explanation.

"Because, at the time, I believed your story. Besides, you did a pretty good number on them." He chuckled then pulled a banana from the plastic bag. "I didn't get the call until I locked up and headed out. What'll it be?"

"I'm still going to call."

"Go ahead, Tessa Marie Scott." He moved like a sloth toward the living room. "I'm getting the kids ready to move. My place isn't far. You got four-wheel drive?"

"Yes. Why?"

"You're going to need it. I brought a snowmobile. We'll take your car in case they find this place. I'll drive."

Tessa held up a finger as her phone buzzed a number at Enigma. Nothing happened. Why wasn't anyone answering? What good was national security if no one minded the store? She clicked off as Handsome spoke over his shoulder.

"Those guys are probably jamming signals."

"Enigma phones can't be jammed," she accused.

"They can if towers are down in a snowstorm. You think Vernon can think of everything?"

Tessa decided Handsome did indeed know a lot about Enigma. Vernon was the Albert Einstein of cyber warfare and little details like cell phones. If only he were here. Heck. If only the whole team was here, even Sam. The constant intimidation she offered sounded kind of touching at the moment. At least she'd be able to take care of Handsome Yeti if he wasn't the real deal.

"Hear that?" Handsome mumbled as he used one of his sausage-sized fingers to pull back the edge of a window shade. "We got company."

"How close?"

"Sound carries over the snow, so three hundred yards."

"Kids, grab your stuff and get in the car. Sean, back seat. Daniel, turn off the fireplace."

Handsome picked up speed as he gathered trash, backpacks, and one little girl under his Goliath arm. Tessa grabbed coats, gloves, and sock hats. They all moved toward the garage door.

"Sean Patrick, help your sister buckle in," Tessa whispered as they moved into action. Whether they sensed danger or not, the children didn't question her.

Handsome slipped out even as the garage door rose. He motioned for Tessa to back out as he pushed his snowmobile inside. She hopped out and let him behind the wheel where he struggled to push the seat back far enough for his huge frame. Fastening her seat belt, she rolled the window glass down to listen. On this side of the house, the forest of evergreens buffered any sounds.

"Let's get out of here. Too quiet."

"Ready, kids?" Handsome sounded cool as a cucumber as he adjusted the rearview mirror. They answered with nodding heads and frightened expressions. "Nothing to worry about. Handsome has taken charge."

Tessa bristled. "Let's not get ahead of ourselves."

CHAPTER FIVE

Chase Hunter sat down at a computer screen next to the rest of his team who studied their own monitors. He held a cup of strong black coffee and decided somebody on staff actually knew how to brew a good cup of joe.

His screen revealed a man in a small room he knew to be down the hall. He'd been there for nearly three hours. There was a cot he used to take a fitful nap, a padded office chair pulled up to a table with another one across from it. A coffee pot had been switched on remotely, thanks to Vernon's warped sense of humor.

Vernon wasn't the most intimidating guy on the team, so he liked to play mind games where maybe the rest of them couldn't. Chase relied on brute strength and posturing for his style. Whatever worked was okay with him. The empty walls gave no indication of date, time, or style of the building where Robert had become a reluctant guest.

"Our FBI friend here yet?" Chase took a gulp of coffee then let his thoughts return to the Grass Valley housewife who had wreaked havoc on his once-orderly life.

"Soon. Said there had been a development," Carter offered with a flatline voice as he stared at the screen. "I hate this guy," he continued, frowning, his forehead creased. "Tessa deserves better." He elbowed Chase. "You know. Like me. We all know she has a thing for astronauts."

"You're an ex-astronaut," Sam chimed in as she zoomed in on Robert's picture. "You're no different than Robert, a lying, cheating, womanizer who can't keep his pants on."

"I didn't hear you complaining the other night at two a.m. when—"

Sam punched him in the side, which only managed to make him laugh. "Shut up, you halfwit. If I ever come to you in the middle of the night, it will mean every other man on Earth is dead and I've had a stroke."

Carter winked at Chase then addressed Sam. "So, I have a chance," he said matter-of-factly.

Chase leaned back in his chair until it squeaked and rocked a little, enjoying the banter between the two. He admired Carter's brain, loyalty, and even his self-inflated ego. Until NASA got fed up with his explosive romances, he had been one of the country's most experienced astronauts. Along with being a playboy, the "no guts, no glory" attitude got him quietly kicked to the curb. He wasn't very good at taking orders from higher-ups who had never been in the trenches or, in this case, the final frontier.

"As I was saying"—Carter doubled his arms across his chest—"Tessa needs to dump the guy."

"Maybe we should hear what he has to say. Kept saying it wasn't what it looked like." Chase sat his coffee cup down after draining the contents.

"I can't believe what I'm hearing. She belongs with us. Full-time. He's holding her back. Bathes in the knowledge the president got her the State Department job. Struts around like a pompous peacock. You could—"

"Enough. She's married and an agent. Taboo. Not interested."

Zoric pulled up a chair on the other side of Sam who scooted over for him to see her computer screen. "I'll remember that the next time she's up to her eyeballs in trouble and you go rushing in like a crazy person to save her."

"I'd do it for any of you. Besides, she's not like us. She's an innocent."

Sam huffed then snorted. "And I'm Mother Teresa. She's tougher than you think and not all gooey and sweet like she pretends."

"Seems to me you got pretty miffed at seeing her husband half-ass dressed with another woman." Vernon blew a bubble with his gum then popped it.

Sam ignored the comment and leaned closer to the screen while removing the red wig and shaking out her ebony hair. In slow motion, she pulled it up, wrapped it in a knot, and grabbed two chopstick-like objects from the desk. She used them to hold the waist-length tresses in place.

The action drew Carter's attention. "Do you enjoy driving me crazy?" he whispered in her ear. Sam continued to stare at the screen without so much as a blink of her cat-like eyes. "You can ignore me all you want, but I know all your teasing means more than you let on."

Chase cleared his throat. "Focus. FBI headed our way."

Besides each team member having a monitor in front of them, the wall was divided into ten large screens. Each one showed the movements of various things going on in the warehouse where they resided. Periodically, two or three screens switched to world maps, global hot spots, or various Washington D.C. streets. Several showed live feeds of Kabul, Baghdad, and Pyongyang. A few other tech-looking people with headphones and pocket protectors wandered in and out. Vernon paid them little mind as they attempted to interact with him by speaking in low voices. Like him, their skin needed a little more sun.

Chase propped his elbows on the table as the door opened to their little slice of paradise with Special Agent Martin joining the Enigma team. His scowl told Chase he wasn't happy about being dragged out in the middle of the night.

The FBI agent paused and put his hands on his hips, pushing his suit coat back. Even at this time of night, the man appeared to be dressed for work. Instead of getting up with a warm greeting, Chase reached back and pulled a chair on wheels up close to his terminal.

"Have a seat, Dennis." Chase nodded to the chair. "Nice of you to drop by."

The agent dropped his hands to his sides and joined him. "It wasn't like I had a choice. And it's Special Agent Martin. No one made us friends." His gaze drifted to the computer monitor showing Robert Scott sitting on the edge of his cot with his head in his hands. "That him?"

"Umm. Guess you didn't meet him in D.C. when the attack on President Austin went down."

"No. I was trying to cover my butt for throwing in with the likes of you guys. I'm sure I'll live to regret it." Chase observed how the agent tore his attention away from the monitor to evaluate the other team members who ignored him. "I see your people practice being invisible even when they're not." The last comment caused heads to jerk in their direction. "And hello to you, too," he quipped. A few nods of greeting and a chuckle from Chase was the extent of the warm fuzzy reunion.

"They don't talk much," was the extent of the Chase's explanation.

"If you ever want to train a bunch of pit bulls, let me know. You obviously are good at calming the savage beasts." Agent Martin sounded a little snarky.

Zoric stared with his dark, dead eyes at Agent Martin then took out his switchblade and clicked it open and closed.

"Is he even in this country legally?" the agent asked, holding eye contact with the Serbian.

Chase glanced at Zoric's and raised his chin. "Probably not. Maybe you two can chat about those possibilities later." He couldn't resist a sinister smirk.

"Did you take his leash off with Reeva Kaplan?"

"Meaning?"

Agent Martin took a couple of photos of a woman from inside his coat pocket.

Carter reached for the photos and grimaced then shared them with the group. The image of a familiar woman lying on a tile bathroom floor, her body covered in blood stuck with him, though. "Reeva Kaplan."

"Wrists were slit, nice and neat." The agent stared at Zoric peering at the photos before passing them along to the others. "She wasn't in this guy's room, either." He nodded at the image of Robert on the monitor. "Was in a room at the opposite end of the hall." Sam handed the pictures back to him, and the team once again faced their screens as if the agent no longer existed.

Chase slowly shook his head. "We didn't do this. She was bound and gagged in numbskull's room. Someone was coming off the elevators at the opposite end when we made our exit. What about his stuff? Did you get it?"

"Of course, we got it and wiped down the room, like you asked. I understand your hacker"—he faced Vernon— "removed him from the guest list. All nice and neat, if you ask me."

"It's what we do, Agent Martin." Tempted to call him by his first name again, Chase thought better of it since he wasn't finished with him yet. "So, I need you to go in there and find out why the honorable Robert Scott was meeting with a character like Reeva Kaplan."

"Sure it wasn't for a little slap and tickle? She had a reputation for roughness in the bedroom. Maybe Robert wasn't getting any at home, if you know what I mean. Heard the wife likes the bad boys."

Carter and Vernon stood up at the same time, their nostrils flaring, hands closed into fists.

Chase shifted his eyes from one to the other.

"I don't think they like your insinuation, Agent Martin."

The agent's lips twisted in a half grin. "A little touchy about Tessa Scott, are we, boys? No disrespect intended. She's a nice lady and did a heck of a job for President Austin. Relax. I didn't know she was back in the field so soon after Afghanistan is all."

"Long story. Let's get this over with."

Chase didn't want to talk about Afghanistan and Tessa Scott in the same conversation. He'd nearly lost her forever thanks to a drug-running scumbag who'd tricked her into believing he was some kind of knight in shining armor. The whole scenario still caused his hair to stand up on the back of his neck.

"You all really are thicker than thieves, aren't you?" Agent Martin groaned as he lifted his body out of the chair then pushed it under another desk. He straightened it before walking toward the door. "You owe me for this one. And don't call me again to clean up after the wild bunch." He raised his chin at the other Enigma team members watching him with suspicion.

~~~

"They're asleep." Tessa rubbed her face, fighting fatigue as she watched the hulk of a man wearing an apron too small for his girth.
~~~

Handsome continued to stir something in a Crock-Pot. "Cooked these beans to mush. Want some?"

"Maybe some of the cornbread. My granny made the best cornbread, and mine has the consistency of cement."

He pointed to a pan on the stove. "Help yourself."

"You work for Enigma, huh?"

"Not exactly," he said with a flippant disregard tone.

Tessa picked up a piece of cornbread. "Meaning?"

"Meaning I owe them a couple of favors, this being one of them."

The only light in the small house came from an LED lantern the size of a flashlight, sitting on the kitchen counter next to the Crock-Pot. After scooping up a bowl of beans, he pried a piece of cornbread from the iron skillet and joined Tessa at the table. He didn't appear to be interested in conversation as he ate with the finesse of a trained chef savoring each bite.

When he finished, Tessa stood. "You fed my kids, so I'll do the dishes. Okay?"

The chair creaked under his large frame when he sat up straight then dabbed a napkin at his mouth like he'd eaten at a five-star restaurant. "Thank you."

Tessa wanted to make sure her new friend had enough time to let his supper settle before she started the barrage of questions again. She took great pains in wiping down the sink then folding the towels across the lip of the counter before joining Handsome at the table again.

"Those men. Do you know who they were?"

"No." His calm voice unnerved her.

"Can they find us?"

"Not if we stay off-line and shut down your phone." He took a deep breath and pulled himself up by grabbing the edge of the table. "Where is your phone?"

Tessa retrieved her purse from a worn chair inside the living room and dug some of the contents out, dropping the makeup bag and checkbook and a thumb-size flashlight, on the floor, only to be snatched up by the man who followed close behind.

"It's not here. I could have sworn—"

He moved into the darkness where the children slept.

"What are you doing? Stop," she ordered as he lifted blankets and shone the flashlight over Heather who cuddled her pillow like a favorite stuffed animal. He moved to Daniel next.

"It probably fell out somewhere in here when we rushed inside." She touched his arm in hopes of stopping his suspicion. "My children would never—"

Handsome reached down and lifted a phone from the floor next to her oldest son. He tossed her the flashlight and scrolled through her network. In a few seconds, he stopped, read something then showed Tessa.

Dad! Mom & us are in trouble. Can't leave Tahoe. Danger. Help us.

"Oh. My. Gosh," she gasped as her hand flew to her mouth.

It was then she heard the sound of crunching snow outside the cabin.

CHAPTER SIX

Agent Martin adjusted the earwig again before entering the room to confront Robert Scott. Captain Hunter would evaluate every word, sigh, eye roll, and mouth twitch of this man. Chances were good he'd written a list of questions to whisper into his earwig during the interrogation. Being called in to clean up an Enigma mess topped the list of things he disliked. If his superiors knew about the extent of his involvement with the secret security force, he'd be out of a job, pension, and a career. Even though Director Benjamin Clark promised to protect him if it ever came to that, he doubted the truth of it. Enigma was whispered in the halls of Langley and Homeland Security. If the Justice Department got wind of what they really did for the president, all hell would break loose. He'd once mentioned his concerns to the captain. The smirk he received in reply still gave him chills.

"Hell would be the least of anyone's worries if someone tries to stop us. Besides, you're in over your head, so why not enjoy it? Nobody will touch you as long as you're in the director's good graces. Oh, and the president's, of course." Chase downed a whiskey, his eyes the color of obsidian. "You'll hardly ever know we're around. And when you do—stay out of the way."

Staying out of the way became his mission in life, until tonight.

He pushed into the room that smelled of coffee and disinfectant then switched off one of the pair of glaring fluorescent lights as Robert Scott rose from the side of his bed.

He reminded him of a pathetic guy caught in a life-changing event. His bloodshot eyes widened once the light dimmed. He needed a shave, and his bed hair showed some early signs of graying. Rumpled clothing hung from his frame.

"Agent Martin. FBI." He stuck out his hand, surprised at the man's firm grip. His father measured a man by his handshake. In this instance, his dad would have said Robert had a Baptist grip—not a bad thing. "Please. Sit down, sir." It paid to be polite.

"I don't understand. What is going on? I haven't done anything wrong. Where is Reeva?"

Agent Martin laid his black file folder on the table as if it were a day-old baby. He folded his hands on top before cocking his head in faux concern. "What do you think is going on, Mr. Scott?"

He ran his fingers through his hair nervously. "No idea. One minute, I was cleaning myself up from the coffee Reeva spilled on me then—"

"She spilled coffee on you?"

"Yes. There was still some in the pot I made earlier. You know those little ones you find in hotels." The agent nodded. "I forgot to drink it until she arrived. She wanted a cup. Thankfully, it was a couple hours old, or I would have been scalded."

Agent Martin heard a whispered question in his ear. "What happened?"

"She tripped? I don't know. When she ran into the bathroom for a towel then patted me down, it got a little weird, if you know what I mean."

"Why don't you explain it to me, Mr. Scott?"

"I took the towel from her and backed into the bathroom to change my shirt. She kept talking to me as I washed the coffee out and used the blow-dryer on my pants. I turned the shower on to get the rinse stains out of my shirt. I hadn't brought another shirt into the bathroom, so I planned to slip out and grab one from my suitcase. It was a little embarrassing. I realized as I came out that Reeva wasn't talking anymore. Next thing I knew, a bunch of thugs were manhandling me, and poor Reeva was all tied up with tape over her mouth. Her blouse was unbuttoned. I'm not sure if they…" He shook his head and lowered his face into his hands. "Terrifying."

"How many times have you met Reeva in this manner?"

Robert jerked his head up and pointed a finger at him. "Wait a minute. I see where this is headed. It's not like that."

"Like what, Mr. Scott?" This would be where the agitated sap tripped himself up and spilled his guts. He'd seen it before, too many times to count.

"You think I was having an affair," he snapped.

"Were you?"

"No," he yelled. "Reeva was a client."

"Another name for hooker."

"No," he insisted, sounding on the brink of tears. "No." He took a deep breath and let it out slowly. "I'm a lawyer. She came to my firm. Wanted some work done concerning international and commercial law. They recommended me. Said I had a reputation. I was at this conference, so she drove down from Sacramento to meet me."

"And this pleased you?"

"Yes. I was flattered. I don't usually get such a high-profile case."

"What did she want?"

"Something to do with a diamond mine in South Africa, maybe some other country. Originally, we were going to meet the next day, but she called to say she was flying out in the morning, and could we meet for dinner to get better acquainted."

"Convenient."

"What does that mean? You think I'm lying? I'm not. I'm happily married."

"Really? Because"—he opened his folder and glanced over some paperwork in the file before closing it again— "I understand you and a Ms. Honey Lynch shared some quality time at Lake Tahoe a couple of years ago."

Robert banged his fist on the table. "She was undercover as a park ranger. Besides, you know perfectly well she was working with you."

"I assure you, Mr. Scott, she was not working for us." Robert's going pale gave him immense satisfaction. Of course, he did know of Ms. Lynch, and she didn't work for the FBI. She was a contract killer who liked to play both sides of the law, another friend of Chase Hunter and Enigma. Even so, this was the part he enjoyed, crushing the suspect into confession.

"I don't understand. I was told she worked for the FBI." The man's forehead pinched over his nicely trimmed eyebrows and perfect nose.

"We're getting off topic, Mr. Scott." He paused to make eye contact with Tessa's husband. "Why did Reeva Kaplan come to your room?"

The man squirmed. "We had dinner. Talk drifted to the diamond business. It sounded like she wanted a little more protection for her investments."

"The Treasury Department fondly refers to these kinds of deals as money laundering."

"Money laundering." He choked. "No. It wasn't some kind of shady deal. Or at least we didn't discuss things in depth. She said she wanted to meet me and make sure I would be easy to work with before she decided on the firm representing her interests. Then we had dinner."

"So, dessert was to be served in your room?"

"You listen here. I don't like what you're implying." The agent locked his fingers together on top of the folder, glaring at Robert Scott. A drop of perspiration formed where his sideburns should have been. "I told Reeva I wanted to surprise my wife with some diamond earrings for Christmas." Robert stuck his index finger beneath his collar and pretended to loosen it. Another indication of guilt.

"Christmas?"

"I know it's months away, but I thought it would give me plenty of time to pay for them. Besides she said she could make me a really good deal. She actually had some samples with her. She didn't want to take them on the plane because of something about having to explain things in customs or too much trouble. These were the only ones she had left after visiting several jewelers' conventions."

When the agent chuckled at the remarks going on in his earwig from Chase's team, Robert rubbed his throat where a bruise showed. No doubt from an unhappy captain who had the reputation for being a little overprotective of Tessa Scott.

"And you saw the diamonds?"

"Yes. Then everything went sideways. She was coming on to me, or I thought she was. I'm not sure. I got nervous. She spilled coffee, and I escaped to the bathroom. When I came out, a bunch of thugs were in the room. One of them spoke with an accent like Reeva's. The others didn't say anything. They seemed surprised to see me. One of them hit me upside my head." He touched the bruise near his temple then dropped his hand to the table.

More chatter in Agent Martin's earwig. Their dry sense of humor, although inappropriate, managed to amuse him.

"Does anyone know about Reeva? Is she okay? She can verify all of this. Do I need a lawyer?"

"You tell me, Mr. Scott." The agent opened the folder again, and pulled out the picture of Reeva covered in blood on a bathroom floor then shoved it across the table.

After only a glance, Robert jumped up so fast his chair flipped over. "Good, lord!" he moaned as he backed up and fell onto the bed. "What happened? Lord. She was fine when we left."

"Yes." He pulled the picture back with one finger then examined it as if he'd not seen it earlier. "Lucky for you, she wasn't found in your room."

Robert wiped his face, dotted with perspiration, on the sleeve of his white shirt. "Who could do this?"

He shrugged nonchalantly. It was a cruel gesture, considering the gravity of the situation. "We're looking into it." Another one of those phrases that tended to drive suspects and victims to the brink of despair. "Didn't find any diamonds. Unless you purchased a few, I guess they were stolen."

"Those thugs must have gone back to finish the job."

"Maybe. But unlikely."

"I had nothing to do with her death, Agent Martin. I swear."

He paused to listen to the Enigma team mocking Robert with whining voices, except for Chase who remained strangely quiet with only an occasional question. With a glance at the wall clock, he realized dawn grew near. Time to wrap up.

"Do you know how you got here, Mr. Scott?"

"How could I? Those thugs bound and gagged me. We rode for a while. I don't know how long. I heard a railroad crossing guard signal, horns blowing, and a couple of dogs barking when we stopped. Next thing I knew, I ended up in this room. The big guy with the accent shoved me down on the bed and held a gun to my head. If he works for you—"

"He doesn't, Mr. Scott. I don't know who brought you here. The FBI got a call about Reeva and this place. Seems to me someone wanted to make sure you were found safe and sound. As to the gun to your head—we don't operate like hooligans." He spoke slowly, adding a hint of disdain to let Enigma understand he disapproved of their tactics.

"So, you believe me? I can go?"

"I believe you were duped, Mr. Scott. I don't believe you're totally innocent or have been completely honest with me. However, we know where to find you if the need arises. I'll get your release papers together and bring them in for you to sign. How does that sound?"

Robert took a deep breath and let it out all at once as if a huge weight had lifted off his shoulders. "Yeah. Yeah. Sure. Sounds good. Thank you." A timid smile played at the corners of his chapped lips. "I don't know where I'm at or where my car is…"

Agent Martin stood. "I can take care of everything, Mr. Scott. I'm hoping I can count on your discretion. Do not discuss this with anyone at your law firm. There are still a number of things we'd like to check out, including your story."

He placed his hands on his hips and nodded like a bobblehead toy from the ballpark. "You got it." He pretended to lock his lips and throw the key over his shoulder. "I don't want any more trouble."

The agent put his hand on the doorknob and twisted. "I apologize for any inconvenience, Mr. Scott. Would you like a bite to eat? This will take a little longer to locate someone to return you to your car and sign the papers. Please let me do this for you."

"Sounds great. I am a little hungry."

"I'll be right back." The agent offered his best smile then removed it as he left the room.

Another man who had waited for him earlier when he arrived prepared a tray with several sweet rolls, juice, and a cup of steaming coffee. The cloth napkin and stainless-steel silverware was a nice touch. The agent remembered him from Washington D.C. when he assisted in cleaning up the mess with President

Austin. Sergeant Ken Montgomery was a former Ranger buddy of Chase Hunter. He raised his chin in acknowledgement of his presence then lowered his head as if to evaluate him with disdain. Another man, a former Marine, appeared from the closed room where the Enigma team waited with some papers he'd hand Robert to sign.

"Tell him to sign the papers, fold them, place them in the envelope then seal it," the Marine said in a matter-of-fact tone.

"Just like that?"

The Marine was Tom Cooper, not known for his witty conversation. "Exactly."

"Screw you," the agent growled as he snatched the papers from the Marine's large hand. The former Marine made no further attempt at conversation.

Agent Martin carried the tray with one hand, pinning the release papers underneath, so he could open the door of the interrogation room. Robert Scott thanked him and took a sip of juice.

"Read over the papers, Mr. Scott. I think everything is in order. Take as long as you need. After signing them, please fold them and slip into the envelope. For your own protection, we'll let you seal the envelope. My supervisor will be here shortly. You can hand the envelope to him."

Robert pulled the chair out at the same time he lifted a sweet roll to his mouth. Indignation and you're-going-to-pay-for-this scowl replaced the scared nice-guy expression as he examined the papers.

~~~

"Take a load off, Dennis." Chase shoved a wheeled desk chair at the FBI agent coming through the door. "Oh sorry. Special Agent Martin."

He plopped in the chair and loosened the striped tie. "You guys are a bunch of clowns, you know that? And very unprofessional, I might add."

"Why thank you, Agent Martin," Carter Johnson's Texas drawl came on top of a chuckle. "You FBI types tend to be a little serious, so I'm glad we could tickle your funny bone."

He pushed back in the chair to relax his shoulders and watch the
~~~

computer screen where Robert read the three-page document. "How many times has he gone over them?"

"Three. Maybe four." Chase smiled as Tessa's husband folded the document and placed it in the envelope then licked the seal. "Won't be long."

"Clever, putting the sedative in the seal on the envelope." Agent Martin sniffed as he rocked in his squeaky chair.

"My idea," Vernon chimed in. "The Pentagon does it all the time to subversives."

"And you would be the conspiracy expert," the agent said drily.

"Damn straight. And there he goes," Vernon said pointing to the computer screen. Robert laid his head down on the table, snoring almost immediately.

Chase smiled. "You're a genius, Vern."

"Thanks, Boss. Cooper and Montgomery are handling the return. They moved his car to another hotel."

"So, Agent Martin, what did you think of Robert Scott?"

"I think he's hiding something." He stood and stretched. "Hard to believe this guy is Tessa's husband."

"Hmm. Go figure." Chase's face remained serious.

"And you put a gun to his head?"

"I didn't pull the trigger."

"What an improvement. I'm surprised your ghoul didn't carve his initials in his butt." He glanced toward the Serbian, "No offense, Zoric."

"None taken." Zoric used his switchblade to clean under his fingernails.

"See you guys—never, I hope." Agent Martin excused himself from the room.

"Hey, Boss." Vernon forwarded a message to Chase's computer. "Better take a look at this. Came through on Tessa's regular phone to Robert several hours ago."

Chase read the distress message. "Must be from one of the kids. Vern?"

"Agreed. I finished a scan on their home computer. Somebody has been snooping around Robert's law firm." Vernon switched screens. "The call center reported a distress call from Tessa. They sent her some help."

"Who?"

"You're not going to like this, Boss."

"Why?"

"It's Handsome Jones."

Everyone scrambled to their feet. "We leave in five," Chase ordered.

CHAPTER SEVEN

"**D**id you hear something?" Tessa whispered. Handsome's frown deepened before he took up a position at a narrow window while still holding the phone. How someone so big could move like a tiny ballerina amazed her. She remained frozen in place as she observed him separate the blinds with a sausage-sized finger and lower one eye to get a better view of the outside. She joined him and laid a hand on his forearm. "I'm scared, Handsome."

He glanced down at her hand touching him then pulled away before speaking. "Pretty late for a visitor. Could be a bear snooping around. Nobody knows this place." He shifted his attention back down to the phone. "Could have followed the ping off some tower."

"Tower? I can hardly call out to order pizza when we visit Tahoe, unless I'm in town. How is this possible?"

"If someone was monitoring your husband, it could be done, especially if they're wanting to find you."

"Why me? I'm nobody. I study maps or follow economic patterns all day. My picture is next to the word boring in the dictionary."

Handsome separated the blinds again to peer out. "We both know this is far from the truth, Mrs. Scott."

When Tessa swallowed, it sounded like a gulp gone bad. "Okay. So, I've gotten into a little trouble in the past." She pushed at his arm to move him aside so she could scan the area. It felt like moving a piece of furniture. The fallen snow glistened with the moonlight pushing out from behind the clouds. "What do we do? I don't want to scare the kids for nothing."

The big man removed his coat from an antique hall tree by the front door. His movements reminded her of a sloth coming down to the rainforest floor in some Disney film. The urge to help him created an overwhelming sensation of dread in her gut. She chewed the inside of her jaw to maintain calm.

"Do you have a gun?" she whispered when he pulled on a hat with earflaps the color of snow.

"Don't need one."

"How do you know? You can't go running about in the night when some armed bad guys might be lurking behind a tree, Handsome," she snapped, watching him pick up gloves resembling oven mitts.

He stopped and smiled down at her. "Bad guys? Lurking? You watch too much TV. Besides, I'm a pacifist."

"Boy, are you in the wrong line of work. We need you in here."

"You'll be fine. Lock the door behind me. If I don't come back in ten minutes"—he tossed the phone to Tessa— "call the number I programmed in for you."

She glanced at the phone, suddenly irritated her son had put them in further danger. "Who is it?"

"The good guys." Again, he smiled then unlatched the door. He stopped before stepping outside and glanced over his shoulder at the sleeping children. "It's going to be all right, Mrs. Scott. No one will get in."

He pushed out into the night like it was a walk in the park. Since the door lacked a window, she couldn't determine what might be happening. Considering his ability to move in slow motion she wondered if he'd even appear in time to warn them of danger. She didn't have much hope of seeing him out the window against the snowy backdrop, but she peeked out anyway. After waiting twenty minutes, instead of the ten he'd instructed, she dialed the number he'd programmed into the phone.

"Tessa?" Chase Hunter sounded surprised. Thank you, God, she prayed. "Are you okay?"

"Yes." His deep voice gave her strength and confidence things would work out. "Scared."

"Where is Handsome?"

"How did you know—"

"Doesn't matter. Is he there?"

"No. He went to check on something outside. We heard a sound."

"And the kids?"

"Asleep. I didn't want to alarm them if I didn't need to. What is going on?"

"We're on our way—"

"On your way." She couldn't keep the panic out of her voice. "All of you? Good lord! How much danger are we in?" When Chase didn't respond, she realized how fast she'd been talking. He frowned on a lack of control from an Enigma agent. "Chase?"

"You'll be fine."

"So I'm told."

"Keep your doors locked. Do you have a weapon?"

"Brought my winning personality and wit." She heard him chuckle. "Of course, I don't have a weapon. I'm with my kids, for crying out loud!" With another peek out the window, the only thing she could see was the occasional drop of snow from a burdened tree branch. "Handsome hasn't come back. I bet he's in trouble—or hurt—or dead—or…"

"Stop it. He can take care of himself."

"I'm not so sure. He seems like a gentle giant." She paused at an eruption of laughter in the background. His team caused mayhem while they tried to save the United States or, in this case, her. One of these days, they might decide to throw her to the sharks and watch her bleed out. Heaven knew she deserved it. It remained a mystery why they put up with her.

"Don't let him back in the house." Chase's voice took on a tone of sinister warning.

"I can't leave him out in the cold. He came to our rescue."

"Yeah, about that… Do as I say."

"I will not," she fumed. "He could freeze to death. And, besides, the interstate is closed, and you won't be able to get here."

"The highway never closed."

"A sign at the convenience store said to find an alternate route. Several semis turned over and were blocking the road."

"Nope. Other than traffic moving a little slower because of the snow, the road crews have kept the highway clear in spite of the storm."

"Strange. Handsome worked at that gas station. Filling in for a sister, I think."

"Handsome doesn't have a sister, or any family to speak of. His mother died in childbirth, and his father took off not long after. He grew up in the foster care system."

A chill ran up her spine. "But he said—"

"Don't open the door. Can you tell me where you're at in case Vernon loses your signal?"

Although she remembered the route she'd followed to the safe house, how they got to this place was a little fuzzy. She had tried to keep the children calm, focused on them as Handsome drove their car. It hadn't seemed very far at the time. She told him what she recalled. Why hadn't she paid more attention? Her kids' safety, maybe their lives, depended on it.

"That's not much to go on, Tess. The road is only wide enough for one vehicle?"

"Yes. He had to use four-wheel drive to get back here. He's a good guy, right?"

"He can be."

"Great. I'm stranded with three kids, this big guy who came to our rescue, who may be more dangerous than whoever came after us…"

"Doubtful. Whoever came after you won't want to cross him. He's not a very patient person."

"I think we're talking about two different people. Doesn't he work for Enigma? This means he's a good guy. Right?"

Another burst of laughter from whoever rode with Chase. Considering all of their backgrounds, being a good guy might be a bit of a stretch in the character department. She was the token girl-next-door person. At least she used to be. Things had changed over the last year to tarnish her once-flawless image.

"Do as I say, Tessa. This once, can you follow orders?" Chase's voice carried exasperation, meaning an I'm-going-to-kick-your-ass tone. "Do you have someplace to hide there?"

"It's a tiny place. A closet, maybe."

"Keep that option just in case."

"In case of what?"

"Tessa, I need you to put your big-girl panties on and think this through. If someone is after you, then use what is there to protect yourself. I can't imagine Handsome wouldn't have some kind of weapon. Search the place. Stop being a nervous Nelly."

"Don't talk to me like I'm a baby."

"Then stop acting like one," he growled. "You fought the Taliban, saved the president's life, and beat the hell out of a Libyan terrorist with a rolling pin. This is no big deal for you."

Tessa rolled her shoulders before taking a deep breath. "You're trying to sweet-talk me."

A few more chuckles in the background, but none of them from Chase. "It's been a long night. We'll be there in another hour. In the meantime, I'll see who else we've got to search for you."

"Thanks, Chase. I'm sorry about this." They'd become like family to her. Even Sam, who usually tried to undermine her and make life a living hell, had taught her how to survive in a pinch. If she had been dragged into this against her will, there would be consequences—like walking over a bed of burning coals.

"Not your fault."

She looked down into Daniel's cherub face and sighed.

"I think we may have a problem with your number two son."

"I think he's been hacking again."

"He's a genius." Coming from Vernon, this gave her more pause than pride. The Enigma computer whiz managed to tick people off at the NSA and the Pentagon on a regular basis. "I'm taking the kid under my wing when this is over."

She guessed Vernon Kemp thought he had another way into her life and especially her heart. "Okay, Vernon. Nothing illegal."

Chase butted in. "Daniel does okay in that department all by himself."

"What were you guys doing tonight? I thought you'd be in San Francisco for another day or so. I've been out of the loop since I brought the kids up here. Business or pleasure?"

"A little of both."

Usually those words meant he enjoyed scaring the crap out of somebody deserving a bullet to the head. This is how it went with

Enigma. When you thought they were a normal bunch of freedom fighters for the United States, they put on their demonic sense of justice badge and wreaked havoc on any unsuspecting terrorist, conspirator, or criminal.

"What does 'a little of both' mean exactly, or can you tell me?"

"Tracking a woman who was involved in the conflict diamonds' business. Planned to confront her but ran into a problem we had to solve first. Before we could resolve the issue, someone decided to make her unavailable. Permanently."

Two years ago, she would have been horrified at such casual conversation about a dead woman and conflict diamonds. Not anymore. "What stopped you?"

He exhaled long and slow. "She was with an innocent. Had to get him out of the way before we took her down or whoever she planned to meet later. Didn't go as planned."

She moved to the window to steal another glance at the whitescape outside. Having Chase on the phone gave her confidence. The sound of his voice always drove her into a black hole of emotions she held off exploring, but loved the way it warmed her nonetheless. He managed to instill a sense of fearlessness in her whenever these kinds of situations popped up.

Her thoughts drifted to her husband, Robert. His trip to San Francisco had prevented him from coming with them to ski these last few days. It hadn't been easy to return to being the devoted wife again after escaping Afghanistan. Recently, with therapy, she had begun to enjoy being his wife again, even though she carried the secrets of the things she'd done in such a godless land. For all he knew, she was rescued by a bunch of Special Forces after getting lost in the wilds of a war-torn country.

"Tessa?" With her in need of his support once again, Chase's voice reminded her without him, she would still be the captive of a mountain tribesman.

"Yes. I'm here. Took a peek outside. Nothing."

"Keep me on the line as long as you can. Vernon is tracking your signal."

"Are you still on speaker phone?"

Silence ensued for only a second. "Not anymore."

Tessa closed her eyes as if he stroked her face. "I'm sorry we haven't been getting along lately, especially since Afghanistan. It had nothing to do with you. I've been distant and cool toward you. I appreciated everything you did for me, for bringing me home to take up my life again. You are everything to me, Chase. I hope you know that. I miss our long talks, our lunches together at the university, everything."

"Me, too. We'll discuss it later." Of course, she knew he couldn't say too much because chances were, everyone would be straining to hear every little word. "You're welcome, by the way."

"If I hadn't been kidnapped…"

"Then things would be different." His voice resembled reading a stock market report. She guessed it meant he didn't want the others to know the two of them had nearly crossed the line of ethical work relationships. Chances were, they wouldn't discuss it later. Something always got in the way of talking about their special friendship because of being sidetracked by world events.

"Chase, you must know how I…" She froze.

"Tessa? What's wrong?"

"Someone is trying to get in. The doorknob rattled."

"Tessa? Tessa!" Chase snapped a little harsher than he'd intended. "Sam, check to see where the Highway Patrol is and if they can spare a man. Next, call the police at Truckee to do the same." He pushed the phone tighter to his ear to hear the slightest sound.

"A step ahead of you. Already tried Truckee while you were stroking Betty Crocker." Chase leveled an irritated gaze to silence the insults. "All units are out on calls of one degree or another. Highway Patrol has me on hold. She won't be a priority."

"Take the next exit, Carter." Vernon sat in the back seat and stared at his laptop. "I think I found a shortcut."

Carter took the exit a little too fast and swerved into a slide to correct. He let out a banshee howl then laughed. Chase frowned over at his teammate, never amused at his antics, but still wishing he could possess his zest for living life to the fullest. He guessed if you'd spent longer on the space station than any other astronaut besides Scott Kelly, you experienced things with a little more gusto, or maybe stupidity, in his case.

"Oops. Overcorrected. Let's have it, Vern," Carter chuckled as he stole a glance at the young computer genius. "Why, Vern, you're as pale as a ghost. Better stay close when we get out, or we might lose you in all this snow."

"Tessa?" Chase asked again. "Talk to me."

Nothing.

He tossed his phone to Zoric next to him. "Damn woman is going to make me lose my mind one of these days."

"I think you enjoy her careless disregard for authority." Zoric wiped at the moisture forming on his window. "We all do. It's so—innocent."

Chase tapped Carter on the shoulder and pointed to a gas station with a sign still announcing the highway had been shut down. He nodded and kept driving as Vernon offered directional changes intermittently. Usually, he didn't sit in the back seat. He wanted to be the one driving or giving orders from the front. Carter, his second in command, suggested the change since Chase remained agitated over finding Tessa's husband with another woman.

"Innocent? There isn't one thing innocent about her," Samantha grumbled from the rear seat. "All of you are seduced by the smell of chocolate chip cookies and her 'aw shucks' mentality. She is playing you." Chase listened but continued to stare through the space between the front seats and out the window. "If you'd give her hell then bend her across your knee, there'd be none of this nonstop insubordination."

Carter took one hand off the wheel to snap his fingers. "A great idea, but only if I can watch."

"All of you, shut up and focus."

Chase knew he went easy on the Grass Valley housewife. From the moment he'd laid eyes on her, there was something he couldn't resist. For some reason, she helped him see humor in the simplest things, believe in the possibility of a higher power, and instilled a desire to be a better person. Tessa's ability to find trouble gave him plenty of opportunities to rush in and be the hero.

He'd never acted on his feelings. Somewhere during his career, he'd committed to never toying with the affections of a female agent or a married woman. Unfortunately, Tessa fit in both those "off-limits" perimeters. It didn't keep him from falling in love with her or finding reasons to be alone with her. When both of them ended up in Afghanistan under a dark cloud of corruption among American officials, their attraction for one another threatened to make them throw caution to the wind. The call of duty demanded he delay crossing the moral line he'd had every intention of destroying. Someone else stepped in to take advantage of his absence, changing her forever.

Now, here he was again, coming to the rescue. Maybe one of these times she'd insist on showing her appreciation in a way besides her chocolate chip cookies. With so many complications in her life, he postponed the first move. On the other hand, if she decided…

"Hey. We're coming up on the safe house," Vernon said as he glanced back at Chase.

"Try calling her again, Zoric, so Vern can pick up a signal."

Zoric handed him the phone. "Ringing."

~~~

Tessa bit her lower lip so hard she tasted blood. Only the glow from the fireplace lit the room as she picked up an iron poker and moved behind the door. The doorknob turned so slowly, she doubted she'd seen it move. One of the kids exhaled and rolled over, drawing her attention. Heather mumbled in her sleep, and a log shifted in the fireplace. Any other time, she'd have loved those sounds. Now it scared her like the click of a gun in a dark room.

She reassured herself by touching the lock—still bolted. Nothing else happened as she stared at the door, holding the poker like a samurai sword. After a few minutes, she exhaled several large breaths as if they'd struggled to be released.

"Where are you, Handsome?" she whispered. A step toward the children drew her attention to another sound at the back door. "No. No. No."

She stumbled her way through the kitchen and managed to trip over a chair in her rush. The door creaked open as a gust of cold air pushed into the small attached mudroom lit only by a nightlight. The outline of someone stepping inside propelled her to take action. Lunging into the cramped area, Tessa swung the poker across what she hoped would be a sensitive and vulnerable area.

The figure staggered back, hitting his head against a board with coat hooks. A grunt of discomfort reached her ears when she reared back the poker to take another swing. He caught it midair and jerked it from her hand. She jumped back as her phone vibrated in her pants pocket. Shaking his head, the figure
~~~

straightened to his full height. Tessa pivoted to escape, only to feel a hand catch the hem of her sweater. He yanked her backward. A frantic attempt to dig out her phone caused her scream to sound more like a choking sound, only to have it slapped from her hand.

~~~

"Tessa?" Chase could hear noises, maybe even a gasp, or was it a cry for help? He continued to listen, switching to speaker mode.

Everyone strained to listen to the chaotic commotion. Even Carter slowed the vehicle and cocked one ear.

"Got her." Vernon's voice, although barely above a whisper, sounded encouraged. He gave Carter new directions before evaluating his computer screen once more.

"How long?" Chase grabbed the back of Carter's seat.

"With the road like this, maybe half an hour."

Silence followed. Chase knew the urge to curse, grumble, or complain would not get them there any faster. Instead, he formulated a plan of attack. Too many missing variables in the current situation to know the number of intruders—how many outside and inside. What had happened to Handsome, and where were the children at this moment?

It rubbed him the wrong way when kids got hurt. The Scott children made Tessa a little crazy at times with their bickering and propensity to be mischievous. He'd told her on more than one occasion they came by it honestly, so stop worrying. She managed things all right. The little girl, Heather, was the spitting image of her mother, but the boys favored their father. Hopefully, they wouldn't grow up to be a jerk like him. He was keeping an eye on Sean Patrick who demonstrated some leadership skills, even at a young age. Tessa said he dreamed of the military academy. Daniel was a brain, and Vernon monitored his activities on the internet when his own workload allowed. Probably should have been more diligent, considering he snooped on the wrong people.

He didn't want anything to happen to Tessa on a variety of levels, but the number one reason was because children shouldn't be terrorized by crazy people. If anything happened to those kids, someone would pay.

"Up ahead, Chase." Carter put the Suburban in park but left the
~~~

engine running. "See a late model SUV at our two o'clock."

"Kill the engine," Chase instructed as both he and Zoric lifted their binoculars. "No one inside it."

A rattling sound emitted again from the phone in Tessa's possession. Mumbling carried through to them. The words, "stop it, no, my kids, and help," faded in and out without any way of putting it in context. Chase could feel himself tighten up like when he confronted an enemy in battle. Every muscle, nerve, and brain cell prepared to eliminate the threat. The sound of a weapons check and zippers closing followed by car doors quietly being opened, found the group of Enigma agents moving a short distance to hide behind a bush or tree before taking further action. When Chase pointed in several directions with his trigger finger, the group fanned out toward the cabin.

~~~

"Stop it," Tessa snapped as she applied a disinfectant to the cut on the back of Handsome's head. He jerked from her touch one too many times. "You gave me a scare. At least my kids didn't wake up during the excitement." Both she and her new protector glanced toward the living room where the children continued to sleep.

"Maybe you should sleep for a couple of hours. I'll keep watch." Handsome pushed her aside and stood.

"Help is on the way. I talked to Captain Hunter not long ago."

The stranger's frown deepened at the sound of Chase's name. From the way he puffed out his cheeks and bit his lower lip, she got the feeling he wasn't too happy about the thought of the cavalry showing up.

"What's wrong? You said to call them if you didn't come back."

"I came back."

She rubbed at the goose bumps rising on her arms to fight off the chill of suspicion. "What did you find outside?"

"Two men. Same ones at the gas station. White South Africans."

"In Tahoe? How do you know they were South Africans?"

He moved to the kitchen window and used one finger to push the curtains open enough to peer out. "I know."
~~~

"Where are they?" Tessa took a step backward in the direction of the living room.

He dropped the curtain and shifted his bulbous eyes to her then flicked a glance toward where the children slept. "They were bad men." He pulled out a drawer and withdrew a large butcher knife. "You should go in with your children now."

Her body refused to breathe. She held the air tight in her chest as her hands went to her mouth to suppress a scream. The lights over the stove and sink flickered then extinguished. Only the light from the fireplace danced around the room. Still, the children remained asleep.

For such a large man, Handsome continued to move like a ghostly apparition. He held his free hand to his mouth and indicated she should be quiet as he moved toward the back door. She hadn't heard it before, but there was certainly something or someone trying to get in. He had closed the door then placed a ring of antique keys around the doorknob. The sound of their slight quiver must have alerted him.

There came a moment when a rush of winter's blast swept in around her feet, yet she remained frozen in place as she watched Handsome press his back against the wall going into the laundry room. Someone dressed in a light-colored jacket and sock hat slipped through the doorway into the kitchen. Both hands gripped a weapon as he paused for a second. He straightened when his eyes fell on her. Once again, she hadn't followed orders, this time Handsome's orders. The weapon lowered slightly as she recognized the stance of the man who never failed her.

"Watch out." Tessa threw her hands forward, as if by doing so she could stop Handsome.

The giant of a man knocked the weapon from Chase's hands then grabbed him around the throat and slammed him against the refrigerator. He lifted the Enigma agent about six inches off the floor as Chase pawed at the stranglehold.

Tessa stepped up behind Handsome and felt his strength when he pushed her back with his free hand. Chase managed to touch the floor again but remained in the giant's grasp.

"Handsome, let him go." Tessa tried to step closer but was held at arm's length before his attention returned to Chase.

"Nice to see you, Handsome," Chase croaked as he blinked then wrinkled his forehead as if in pain. "I see you are keeping fit."

Handsome removed his grip on Chase's throat but took the opportunity to slam him against the refrigerator door again.

"Handsome, you're going to wake the kids!" Tessa fumed.

Chase narrowed his eyes at her. "Seriously? That's what you're worried about?"

Tessa moved closer, avoiding Handsome's outstretched arm. "Oh. Sorry. Handsome, let him go."

"No." He continued to glare at Chase, nostrils flaring, his chest rising and falling as if he'd been running. He then applied more pressure to Chase's chest. The agent cringed.

"You aren't still mad over our little misunderstanding in Tunisia, are you?" Chase gasped for more air and tried to pry Handsome's hand from the middle of his chest. "I swear I didn't know you'd end up in prison."

"Handsome, please." Tessa also tried to pull him away, but he shoved her back with his elbow. "Let's talk about this. I'm sure Chase never meant to hurt you." She stole a glance toward the living room. Then she let her mom voice come through. "I swear, if you wake my kids, I'll take a baseball bat to that thick head of yours. This is the first time all day I've had a minute to myself, and you're ruining it!"

Handsome's frown deepened as he glanced over his shoulder to where the children were sleeping. Then a click sounded as another gun pressed to the man's temple.

CHAPTER NINE

"**H**ello, Handsome," came an East European accent. "I see you are misbehaving again."

"Zoric," he said flatly. "I should have smelled cigarette smoke when you slithered in like the snake you are. Guess you decided to take a shower and put on clean clothes." Handsome did not remove the pressure from Chase's chest and lifted the butcher knife from the counter with his free hand.

Zoric gave a snicker then pushed the barrel of the gun tighter to Handsome's head. "Stand down."

"What? Are you going to shoot me in front of this lady and her children? Very messy."

"So right," the Serbian smiled as he pulled a switchblade from a pocket and pushed a button to flip out the blade. "But I came prepared."

"Oh, for crying out loud!" Tessa snapped. "This place reeks of testosterone."

Samantha tiptoed inside the kitchen and, after evaluating the situation, slipped her weapon back into a holster. Handsome refocused his attention on her. For once, Tessa was grateful the woman was probably the most beautiful creature in the world, not to mention deadliest. Sam offered a brilliant smile as she placed her hands on her hips then blew Handsome a kiss.

"Hello, Handsome. And I do mean handsome. You old dog. You were supposed to call me if you ever got to California.

Remember? I told you I'd buy you dinner. I must be losing my touch." Samantha cocked her head then winked. "I like a man who plays hard to get."

"Let's face it, Sam," Tessa huffed as she folded her arms across her chest, "there isn't much about any man you don't like."

"You're not helping, Tessa," Chase growled through clenched teeth.

Sam pushed her face into hers, and sniffed. "Ugh. You still smell like cookies. Shows on your hips, Betty Crocker. How about a gym membership as an early birthday gift? My treat. Lord knows you need it."

"Bite me," Tessa retorted, but her rapidly batting eyelids revealed her intimidation.

Samantha flashed a brilliant smile. "Nice comeback."

Handsome watched the two women go back and forth. The distraction caused an involuntary loosening of pressure on Chase's chest. In a split second, Chase slipped out from under the large hand and landed a hard blow to Handsome's solar plexus. Taking a step back, a surprised expression crossed his face. His hand flew up and knocked the knife and gun from Zoric's hands, but barely flinched at the punch. He swung his own knife at Chase and dodged a second blow. Chase managed to catch hold of Handsome's thumb then bend it back until the knife clattered to the floor.

Samantha scooped up Zoric's weapons in a fluid, graceful move then sighed. "Oh, Handsome." She handed the Serbian back his weapons as Chase kicked the second knife away then reached for his gun on the floor next to the stove. He shifted his attention to the two women in time to see them do a fist bump. "Good job," Sam offered sarcastically. "It seems men everywhere enjoy a good cat fight."

Tessa rolled her eyes and reached out to pat Handsome's arm.

"What is going on between you two," Zoric grumbled as he put away the knife. "Fist bumps?"

"Don't get used to it." Tessa took in a deep breath.

"Mommy?" It was Heather standing up by the couch, rubbing her eyes. "I gotta go potty." The little girl wobbled around the end of the couch and rubbed her eyes.

Tessa waved the others back as she scrambled to reach her

daughter. "Okay, baby. Come this way." She took the little hand in hers then led her away. In a few minutes, she returned carrying Heather in her arms, pressed against her chest.

"Where's Handsome?" Heather mumbled through a yawn.

Handsome came up alongside Tessa. "I'm here." Heather pushed back from her mother and offered a sleepy smile at the giant of a man. He tenderly touched her curls. "Go to sleep. Mommy needs her rest. Okay?"

She nodded then fell back against Tessa. "Okay," she whispered.

Tessa tucked her under the covers on the couch then took a moment to gaze on her sweet face. She fussed with the covers on the boys before touching their heads with a kiss she placed on her fingertips. The feeling of love nearly overwhelmed her, remembering how she'd nearly been lost forever in a wild land, void of humanity and respect. If it hadn't been for two dangerous men, she never would have returned to love and cherish her family.

"Asleep?" Chase whispered as Tessa and Handsome returned to the kitchen.

"Yes. Keep your voices down or all of them will be up. I don't want them to know about any of this." When they exchanged glances, Tessa understood there would be no more arguing or posturing, at least inside the house.

The lights over the stove and sink flickered back on, illuminating the kitchen with low light. She could feel Chase's eyes on her as she moved to make coffee for everyone. Their relationship had suffered because of the things she'd done in Afghanistan. Overwhelmed at being in a war-torn country, she had been on the brink of breaking her vows to Robert, a good man who remained clueless concerning what she did for a living.

She pictured Chase all action and fireworks, where Robert was hot chocolate and a good romantic comedy movie. Until she'd been dragged kicking and screaming into Enigma, Robert had seemed like a rock star to her.

Things grew complicated as she transformed into an action junkie. She always survived by the seat of her pants, thanks to a bunch of sketchy agents promising they were doing good for the country. Robert would never understand the risks she took when it could jeopardize their family. Something needed to change. Should she leave Enigma and go back to a life where the most exciting thing she did was find a new toilet bowl cleaner for messy boys? Thankfully, until today, the children were not exposed to the things that really did go bump in the night.

"I need to know what this is all about." Tessa poured a cup of coffee and handed it to Chase.

Sam, Zoric, and Handsome slipped out the back door, informing him they were going to have a chat with the prisoners in the shed. Carter and Vernon needed to get in out of the cold as well, so they were going to relieve them. "Conflict diamonds. I think."

"I'm being followed because of conflict diamonds?"

"Not sure." He took a sip of coffee then rubbed a spot on his chest.

Tessa had seen him do the gesture so often she almost forgot this time it might be because Handsome had hurt him. She stepped closer, pretending it was concern, knowing it was because his existence was magnetic. "Are you hurt? You keep rubbing your chest." She longed to touch the spot, but he'd only move away. Enigma agents didn't always like to be touched unexpectedly.

He took another sip then narrowed his eyes at her. "I'm good." He stepped away to top off his cup. "Handsome doesn't know his own strength." His back was to her. "About the diamonds…"

"This seems a little odd to me, considering this is California and conflict diamonds usually are associated with African interests. The Kimberly Process has reduced much of the conflict trade, maybe as much as 90 percent. The United Nations data supports this."

Chase rested his back against the counter, smiling.

"Why are you smiling? What's so funny?"

"You. I love it when you morph into an academic and get incensed about the injustice in the world." He chuckled then took a long drink of his coffee before peering over the edge of his cup at her, as if masking an emotion threatening to rise to the surface.

The *love* word took her by surprise. She nervously rubbed the side of her jeans while raising her chin, in what she hoped was a defiant pose. "Glad you find me amusing."

"I find you a lot of things," he offered as he stared at her with laser-like focus. "Amusing is only one part of you I—"

"Hey!" It was Vernon coming through the mudroom.

"Shhh!" Both Tessa and Chase held a finger to their mouths as they nodded toward the living room.

Vernon shrugged and offered a lopsided grin before whispering, "Sorry." He spread his computer gadgets on the table and sat down to work.

Tessa shifted her attention back to Chase and dared approach him until she stood about a foot from his body. "You were saying?"

Chase set his cup down then folded his arms across his chest. He let his gaze caress her hair and face. His deep-brown eyes showed no emotion; only his high cheekbones tightened and released as he appeared to mull over what to say. When his eyes darted to Vernon then back to her, she knew the chance of an honest conversation about his feelings had evaporated.

"Yeah. Conflict diamonds. We got word someone at the UN might be on the take. In the last two years, four hundred fifty thousand carats have been funneled out of Africa. They've been difficult to trace."

"What do you want me to do?"

"This is not my area of expertise, and you are all over geopolitical conflict issues."

"Why haven't you spoken to the State Department or, I don't know, maybe the CIA about taking an interest?"

"Our Enigma benefactors are nervous. They don't trust the government, and we don't want to tip our hand. They aren't big fans of the UN to begin with, so I couldn't even bring in other geographers from the university."

Tessa had learned early on wealthy business men throughout the world, mostly the United States and Canada, controlled the purse strings at Enigma. Even though the FBI, CIA, and a multitude of other government agencies knew of the allusive organization, none of them suspected it was privately funded, except for President Buck Austin. It had been his brainchild, and it didn't take much to encourage others to foot the bill. The catch was the benefactors had no say. Other than being watchdogs to what they deemed a threat, their interaction with the group was nonexistent. What they received was justice, security, and the ability to continue propping up the economies of the world, therefore preventing it from falling into chaos.

The possibilities stacked up in her head as she toyed with the search avenues and scenario strings she'd follow. She envisioned a political domino game with all the pieces stacked perfectly straight until something tipped the very first piece.

She blinked away the thought to discover Chase staring at her again. "Thinking."

The corner of his mouth lifted. "I know."

"I still don't understand how or why I was targeted, Chase, or why you guys rushed up here."

Vernon clicked his tongue and showed her Handsome's mug shot and criminal record on his computer screen. "Might want to read this before he gets back inside." He stood up and offered her his chair. "Anything to eat?"

She pointed to the Crock-Pot smelling of overcooked beans. Easing into the chair, she propped her elbows on the edge of the table then read the report. Several times, she glanced up to see Chase watching her even as Vernon chatted in his ear and took a spoonful of beans.

A chill engulfed her as she continued to read one report then another about the man she'd allowed in to protect her and the children. She'd even gone into the dead of night through a blizzard to this high mountain cabin, trusting he was one of Enigma's finest. But was there such a thing? She knew the kinds of things these people did for a living, and having a heavy conscience was not a job requirement.

They often joked she was their moral compass and how annoying it was at times. Their ideals were black and white. Hers were shades of gray with blurred lines leading to the belief that good trumped evil. But she'd come to realize it took people like Enigma to give good a chance.

Carter came into the kitchen and quickly removed his coat then joined Tessa. She was never easy about him standing so close. His reputation as a lady's man and thrill seeker hadn't helped him at NASA when serving as an astronaut. After getting the boot for his antics he fell in with Enigma; a perfect fit. But even so, she found him irresistible and couldn't help but feel affected by his boyish charm.

He whispered in her ear, "What, no hello kiss or thanks for the rescue?"

Tessa reached up and patted his cheek. "Go away. I'm busy."

He laid a hand on her shoulder for a moment, his way of showing she belonged. Even though he hit on a wide range of female types, he'd pretty much given up on her, thanks to Chase. He chuckled, and her gaze darted to Chase, his expression stone cold.

"How's it going out back?" Chase asked as Carter joined him at the coffee pot.

"Oh, the usual. They resist. Zoric gets excited about cutting something and scares the hell out of them. Throw Sam and Goliath into the mix, and I wouldn't want them sitting in my car unless they had a change of clothes." He chuckled in his good-natured way then faked a punch at Vernon who dodged and fell against the counter, rattling some dishes.

"Shhh!" Tessa warned.

"Why am I always the good guy," Carter mumbled as he picked up a metal toaster and peered at his reflection. After he gave himself a wink, he grinned at Tessa. "I still don't know how you resist this."

Tessa continued to read but uttered softly, "I'm not good enough for you, Buzz Lightyear." She glanced up to see Carter elbow Chase, who pushed back.

Almost everyone tiptoed around Chase when it came to business, but not Carter. Life was one big opportunity to rub someone the wrong way. Sometimes Tessa enjoyed his cavalier attitude. It took the edge off many a serious situation.

Sam returned. She dusted off some flakes of snow from her long black hair pulled up in a ponytail. "Got word from the Highway Patrol. Filled them in on our situation. Said they'd be glad to take our prisoners into custody and transport them to Sacramento in the morning. On their way."

"Good."

"Not really. They already knew our location. No way I would give that information out, nor could the Highway Patrol ping off my phone. They don't have the equipment in the field. It's someone else. Better get ready." Sam jerked her chin up and cast a disgruntled gaze down her narrow nose at her. "Get your gear, Betty Crocker. We need to move your kids. Now."

CHAPTER TEN

Robert Scott discovered his bags in his car when the FBI delivered him back to his hotel. He'd fallen asleep in their car so he couldn't determine the distance from his hotel to the place of detainment. Maybe the feds had put something in his food or coffee to make him sleepy so he wouldn't know.

Although the driver of the black SUV dressed like the other agent he'd met, there was more of a military demeanor about him with the broad shoulders and short haircut. The only words he spoke were to answer his occasional question.

Yes. No. Maybe. We'll see. Hmm. Almost. Then repeat. His voice sounded raspy as if he weren't used to talking. The guy riding shotgun stared out the windshield as if in some hypnotic state of mind. He also appeared former military, especially with a couple of days' stubble on his face. All the feds he'd ever seen were impeccably groomed. After a while, Robert decided to lay his head back and doze.

The sudden jolt of braking and shifting the car into park snapped him to alert mode. He spotted his car instantly with the realization it had been moved to a more isolated area underground. It wasn't even the same parking garage. No matter. In two minutes, he would put this nightmare behind him and figure out what was going on.

"Your bags are in the back seat, Mr. Scott. You're gassed up and ready to go," the driver said as he opened the driver's side of the sedan.

"I need to pay my hotel bill." Robert stepped back, planning to head for the elevator.

"Unnecessary," the driver insisted as the guy who rode shotgun took an envelope from inside his suit coat and handed it to Robert. "All checked out."

Robert stared down at the outstretched envelope for a few seconds before relieving him of it. He couldn't decide if he should double-check the charges or trust them. One thing he didn't do was make eye contact. Standing in the dim light of a parking garage added to the unsettled vibe he got from the two men. Both of them were a good three to four inches taller than him and outweighed him, he guessed, by twenty pounds of muscle.

"Okay then. Anything else?" Robert slid behind the wheel and reached to pull the door shut, but the driver remained planted firmly in the way. "Guess I need my keys," he chuckled, knowing it sounded a little nervous.

"Yes. Of course." The driver pointed to the console. "You'll find them in there. Have a nice day, Mr. Scott." He pushed the door shut, stepped back with his sidekick, and continued to stare at him.

Robert turned the key and powered down the window. "I neglected to ask Agent Martin about contacting Reeva's company about her death."

Both the men stood with their hands clasped in front of them, their faces buried in shadows.

"We'll handle everything, Mr. Scott. No worries."

"What will I tell my law firm about all—"

"Mr. Scott, you'll tell them you had a very nice dinner with the lady and she promised to be in touch. Understand?"

Robert had opened his mouth to ask another question when the driver stepped closer and reached through the window to yank him so close he nearly touched the man's nose.

"Keep your mouth shut, Mr. Scott. We'll let you know if there is anything else we need from you. Go home and take care of that pretty wife of yours, play ball with the boys, and rock your baby girl to sleep. I'm sure you don't want Tessa to know you were with another woman tonight."

Robert felt his mouth go dry and sweat form under his arms. "No. No, I don't."

The driver released his collar then patted it back in place like a loving father before straightening his tall frame. "When you exit the garage, you'll need to go right, Mr. Scott. Drive another three blocks, and I'm sure you'll find your way from there."

Robert chewed his bottom lip as he put the car in reverse. He probably drove a little too fast leaving the garage, but he didn't want any more time with those two. Maybe he'd stop on the outskirts of the city to get more coffee to stay alert. It concerned him they knew his wife's name and that he had three children. Should he expect the FBI to be able to find out such things, or was he being paranoid? Either way, he certainly didn't want Tessa to know about Reeva. The whole situation appeared scandalous. He would never make partner at the law firm under such scrutiny.

He found an all-night coffee and donut shop once he'd reached the outskirts of Vallejo. Since it was a well-lit area and a number of cars were already parked near the door, he decided to stretch his legs. Before leaving the car, he grabbed his small shaving bag out of his suitcase and carried it inside with him, flinching at the bright lights.

He ordered two bear claws and a large vanilla cappuccino, found a booth by the plate-glass windows, and set his order number on the edge of the table. Taking a deep breath, he pulled a prescription bottle out of the shaving bag with the label Amoxicillin. His dentist had insisted he take the meds for some infection he found around a tooth scheduled to be pulled in a few days. Squeezing the lid off, he peered inside then dumped the contents into his hand. After he placed each pink pill back in the container, there remained four shiny things.

Diamonds.

~~~

Tessa let Handsome carry Heather to her car as the boys grumbled and plodded alongside. They didn't comment on the others hiding in the shadows, a good sign she wouldn't have to explain why five dangerous-looking people had joined them.
~~~

"Everything okay, Mom?" Sean Patrick yawned as he shivered against the cold.

"Yes, sweetheart. Handsome heard the highway would be open for a while and has offered to take us home." Did she sound as nervous and terrified as she felt?

"How will he get back?" Daniel scooted to the middle of the back seat and buckled himself in. He helped Handsome figure out Heather's car seat safety belts as his big brother squeezed in next to him.

"Not to worry, Daniel." Handsome reached over, patted him on the head, and smiled. "A couple of friends will meet me in Grass Valley. I don't have to work today, so there's no rush to get back." He patted Heather on the cheek and gave her a wink.

Daniel's yawned caused a chain reaction. By the time the car pulled out onto the side road, that required four-wheel drive, the children were once again sleeping.

Tessa rested her head back for only a second to collect her thoughts before speaking. "Not to second-guess you, Handsome, but are you sure about this road being safe?"

"Sounds like a second-guess." His voice held the excitement of someone watching butter melt. "Captain Hunter would not let me take you or the children if he thought you wouldn't be safe with me."

Tessa closed her eyes, fighting sleep. "I know," she whispered. "Sorry. I'm running on fumes. I can't think straight." This time she couldn't hide the quiver in her voice.

"So, is there something going on between you and"

"Absolutely not," she moaned. "Nothing going on with anybody. The captain thinks I'm inept and wouldn't be able to find my way out of a paper bag."

He chuckled.

Tessa sat up straight and frowned at her driver. "Chase tends to be a little overprotective at times. I think he believes if he doesn't treat me like a baby sister, I'll screw up his life and put the team in danger."

"A man doesn't stare at his baby sister like he stares at you." Handsome stopped the car and switched off the engine. "We wait here. If those guys are coming, we'll be hidden. Twenty minutes at most. Then we'll go."

Tessa released her seat belt and twisted around to throw an afghan over the children. The early morning hours remained cold. Snow periodically fell like clouds then cleared to delicate flakes. They were snug in their coats, hats, and mittens, so she believed they would stay warm until they could start the car again. Fear for her children gave her no choice but to trust this man. Her heart pounded in her ears.

"There," Handsome whispered as headlights appeared in the distance. Their white car blended with the snow and was parked far enough back into the trees, there didn't seem to be any risk of being discovered. "It's a Highway Patrol car. Probably the guys Sam warned us about."

"What if they were legit?"

"What if they weren't?" Tessa watched him track the passing vehicle then turned to her. "You second-guessing her, too?"

"I've always found it healthier to second-guess Samantha Cordova. She would like nothing better than to get rid of me."

"She's a piece of work, all right. Don't trust her, either. Somebody who is that beautiful and carries a gun means trouble."

"I know! Right? I knew you and I had something in common." Tessa wanted to believe her comment, but it came out like a half-hearted compliment. "Tell me. How do you know these guys? Were you recruited in college or the military?" He didn't seem like the college type and didn't act disciplined enough to be military. Whatever had brought them together turned out badly, it seemed. The CIA popped into the rational side of her brain, but she decided not to ask such a direct question. He'd only lie.

Handsome gripped the steering wheel. "Recruited? More like blackmailed. I was doing a little freelance work in Africa a few years back for some diamond brokers. Wanted me to get their goods past the UN sanctions so they could increase their profits."

"Conflict diamonds," she whispered.

"Some thought so. I believed they were greedy and wanted to bypass a process targeting their countries for possible conflict diamonds. After all, there were outbreaks of fighting in those areas. It wasn't like they cared who was fighting who or even the reason. They only wanted the profits. It might surprise you to know there are actually people who will pay top dollar for conflict diamonds."

"Why on earth would they want conflict diamonds knowing the pain and suffering they inflicted?"

Handsome shrugged and started the engine. "Some kind of romantic notion, I suppose. Money to be made." He eased the vehicle forward. The sound of crunching snow and the click of Tessa's seat belt mingled with the soft snores of her children. "Things were not so good back then. I was not sure of my direction."

"And here you are, shepherding us to safety."

"Don't give me any wings or a halo. I'm doing this to help myself. The folks of Enigma tried to recruit me because I have certain contacts and skills. They got me out of a hellhole prison in Tunisia."

"What did you do?"

"Doesn't matter. I will tell you I was framed by your boyfriend Captain Wise-Ass Hunter. All a setup so I'd come to work for Enigma."

"For one, he's not my boyfriend. Two; they don't set people up to work for them."

"Really?" He waited before pulling out onto the partially cleared road. "How did you come to work for them?"

"Totally different." Tessa experienced a couple of flashbacks of their tumultuous beginnings.

"You keep telling yourself that. Pretend you have a choice. Try to leave them sometime and see what happens to you."

"I have the ear of the president."

He chuckled in a sinister tone. "Yeah. We all do." He glanced over at her.

She realized her mouth had dropped open to speak but nothing came out.

"What? You think you're the only one who the president strokes to get what he wants?"

"Let's talk about you, not me. What did they do to you?"

"I'm done talking. Get some sleep. I'll take you home, and life will be good."

Tessa didn't want to hear anything questionable about Chase or the rest of the team. She decided it might be better to take it up with him the next time they met. For all she knew, Handsome Jones was a liar or worse. She trusted the team. If they held back information from her, then it was for a good reason. With all they'd been through together, Enigma had earned the right to demand her loyalty and trust.

As her eyelids grew heavy, she considered Robert. How would she explain Sean Patrick's call for help? Letting a strange man into her car, escaping into the night to some unknown cabin in the woods, a car chase ending with her stabbing car tires… How would she give all that a positive spin? Robert would listen to the children babble on about their skiing trip then move to the adventure that followed. She needed to be prepared for her husband's reaction.

She didn't deserve such a good man. He loved her. There were no surprises to come back to haunt him. If he knew all the chaos and mayhem she'd been involved in the last two years, he'd put his law degree to good use and divorce her. All he knew was President Buck Austin was extremely grateful she'd saved his life and ensured she got a plush job with the State Department while she worked on her Ph.D. in geopolitical conflict.

When work got crazy at the law firm, he bordered on being an absent father. The boys learned early on their father couldn't be counted on to make every game or even practice some old-fashioned catch in the evenings because he was too tired. But he loved his children and often bragged on them. Heather managed to weave some kind of a spell over him, like little girls do. She pouted if he didn't swing her up in his arms when he came home at night. Even when he tried to discipline her, it never worked out like he planned.

"I love my family," Robert would say when he kissed her good night.

"And we love you," she responded.

Their love had been tested in the last two years, with Enigma placing demands on her life that became difficult to handle even when nothing went wrong. Something took over her common sense when it came to doing their so-called "patriotic duty," to make life safer for her children. The reality of her situation was she loved the adrenaline rush that resulted from being on the edge of chaos and danger. For the first time in her life, Tessa felt alive and cherished every single moment.

The relationship with Captain Chase Hunter remained

complicated. Part of the time she considered him a bully with a god complex. Other times, he morphed into an action hero you might see pictured on a video game. She'd lost count of the times he'd pulled her from the fires of destruction. Strong, ethical, dangerous, and a military hero didn't seem to cover how she really thought of him. Yes, she understood her hero worship was a slippery slope, especially when there were times he implied he'd like to explore other avenues of pleasure.

But the desire in his eyes faded after she returned from Afghanistan. With the horrible acts she'd committed to survive in such a godforsaken country, it had taken a great deal of therapy to regain some of her old self. Then there was the tribesman who'd stolen her heart when she thought all was lost. No matter the amount of therapy, she wasn't likely to forget him anytime soon.

Chase had rescued her from a life of hardship and insisted she face her sins. He risked his own life so she could return to her Mayberry-type life in Grass Valley. Thankfully, Robert remained clueless as to the seriousness of her situation when abandoned in Afghanistan. He continued to think of her as the perfect wife and mother. Chase ensured her husband remained in the dark. With life getting back to normal, she still couldn't prevent Chase from appearing in her dreams at night.

"Mrs. Scott?" Tessa jerked up straight in her seat and rubbed her eyes. "We've got company."

CHAPTER ELEVEN

Tessa fumbled for her phone in her purse and realized she had no service. She tried to access the same button in the glove box her son had used the day before.

"Mrs. Scott? How can I help you?" The voice was male, with a slight British accent.

"I'm being followed by someone impersonating Highway Patrolmen."

"Okay. Our satellite is having trouble seeing you because of the dense cloud cover, but you are on our radar. Let me see if there is help nearby." In a few seconds the voice returned. "If you can lose them, there is a side road on your right about a half mile ahead. There should be cover not too far in."

Tessa glanced over at Handsome, who nodded then sped up.

"There is a note on your account. Did Mr. Jones locate you earlier?"

Handsome seemed to be concentrating on the road.

"Yes. He was able to secure a safer location for us. He's with me."

There was a pause, some static, and a slight cough. "Very good, Mrs. Scott. And the children?"

Tessa glanced back at her sleeping angels. "Asleep. I want to get them home where it is safe."

The voice deepened, and the British accent disappeared. "Then you probably shouldn't be riding with Handsome Jones, Mrs. Scott."

Handsome faced her for only a few seconds, revealing an angry frown and wide eyes. "Disconnect!"

Tessa obeyed and began a frantic back-and-forth twist in search of trouble.

"We may need to switch cars. We're not following those directions. If they are tracking us, we need to hustle."

"But we don't have another car."

"I have one not far from here." Handsome took a sharp turn into a narrow dirt road.

"I thought you came to find us on a snowmobile." It had all been a lie.

He shook his head. "I did, but… You're a very trusting person."

~~~

Vernon tapped his keyboard for the third time. "Sorry, Boss." He closed the laptop. "Someone has blocked my signal. I can't find them. I backtracked to the help-and-rescue line, and they haven't heard from them, either."

"Maybe it's good if they haven't asked for help." Chase chewed on his bottom lip as the rest of his team came in from searching the area.

"You're probably right. But they did say their system was down about five minutes with some unknown interference. They checked, and no distress calls came through during the span of time we needed. I asked if they could locate them."

"And?" Chase growled his impatience.

Vernon avoided his narrowed gaze by packing up his equipment. "She said it appeared they were being followed. She tried to call Tessa, but the line went dead."

"Dead? So, what you're telling me is someone has hacked into our secure system and is about to intercept Tessa and her kids?"

"Guess so. And I think Handsome knows it."

"Explain."

"Dispatch inquired about Mrs. Scott because the first person they sent to help her ended up in a ditch after taking a sharp turn.
~~~

Snowplow spotted him after seeing a light-colored late model sedan run up on him and give him a little nudge into a snowdrift. They were able to get him some help. He was unconscious when the ambulance took him away. If they hadn't come along when they did…"

"I get the picture," Chase snapped.

"That's when Handsome got the call. He, and you'll like this, was already in the neighborhood. Maybe he pushed the first guy off the road."

"So, we have double trouble. We're assuming our mystery trackers are after whoever hacked their system and Handsome is mixed up in this somehow."

Sam and Carter packed up what little gear they'd brought in while Zoric returned to keep watch outside. Even though they didn't comment, their sideways glances indicated a rising concern.

"We should never have left him in Tunisia." Vernon pushed his glasses up on his nose before pulling on a sock cap over his mop of unruly red hair falling to the bottom of his neck. When he noticed Chase glaring at him, he gathered up his computer bag and backed toward the door. "I'm saying maybe we should have investigated the story about Handsome's real identity."

Chase stormed toward him, only to brush past so fast he fell back against the refrigerator. "Let's go. Not waiting."

This time, Chase got behind the wheel. Driving helped him focus. It didn't matter if the weather sucked, the music blasted, or if conversation bordered on confrontation. The road gave him clarity. Nothing distracted him when the engine roared to life. He loved cars, especially old ones he could tinker with or restore. He'd realized years ago, engines could be controlled, manipulated, and improved—unlike the human elements he dealt with on a daily basis. With a vehicle, the unexpected could be evaluated or explained. Now he would think, plan, and anticipate the unknown enemy. What he refused to do was let Tessa Scott cloud his judgment.

~~~

Robert pulled into the garage and switched off the ignition. He sat there pondering his next move. What would he tell Tessa about
~~~

the evening's events or even why he was home so early from the conference? She would flip out over this with her little-Miss-Perfect attitude. He had to admit the decision to let a strange woman into his room to examine diamonds had disaster written all over it. Once again, he'd let the prospect of bringing in a big account to the firm, thus increasing his year-end bonus, overtake any hope of common sense. Why did he do these kinds of things? Because he was stupid and greedy. He banged his fists on the steering wheel and gritted his teeth.

His parents had been thrifty to a fault. Even so, there was never much money; his clothes came from end-of-season sales or discount stores. Money meant success to him, along with what you had to show for it. He invested religiously so the kids would be able to go to college. He'd paid off his own school loans only recently. Tessa had fallen in love with their urban country house with a touch of Victorian charm, and he'd managed to get it in a short sale for half its original price. Even so, with three kids, a mortgage, and a wife who wanted to be a stay-at-home mom, he seemed to be always paying bills.

When she took the job at the university in Sacramento with a very hefty salary, things got easier. Several times, he'd feared she'd quit, especially after returning from Afghanistan. Whatever happened over there, she avoided talking about it to him in spite of his encouragement to share. A therapist by the name of Dr. Wu, who worked at the university, brought her back to the cheerful, loving wife he'd married. There were still issues in the bedroom, but he didn't want to rush her. He imagined some horrible things she may have witnessed or experienced in such a godless land.

For some unknown reason, the President of the United States opened doors for her Robert thought impossible to open. His chief of staff called several days after she'd returned from Afghanistan to check on her condition on behalf of the president. Robert sometimes felt like he walked in his wife's shadow. All he wanted was for his wife to be happy and love him, in spite of his faults. The last year had helped him realize how precious and special others saw her. Yet, there remained something elusive and secretive about her that only managed to make him love her more. Maybe she realized, after working occasionally for the State Department, she could do better than him.

He needed to step up and do more as a husband and father. Truth be told, he wasn't very good at it. Tessa never tired of playing with the kids, preparing lunches, planning meals, and managing the household responsibilities besides working on her Ph.D. in geopolitical conflict. When he got home from work, all he wanted was to veg out in front of the TV and watch the news or his favorite show.

Even though he adored his kids and dreamed of bright futures for them, he struggled with communicating his feelings. He'd grown up in a home where his father never expressed love toward him, although his actions proved otherwise. Sometimes he wished he was still alive to talk to him about it. His mother, kind and loving, reminded him of Tessa.

Something had changed between them. What had he done to make her act so independent? Not so long ago, she'd needed his advice and reassurance on almost everything. Perhaps he'd taken advantage of her insecurities. She'd been a country girl from Tennessee when he'd married her. He had been her first real love and certainly her first sexual experience. Nothing prepared him for the love she showered on him at every opportunity. The feeling of devotion waned between them, like an old married couple, more friends than lovers.

He was scared he was losing her.

As the garage door lowered, he pulled out his cell phone and noticed a missed call hours earlier from Tessa. His eyes darted to the empty space in the garage where her SUV should be parked. Where was she? He retrieved the message, but it was too garbled to understand. The text message indicated they'd decided to stay one more day.

"What a relief," he groaned out loud. "I can pull myself together."

Maybe he'd surprise Tessa and have dinner ready when she got home, or do a load of laundry. She'd be thrilled to have one less thing to do. First, he wanted to take a shower and maybe a nap. The long night of unexpected terror had left him exhausted. A yawn took over as he exited the car and stumbled toward the back door. He had time to get things in order.

~~~
~~~

Tessa stared in horror at her driver. "Handsome? What was the guy talking about?"

"No idea. But as I said, we're not taking his directions."

"That wasn't Enigma I was talking to, was it?"

"Not likely. Could be the center has been breached."

A gulp escaped into the icy air as Handsome glanced over at her, anger playing at the corner creases of his eyes. "Who are you?" she whispered.

"Nobody." The car slowed and pulled into the driveway of a large log cabin. He managed to maneuver the car around as he pulled off into a stand of trees behind a large boulder. "I'm nobody," he sighed again.

Tessa reached in her purse for her phone, only to have him snatch it away.

"I want to call Chase immediately. Give me the phone or—"

"What? You going to try and take it from me?" He released his seat belt and faced her. "I mean you no harm."

She couldn't keep her voice from quivering. "My kids—I need to know you won't hurt them."

"They are safe with me." His voice held the emotional depth of a slice of cheese.

She closed her eyes to say a quick prayer only to have the image of Captain Hunter loom up in her memory. Something warm and wonderful sprang up between them for mere seconds when they'd left the cabin.

"It's going to be okay, babe," he'd whispered as he slipped his rough hand around the back of her neck and squeezed.

A gentle rub to her shoulder blade followed as he let his palm come up to touch her cheek. His eyes had mellowed, as if he wanted to share something more personal. He hadn't called her "babe" for a long time. He used the endearment when they found themselves alone and he let the mask of superhero expose his more human side.

The boys had called to her from the back seat or she would have laid her hand on his, to show him a hint of the affection welling up inside her. He stepped back so not to be spotted. Handsome had tapped on the roof of the car, drawing their attention then tilted his head for her to get in the car. She opened the door and shifted her gaze to Chase and mouthed the words, "Be careful." He nodded as the others came up to stand beside him. They would take care of the threat headed their way. They never failed. Never.

A tear squeezed from her eye as she wondered if they'd been misled as to where the danger really intended on going.

"Stay here." Handsome opened the car door.

"What? Where are you going?"

He continued to push himself out of the vehicle then bent down to glare at her. "Lock the doors. I'll do what I can if they come. Get behind the wheel and run over anyone who gets in the way. Can you do it?" She opened her mouth but nothing came out. "Can. You. Do. It?"

She nodded and threw her leg over into the driver's side, attempting an awkward transition. As she righted herself, he quietly shut the door and waited for her to secure the locks. Tessa moved the key in the ignition before stealing a glance at Handsome who continued to watch her, his nose nearly pressed against the window. Then he jerked upright to stare out into the darkness from which they'd come. She couldn't see because of the boulder and stretched to the passenger side in hopes of getting a glimpse of whatever spooked him.

When she straightened again, Handsome had disappeared. Her right leg trembled as it pushed on the brake.

With an adjustment to the rearview mirror, she noticed Sean Patrick staring at her with wide eyes. His contorted expression helped her realize she needed to solve this problem all on her own. One last time she tried to see where Handsome might be hiding, but something so big couldn't stay hidden. He'd left them alone to be bait, to delay his capture. Was someone coming for them, or did he want to avoid capture if she got caught? She and the children could possibly be collateral damage if this were the case. Whoever these people wanted, her children were in danger.

Putting the car in reverse, she backed into the driveway so she could head straight out to the highway if need be. The coast remained clear as the headlights beamed ahead to give her confidence.

Then she approached the highway when a patrol car entered and paused. She braked slowly, bringing the car to a stop. Maybe they really were Highway Patrolmen, and she was safe. These could be the real good guys come to rescue her.

Suddenly they barreled toward her, and without thinking, she threw the car in reverse and hit the gas. She let loose a squeal of terror as Sean cried out.

CHAPTER TWELVE

The car plowed backward through the snow at a speed Tessa feared she couldn't control. On some level, the awareness her son, Sean Patrick, staring at her with eyes the size of quarters, drove her to concentrate then swerve the car where it angled into a narrow opening between two trees. No way would she be able to open the door in such a tight fit. The patrol car fishtailed when a tire hit a clump of snow turned to ice. To close the gap again, they accelerated as she backed between the trees. The unexpected trick caused them to slide past her as their brake lights came on.

Holding her breath, she floored the gas and spun out onto the drive once more. She caught a glimpse in the rearview mirror of the patrol car trying to circle around. She heard something thud against the back of the car then again when her side mirror shattered. A scream caught in her throat as the next shot hit her tire. She careened to the side of the road, burying her good tires in a snow drift.

Pushing the button to engage the four-wheel drive only produced a grinding sound and rocked the car enough to wake the other two children. She heard yawns and sniffles when Sean Patrick spoke softly to his siblings about going back to sleep.

The patrol car eased alongside her and almost stopped but

continued forward to block another attempt at escape. Both sides of the patrol car swung open their doors. They took their time exiting, probably having already noticed she didn't have Handsome with her.

Their brightly colored jackets almost glowed in her headlights as they stopped and stared at her. They exchanged words, the result being they each pulled out a gun then lowered it to their side. She hit the gas again without positive results but drew cynical smirks from the two.

When they proceeded in her direction, a huge figure stepped out of the woods behind them. Handsome. Covered in a white parka, he could've been invisible if not for the round, black face creating such a contrast. His steps lumbered forward, as he swung his arms to match the Michelin Man image he projected.

Tessa took a deep breath as her hands tightened on the steering wheel.

"Sean Patrick, can you get Heather and Daniel down into the floor?"

"Mom?"

"Sean Patrick!"

"Yes."

The click of release to his seat belt then two more followed. Daniel asked his brother sleepy questions as Sean Patrick pulled his sister down to the floorboard. He told Daniel to shut up, he'd explain later, and to stay quiet. For once, her second born didn't initiate his usual litany of absurd questions, which, depending on the answer, would follow with, "What if…"

Turning her attention back to the approaching threat, she waited until they reached the front bumper then laid hard on the horn. The sound covered Handsome's approach. One of the men grabbed her door handle but appeared to get distracted by a noise coming from his partner being tossed like an angry snowball into the ditch.

Handsome leveled his icy gaze on the man outside her window who raised his gun to shoot. Tessa grabbed a wayward straw lying on the dashboard with the wrapper still intack. She ripped the end off with her teeth and lowered the glass. Before he could get a shot off, she blew through the straw, sending the paper into his eye and throwing his aim off. The whish sound of the silencer still surprised her as she quickly closed the window. He stepped away this time as he took aim, but Handsome closed the gap between them faster than she thought possible for such a big man. The stout stranger, nearly as tall as Handsome, seemed able to hold his own as he wrestled to keep his weapon.

The rear doors of the patrol car flew open and two more men exited, ready to take on the big man from behind. Even the one in the ditch rallied and staggered to join in the fray. Tessa knew in her heart not even Handsome could overcome those odds. Apparently, they wanted him alive, or they would have killed him already.

When they'd wrestled him down, she spotted movement coming out of the woods. There was a grunt as one man jumped back then sprawled across the ground; a dark spot formed on the snow packed ground. Handsome was released as his captors diverted their attention to a new threat. Before she could assess the event unfolding, they were laying their weapons on the ground and raising their hands in surrender.

Two of the rescuers gathered the discarded weapons while the other two pointed their AR-15s at chest level. Even with white ski masks pulled over their faces, Tessa recognized the stance of each Enigma team member. She was wondering where Vernon Kemp might be, when a large SUV came down the lane and he hopped out, leaving the engine running.

Her kids rose from the back floorboard to check out the situation. She killed the headlights so not to bathe the scene in too much detail. She twisted in her seat, feeling the pounding of her heart begin to normalize. Even as a slow breath of relief escaped her mouth, she allowed herself to smile.

"Mom?" Sean Patrick couldn't take his eyes off the scene outside. He was her roughneck child who liked to come to the rescue of bullied classmates and protect his siblings when necessary. "What is going on?"

"Where's Handsome, Mommy? Is he okay?" Heather crawled up over the console to snuggle in her lap. Their noses touched and Tessa, once more, knew how blessed her life was compared to so many in the world.

"Yes. Everything is okay. We blew a tire. Handsome went to get help and…"

She jumped at a tap at her window, and managed to roll the window down. In spite of the white mask covering his face, she knew by the almost obsidian-colored eyes, Chase Hunter had once again rescued her.

"Everything all right, ma'am?" His voice, deep and clear, sent chills up her spine. Heaven help the person who tampered with his team or his country. And she often liked to think there would be a special kind of hell to pay if anyone harmed her. For some reason, the man had taken a special protective interest in her. Maybe it was because she was an "innocent" as he liked to say, or maybe it was something more personal.

"Yes. Thank you. A little shook up is all."

Sean Patrick stretched over the console and peered at Chase, his forehead creased liked a concerned military general. "Sir? What went down? Were those guys after Handsome? And who are you guys?"

Chase glanced back at the men being fastened into cuffs then to Tessa.

"We're the Highway Patrol, but more of a search and rescue squad." He addressed Sean Patrick and offered his charming smile. "We've been tracking these guys. They robbed a bank in Truckee, stole a patrol car, and hightailed it out of town."

"Wow!" Daniel squeezed himself in front of Sean. "Cool. Why were they here?"

"Probably on the lookout for another car to escape in. Doesn't take long to leave a trail when you stole a patrol car, so they needed to switch before we zeroed in on them."

"Is Handsome okay?" Heather reached through the window and touched Chase's mask then withdrew to lay her head on Tessa's shoulder.

Chase reached in and patted her head. Tessa knew from the way he'd smiled at the little girl he would be an easy target of her sweet manipulation. "Yes. Mr. Jones got a call off from his cell phone."

"Yes. He walked out to get a signal," Tessa quickly added to the lie. "Bless him."

"These guys probably saw your tracks, followed them in, and planned to take your car."

"So, our mom tried to save us?" Sean Patrick jerked his brother back and resumed his place over the console.

"Looks that way." Tessa noted a kind of sarcastic tone in his voice as she met his gaze. "We'll need to take your statement,

Miss—"

"Scott. Tessa Scott." She felt foolish pretending.

"Mommy, I want to go home. I'm tired. I miss Daddy."

Tessa kissed her forehead and sat her in the passenger seat then rolled up the window before removing the key. All she needed was for one of the kids to do something crazy to add to the chaos. "Won't be long." She clicked her seat belt as Chase opened her door. "Mommy is going to talk to this nice man about getting our tire fixed. Why don't you climb back to your car seat and cover up. Boys, help your sister, and you cover up, too."

She walked next to Chase as he moved away from the car. She saw Handsome rise from the ground and thought about some abominable snowman appearing at unexpected times. He shook himself like an animal repelling snow from its coat then rolled his shoulders as one of the team, Sam, talked to him. Even though her face and long hair remained hidden, she was the only one who could come to a fight like she was a million-dollar fashion icon.

"Are you all right?" Chase spoke out of the corner of his mouth as he continued to watch Handsome.

"How did you really find us?"

"When I rubbed the back of your neck, I put a tracker chip on your collar."

A chuckle escaped her trembling lips. "And here I thought you were being affectionate."

He stopped moving. "You'll know when I decide to be affectionate."

She repeated his words in a monotone. "You'll know when I decide to be affectionate."

He narrowed his eyes.

"So, why the tracker chip? If you didn't trust Handsome, why did you let him take us?"

"He doesn't have a beef with you. It's me. Besides, we thought we were in for a fight and didn't want the kids around."

She sighed and nodded. "I'm grateful. But Handsome left us. Told us to stay where we were." She went on to tell him about the voice at Command who sounded threatening.

Vernon nearly lost his footing as he approached, but Chase reached out to steady him. The tech genius listened as she told him about the cryptic message and voice. When she finished, he slipped his way back to the car. If anyone could get to the bottom of this, he could.

From the three faces pressed to the car window, it became obvious the kids hadn't obeyed. When she shook her finger at them, heads ducked out of sight.

"How am I going to explain this?" she asked in exasperation.

"You're a good liar. I'm sure you'll think of something. You always do," he quipped.

"I know you meant that as an insult, but any decent wife and mother has to be ready for a big, fat whopper once in a while to keep things running smoothly." She flashed him a bright smile, but he didn't seem amused.

"I see how marriage works. You lie to each other?"

Tessa sensed the conversation had moved into quicksand again. "I was kidding. You need to lighten up. I don't lie to Robert. We have a good marriage."

"A good marriage." The words came out so flat she thought maybe he was reciting the day's stock market report. "Did you ever tell him about the tribesman in Afghanistan?" She opened her mouth to speak, but he hurried on. "How about the little incident in an alley between me and you?" She stuttered a "but" as Chase continued his onslaught of truth. "And then there is the little matter of Libyan terrorists, the blood transfusion for the president, and me crawling into bed with you one night in the mountains." She could feel her face begin to transform to an angry scowl. "Nothing to say? Wow. Married life is pretty special."

Tessa pivoted to storm off, but he reached out to stop her. Jerking free she spoke through gritted teeth. "And those are secrets I was told I had to keep or Enigma would make my life hell. You guys pretend to be the best thing since peanut butter and jelly to this country, but the truth be told you are a bunch of ego-inflated bullies who like to jump into trouble because you get off on it. I bet you'd do it for free."

Carter walked up with Handsome and nudged Tessa away from her close proximity to Chase. "I don't like it when Mom and Dad fight," he teased. "Handsome, make them stop."

"Is he bothering you, Ms. Scott?" Handsome's voice reminded her of a bass drum in a parade.

Tessa took a deep breath. "No." Another deep breath. Why

couldn't they be civil to each other? She so loved the times they ate lunch together, talked about literature and politics, and even the weather. Those became special moments when they were people working at the university. "How am I going to get home?"

A plan took form between them. "We can get your car out, change the tire, and Handsome can drive you home," Chase said raising his chin toward the car.

Tessa eyed Handsome with concern. "You abandoned us."

"Yes. But I was there when you needed me. I would have been a liability otherwise."

"Okay, Handsome. I guess I have to trust you." Tessa shoved her hands in her pockets and walked away. "I'm getting tired of this nonsense, Chase."

He cut her retreat off. "This wasn't Enigma's fault, and I think you already are aware why." He shifted his gaze to her car. "Daniel stirred up a hornet's nest."

"Is he in danger?"

"We took care of it. But Vernon is going to have to put some safeguards in place from here on out."

"So, he'll be spying on us."

"Tessa, for once, will you let us do our job?" he moaned. When she didn't answer, he stepped closer to whisper. "I'd never get over it if something happened to you and the kids. Please. Stop fighting me so hard."

Her eyes batted in the nervous tic she had when he came too close or touched a nerve. "Under one condition."

"Name it."

"You and me need to straighten things out. I never know if you're my friend or babysitter. I want things to be normal again. Can we try?"

Chase stared at her for several seconds before answering. "We'll see when this is cleared up. I'm not promising anything."

CHAPTER THIRTEEN

Robert stood in the kitchen, trying to make himself some hot chocolate from a mix he'd found in the pantry. The marshmallows were a little tough as he dropped them into the hot brew, so he added a spoonful of whipped topping Tessa kept in the freezer. Then he rolled his eyes as he sipped; it was too cool and needed to be nuked in the microwave again.

He heard the garage door go up, followed by slamming car doors and laughter of his kids. It was a happy sound he appreciated more than ever after his ordeal the night before. Things could have ended up so differently. All he wanted to do was to hold his family close and kiss them, make love to his wife, and pretend nothing ever happened.

Maybe he should fess up to Tessa and tell her everything. Would she understand about being in a hotel room with another woman? Of course not. If the situation was reversed he'd be in a fetal position, crying like a baby he'd been betrayed, followed by hiring a really good lawyer. Better keep quiet. Tessa could be a handful when she didn't understand something which involved their family.

"Hello!" Tessa walked through the open door, carrying a gym bag of what he imagined would be dirty clothes. "Robert?" she called as the children pushed in yelling his name.

Robert set his cup down and scooped Heather up in his arms as the boys gave him a quick hug and talked at the same time, something about hiding, bank robbery, and their mom being a hero.

"Whoa. Slow down," he laughed as he put Heather down and reached for Tessa who appeared a little frazzled. He stepped toward her for an embrace as a huge black man pushed into the room. Jerking her behind him, he stared at the man carrying suitcases and a pink bunny rabbit.

Heather slipped by him and grabbed the bunny. "Thank you, Handsome. I almost forgot Pinkie."

Handsome nodded as his bottom lip jutted out and his bulbous eyes focused on Robert, taking him in from head to toe in a not-so-respectful way.

"Oh, honey, this is Handsome Jones. We ran into a little trouble yesterday and—"

"He hid us from the bad guys," Heather chirped in her singsong kind of voice.

"He helped catch some bank robbers, too, Dad," Daniel chimed in.

Robert pointed to Sean Patrick for clarification. He remained his no-nonsense kid. "Sean?"

He shrugged. "Handsome helped us get away from some creeps stalking Mom."

Tessa gave a nervous laugh. "It all sounds a lot more dramatic than it actually was. Right, Handsome?"

"Yes. Never know about scum coming off the interstate. They were up to no good and—"

"Mom stabbed their tires with Sean Patrick's knife, Dad," Daniel interrupted.

Robert knew his mouth had dropped open and his wife bore a very suspicious grin.

"Anyway," Tessa said shooing the children into the other room. "Long story short, Handsome put us up at his sister's place, fed us, and drove us home." She patted Handsome who still stood holding the suitcases. "Such a sweetheart. We can't thank you enough." She glanced at Robert. "Oh, and we had a flat tire, and I threw a rock that cracked the back window. I may have clipped the side mirror when I tried to back between two trees."

"Tessa." Robert felt both panic and anger.

She lifted a hand to stop him from speaking. "No worries. Already called the insurance company, and I can take it in when I go to work on Monday. You won't have to do a thing." She rose on tiptoe to kiss him on the mouth; the first time in a while. It both surprised and calmed him.

"Handsome," Sean Patrick said, walking back into the open and airy kitchen. "I think your ride is here."

Setting the luggage down, Handsome moved through the dining room then to the living room. When he entered the foyer, he took in the house, which was warm and cozy. Robert noticed he then focused on Tessa who gave him one of her warning looks. This usually held a special kind of control over the kids. He wondered if she'd told the whole story but quickly dismissed it.

"Kids, come say goodbye to Handsome and thank him for driving us home on such slick roads," Tessa encouraged.

The kids thundered to his side and thanked him like polite children should. The boys even shook hands with him. Heather used her index finger to motion for him to bend down so she could hug his neck.

"Thank you, Mr. Jones, for watching after my family. I'm sure Tessa will tell me all about it." Robert slipped an arm around her waist and pulled her to his side, which felt a little like marking his territory.

Tessa extended her hand, too. "Thanks again, Handsome. Take care. Oh, I think your friends are getting out of the car."

Robert could see them through the glass door as they exited the nondescript black vehicle. The driver came around to stand next to his buddy as Tessa opened the front door and waved to them. They raised their chins in greeting then folded their arms across their chests as if they had no place else to go.

Together, Tessa and Robert stepped out onto the wraparound porch to see Handsome lumber down the steps then out toward the waiting car. Heather ran outside waving a colorful picture.

"This is for Handsome, Daddy."

"I'll take it to him, baby girl. Go inside. It's cold." He patted her on the head and shooed her inside.

She smiled and obeyed.

"Be right back, Tessa. Our child has a great future working at the welcome wagon."

Tessa chuckled behind him as he ran down the steps and caught up with Handsome to gift him the picture, when he joined the two standing at the car. He froze when he identified the two men who had driven him back to his car in San Francisco the night before. Without their suits and ties, they resembled redneck brawlers.

"You!" he gulped.

A smirk played on the mouth of the one who had done most of the talking and threatening. The other straightened up, frowning down at him as if he might be used to picking guys like him out of his teeth on a regular basis.

"We meet again, Mr. Scott. Glad your family returned home safe and sound."

Handsome cast one last glance at Tessa standing on the porch then to Robert. "You know these guys?"

"We're old friends, aren't we Robert?" He extended his hand and kept it there until Robert reluctantly took his grip, which hurt like the dickens. It took great restraint not to grimace at the squeeze.

"Get off my property before I call the police," Robert growled under his breath.

The man almost grinned as he dropped Robert's hand and walked around the car to the driver's side. "Remember our little conversation last night, Robert, and you'll be fine."

Robert backed up as they slowly pulled around the circular drive then eased out onto the tree-lined street. He felt his body tense and wondered if he might be suffering a stroke.

When he walked back to the porch, he noticed Tessa staring after them, solemn, with a hint of skepticism plastered on her face. With arms folded across her chest and weight shifted to one hip, she chewed her bottom lip. This often meant she was about to tell him something he didn't want to deal with. Suddenly, her attention shifted to him, and he swore it felt like laser beams boring into him.

As he walked up the steps, Tessa stepped forward and slipped her arms around his waist. "This is a nice surprise. I didn't expect you until tonight. Did all go as expected in San Francisco?"

"So so. How was the skiing?" He really didn't want to talk about his experience. "And tell me about this guy you spent the night with?"

Tessa jerked back. "What?"

"Handsome. I want to hear everything, Tessa. I have a feeling you have more to add to the story." Robert loved feeling her warm body against his. They were getting reacquainted after her ordeal in Afghanistan. Maybe tonight would be the night to rekindle the flames between them. "You're acting a little mischievous."

Rubbing his back then letting her hand slide down to his buttocks, she kissed his lips tenderly. "I love you, Robert Scott."

"Good to know," he said leading her back inside the house. "Because I'm nothing without you. Remember that."

"I'm not likely to forget," she said, shutting the door with her toe. "Trust me."

~~~

Several miles from the university, an industrial center, once vibrant and busy producing everything from ball bearings and lawnmower engines to shelving units and pencils, stood with rusted metal walls. A few boarded-up windows and weeds dared to survive in cracked concrete. It resembled a sad epitaph of *Americans don't make things anymore*. Only the secure fences, electronic steel gates, and hidden cameras disguised as nests and lopsided debris suggested the four buildings had been repurposed for other interests. The few people who worked there also parked their cars inside through a back entry, hidden from the street.

Two of the buildings blocked the other two and held old equipment, cobwebs, and a few curious pigeons that had found their way inside to raise families. The other two buildings were used by Enigma from time to time to meet and set things in motion for an upcoming op. New polished concrete floors, tinted a pale blue, walls adorned with modern art, and skylights allowing light to filter in to keep the jungle of plants alive. Several platforms held work stations dressed with the latest high-tech equipment. Another area had been transformed into a gym.

The building included an open kitchen and enough seating to house twenty people at any one time. The furniture, although black leather, sported textured throw pillows of purple, green, and orange, as if someone wanted it to appear youthful. Wooden
~~~

lockers on the back wall gave an almost industrial feel and housed a variety of weapons and equipment. A narrow hall led to four sparsely furnished bedrooms with their own en-suite bathroom. Another section of the building held interrogation and observation rooms, much like the one on the outskirts of San Francisco.

This is where Handsome Jones was brought by his new handlers.

"Help yourself to the fridge, Handsome." Former Lieutenant Ken Montgomery shut the door behind them as First Sergeant Tom Cooper pointed to the kitchen area for their guests.

Both men were former military. Ken, a Ranger years earlier, had served with Captain Hunter. When his friend made the transition to Delta Force, they'd remained in touch.

Tom Cooper, a former Marine, met the captain on a training mission. Somewhere along the line, he'd been recruited to help Enigma. When it was time to reenlist, the quiet Marine decided to take advantage of Enigma's offer to be permanently on staff.

The two men both had connections to Tessa Scott. Marine Tom Cooper had suffered a blow to the head when she'd tried to escape Enigma custody a couple of years earlier. She'd bested him with nothing more than a broomstick to land him in the hospital. Her escape attempts both embarrassed and impressed him. If she hadn't already locked Captain Hunter in a cell, Tom would have been the butt of a great deal of harassment. He respected her bumbling attempts at courage and decided long ago she was one of the good guys.

Ken Montgomery felt more affection toward the Grass Valley housewife than his buddy since she'd saved him from a terrorist bullet. Although he'd taken a shot to the leg, which could be a killer on a rainy day, he could still remember the crazy-eyed glare of the man bending over him, ready to send him into the hereafter. Tessa, a scared little rabbit, took action to save him then promptly puked in a trash can at her actions. They'd worked together a couple times since then. She'd pulled her weight and then some, in spite of not knowing what the heck she'd gotten herself into. One thing for sure, trouble found her like a heat-seeking missile.

Having to scare the hell out of her husband the night before still rolled across Ken like a sudden hailstorm. Something about the man caught in his craw. He didn't buy the story of why he'd brought a woman to his hotel room. Robert felt like a prickle at the nape of his neck. Trouble. That's what it sounded like to him. In his mind, Tessa deserved better. Hell. They all did.

Now, the two former soldiers lived in this warehouse, transformed into a home of sorts. Neither one desired to live among normal people with normal lives since they'd left the military. They watched over the back door of Enigma, fought when called upon, broke the law when necessary, killed when no other option presented itself, and enjoyed the freedom this life offered to men who couldn't assimilate into society. Their unwavering allegiance to God, country, and Enigma, provided all either needed to survive.

"Pick a room down the hall. I imagine the captain will want you to stick around a day or two to debrief and figure out what this is all about. You can clean up if you like." Ken strolled to the refrigerator and pulled out three cold beers.

"A little early for drinking." Handsome sniffed in distaste.

The former Marine nodded as he grabbed one of the bottles. "It most certainly is." Ken held up his bottle and touched Tom's, as if toasting some accomplishment.

"How do you know Mrs. Scott?" Handsome surveyed the room and walked around the space as if calculating a way out. The Enigma men had seen this behavior before.

When Ken and Tom explained their connections, Handsome grinned. "She's kind of a whippersnapper, as my auntie used to say."

"You have no idea," the former Marine moaned as he touched the back of his head in memory of the concussion he'd received at her hands.

"I'm leaving." Handsome moved toward the exit and rattled the locked door. His eyebrow arched and his mouth puckered when he looked back to his new jailors who smiled between sips of beer.

Ken flopped down on an overstuffed chair then propped his feet up on a coffee table. "Yeah, I thought you might feel that way. Even if you knock us senseless, you won't be able to get out. So, I'd accept you're going to be our guest for a bit. But, hey, go ahead and try to find a way out. We're always trying to find out where our weak spots might be."

Tom rested against the island. "Oh, and so you know, the fence outside is electrified, too, in case you get out. We've also released the dogs to patrol around. Since they don't know your scent, it probably wouldn't be a good idea to mess with them. There are some doggie treats in the back if you want to try your luck."

"The pups need a good workout, Handsome." Ken belched then set his bottle down. "Not sure when the boss will get those two you captured at the cabin here or those other shady characters who seemed to be trying to find you. We've got some special accommodations ready for them. You might want to stick around and see what they have to say."

Handsome lumbered back into the kitchen area. "What makes you think they'll talk?"

Both men chuckled. Ken rubbed the stubble on his chin then addressed the question. "Oh, they'll talk. Zoric has a gift for encouraging people to talk. In the meantime, I'm going to cook some breakfast. How many eggs you want?"

Chapter Fourteen

“So, are you going to tell Tessa about her cheating husband?” Samantha Cordova sat down at the warehouse table across from Chase. “I’d be happy to do it. Please.”

Chase ignored her and continued going through some notes taken on the interrogation of their prisoners. He saved Handsome for last and wanted to make sure the direction the conversation needed to go before confronting him. His agent continued to stare at him over the brim of her coffee cup, as curls of steam lifted in front of her hazel-green eyes. The woman resembled a cat about to pounce on some unexpected prey.

“We don’t know for sure if he was cheating,” he said offhandedly, but not sure he sounded convincing. “Maybe you could tell me why you went for his jugular when you thought he had?” Chase leveled a dangerous glare at her, hoping she’d drop the subject.

Samantha took another sip before setting the cup down then stood up. “I think I’ll go see if Zoric needs any help cleaning up the mess he made in the back.”

“Good idea,” he growled in his usual contemptuous fashion.

Chase tired of the bickering flaring up between the two women on a regular basis. Although Tessa seemed to take the most hits of revenge, she could hold her own on the insults and innuendo in the most innocent of ways. Sometimes he believed each of the two combatants actually admired the other but was too full of pride to admit it. Samantha pretended to want to do bodily harm to the Grass Valley housewife, and Tessa mocked her with an absurd show of fear that only tended to enrage the senior agent.

"You want to talk to me?" The deep, bass-drum voice of Handsome drew Chase's eyes upward as the man towered over him. Something about his stance and doubled fists at his sides hinted at impending bodily harm.

Chase had to admit the man was intimidating enough to give him pause, so he slowly stood to demonstrate his own posturing. Handsome took a small step back. Since they'd tangled in Africa a few years earlier, Chase felt confident his prisoner wouldn't challenge him right away.

"Have a seat." Chase jerked his chin toward a nearby chair. Of course, the man chose a different seat, as he knew he would. "Need anything?"

"Your head on a chopping block," Handsome said casually.

Chase offered a thin smile. "Still pissed over Tunisia, I see."

Handsome remained stoic and silent, staring a hole into the leader of the Enigma team.

"Let's get any misunderstanding out of the way before we move on to other things. You shot the place up, wounding the ambassador's aide and his protection detail. A bomb exploded outside the hotel about the same time you and your band of misfits stormed in carrying automatic weapons. They were dressed like a bunch of ISIS wannabes yelling slogans typical of terrorists in North Africa—"

"What's your point?" Handsome interrupted.

"My point?" Chase gave an exasperated chuckle as he sat down, rocking back in his squeaky chair. "If your CIA buddies had taken the time to give us a heads-up as to the intel and half-baked plan you concocted, to root out the real threat, I wouldn't have hauled you in to the authorities. Not my fault they didn't rush in to save the day. I guess they didn't want to be connected with you, either. Who knew the agency would issue a burn notice on you." Chase smiled ear to ear. "You should be thanking me. I was the one who got Enigma to see some value in you."

Handsome's nostrils flared, but his glare remained sullen. "And what value could someone like me have for the powerful consortium bankrolling the powerful lapdogs of the president?"

"No need to continue the half-witted ruse of being not much more than a part-time employee at a convenience market. What were you doing outside of Truckee when Mrs. Scott needed help?"

"You tell me."

"This is what I know. Our houseguests in the back, who probably will require a few days of soft food and a transfusion, not to mention a change of clothes, indicated you were friends."

"You were misinformed." His body and composure remained icy calm. "They only wanted to take revenge on me because I caught them sneaking around then overpowered them. The ones who came after Mrs. Scott when you showed up seem to believe I owe them money."

"From what they tell me, and these are their words, you owe them about a million dollars in uncut diamonds. Know anything about that?"

"Nothing. Does this mean I soon will need a change of clothing? If so, let me write down my sizes for you to pick up a few things. I'm afraid I didn't bring anything else."

Chase took a deep breath. "I like you, Handsome. You never show fear."

"Thank you. Unfortunately, the feeling is far from mutual."

"You're probably going to like me even less before this is all over."

"You underestimate my feelings of contempt." Handsome cocked his head and raised an eyebrow as his lips moved in and out. "As to the diamonds, it is more like three million. Some unprofessional diamond merchants were stealing from the good people of Botswana, and being of African descent, I thought it my duty to show them the error of their ways." He smiled broadly. "You know, to honor my roots and all."

"You're full of crap, Handsome."

The smile faded from his face as he stared into the distance again.

"Something you aren't aware of," Chase continued, "is a few of your friends lured Mrs. Scott's husband to a hotel room last night. We aren't sure of the intent, but it didn't turn out so well." He pulled out a picture of the dead woman on the floor. "Is this a friend of yours?"

Handsome's eyes shifted to the picture then to Chase. "No."

"So, you don't know who this is?"

"I said she wasn't a friend of mind. That doesn't mean I don't know who she was."

Chase slammed his fist on the stainless-steel tabletop. "Stop playing games with me."

"Are you telling me Mrs. Scott's husband is dealing in illegal diamonds?"

"Right now, we think he is innocent of any wrongdoing except maybe trying to get a good deal on some diamonds for Tessa—I mean, Mrs. Scott."

This brought Handsome's gaze back to him. "I asked Mrs. Scott if the two of you were in some kind of relationship."

"You are a bit nosey. She is my agent, nothing more than a periodic pain in the neck who has endeared herself to the president. Not much I can do to change his mind."

This brought a burst of laughter that echoed off the sixteen-foot ceilings. "I guess that's why you disobeyed protocol and went after her in Afghanistan. Sounds more than a pain in the neck to me."

How did he know about the insane rescue attempt where he nearly got himself killed along with Zoric and Tessa? "And you sound like an incurable romantic. I would have done the same for any of my team."

Another belly laugh ensued then he slapped his hands together. "The mighty Captain Chase Hunter has a weakness, and her name is Tessa Scott. Lord, have mercy! You are human after all." He scooted his chair closer to the table and folded his hands over the dead woman's picture. "Okay. But there is something I want from you."

~~~

Dr. Andre Girard reached for the phone as it rang on top of his clutter-free desk. He closed a yellow folder and stacked it with other pastel folders, each color having a special meaning as to the section of the alphabet it belonged when he lifted the receiver to his ear.
~~~

"Hello. Dr. Girard speaking." He swiveled his chair to face the fading light of day behind him that created a cloud across the window pane. He needed to get those cleaned. "Hello," he repeated as he took a moment to remove his glasses and rub his eyes.

"Father?"

"Louis! My boy, it is good to hear your voice." The doctor pushed his chair back around and pulled a picture of his son from the top drawer. "Where are you?"

"In the States. Everything okay?"

"Yes. Yes."

"I miss you, Father. Are you well?"

"Yes, of course. And you? You sound tired."

The son chuckled. "You worry too much. How goes the practice in Florida? The weather suit you there?"

"I love it. The weather reminds me of the Okavango Delta. I try to go fishing on the weekends."

"Maybe I will join you soon. I miss our time together."

The doctor noted the warmth in his son's voice.

"When do you go back to Botswana to help at the medical clinic?" Louis asked.

"Not for a few months. Will you join me this time?" A father could hope.

"I will try, Father. The time draws near." The son paused, and the father waited. This wasn't the first time he'd received one of his cryptic calls. "Father, some people are searching for me. I want you to be safe. Do whatever you need to do to remain protected. Tell the truth, if necessary. I will be fine. I am in no danger for the moment. I have made some new and interesting friends."

Dr. Girard lowered his voice. "We have a plan. Nothing to worry about."

"And the prize?"

"Safe." He gave his son some directions as to where to find it.

"I love you, Father. Thank you for everything."

The doctor chuckled. "It has been my honor. You are my heart and soul. Without you, my life would have meant little."

"Be careful. I will try and see you soon if possible."

"I know. But there is still much to be done. Go with God, my son."

The caller clicked off.

~~~

Fingers drummed on a plastic sandwich container left on a laminate countertop. Besides a microwave, a mini fridge, coffeemaker, and a caddy of cutlery filled the already-crowded surface. The acrid smell of burnt coffee and greasy leftover pizza permeated the room. A ding brought a quick retrieval of the food from the microwave, followed by the hiss of a soda can being opened.

Robert had waited to eat lunch alone in the break room. Sometimes he worked through lunch so he could meet a deadline or go home early to have dinner with his family. A few times, he took a client to a nearby eatery or went with some of the attorneys from the firm to be one of the guys. He was on track to make partner soon. Why he'd been pushed toward a specialty of contested lands and acquisitions in disputed territories in foreign countries remained a mystery, except no one else seemed willing to take on the job. There wasn't much need for this kind of litigation in California. He'd probably dealt with three cases in the last five years, but he believed in time the specialty might become a lucrative endeavor for the firm. With Tessa's connections to Washington D.C., he hoped other doors might open for him. So he persevered and the law firm crowned him the expert. Mostly, he worked on cases involving commercial law, which was probably why the firm sent him Reeva. Now she was dead.

He couldn't get the image of her bloody body sprawled on the bathroom floor out of his head. Not his room, but whose? And who were those people who burst in on him and Reeva? He could have been left behind and suffered the same fate. Why on earth did they take him for interrogation then release him later?

Was it because the FBI knew of his wife's connection to the president? Unlikely, he reasoned, since the agent appeared to be local. His wife remained adamant about keeping her friendship with President Austin secret. Yet those thugs who returned him to his car knew her. Then they showed up at his house to get Handsome or whoever he was. He could have sworn the quieter of the two stared at his wife. When he'd glanced back, he thought Tess had transformed her body into that haughty stance she took
~~~

when her stubbornness kicked in: weight shifted to one hip, head slightly lowered to level a dangerous glare, and an arched eyebrow that could stop stampeding boys in their tracks. He'd asked her later who she thought they might be.

She shrugged. "Beats me. He said some friends would pick him up. He called someone on the way home. Actually, I dialed for him. You know. No text or calls while driving. I insisted on being safe."

"I didn't like their looks."

Then she kissed him on the mouth, long and passionately, and whispered how happy she was he came home early then promised a few things she planned to do to him after the kids went to bed. The kids apparently liked the big guy, and Tessa didn't appear to be concerned by his friends or him. So, as usual, he got distracted.

"Why so many questions, Robert?" Her eyes went wide. How innocent of the world his wife could be. "You don't think I would ever put our children in jeopardy, do you? I mean—"

"No. No. Lucky he came along when he did. You said the Highway Patrol showed up, right?"

"Yes. Handsome protected us. I'm so grateful. God is good." She sighed and walked away. "Why don't you hurry the children along to bed? They've been waiting for you to read them a story."

She continued to distract him the rest of the evening. Life was good again with his wife. Why muddy the waters with a confession of his lamebrain decision to take a woman to his hotel room? However innocent, the appearance of impropriety would not be lost on Tessa. How many times had she accused him of being a flirt or a little too friendly with the opposite sex?

Robert chewed slowly on his pepperoni pizza before taking a swig of soda. An involuntary hiccup escaped as he put a fist to his chest and burped. Heartburn would follow as he stewed about his future. He'd waited all morning for a tap on the shoulder or a phone call from the FBI or some clandestine entity who would inform him of what he should do, say or not say, so his life could proceed to something without trepidation and misgivings.

Arriving early, before he'd even hung up his coat, one of the partners strolled into his office to congratulate him on securing the diamond accounts from several large African conglomerates for the firm. He pumped his hand vigorously and flashed his glowing, whitened teeth.

"Good job, Robert. I knew you and Reeva would hit it off. Got an email this morning stating how impressed she was with you and her company would be reaching out ASAP." He straightened to his height of five foot five and placed his hands on his hips so his suit coat pushed back enough to reveal a white shirt that blended seamlessly with the smile. The deep-blue tie, crisscrossed in a pale-gold design, impressed Robert as expensive, unlike his own that Tessa had bought him from a local men's shop in Grass Valley.

"Email? Already?" Robert stuck his finger between his collar and neck.

"Yeah. We're very pleased." He landed a fist on his arm. "You didn't hear it from me, but we're going to offer you a partnership at our next quarterly meeting."

Robert stuttered then laughed. "I don't know what to say."

"Remember, mum's the word." Another fist to the shoulder occurred before he headed out the door.

Now, here he sat, alone with his jumbled thoughts about the future. If he told the firm about what really happened with Reeva, he'd not only not make partner but probably lose his license to practice law. Carrying the paper plate to the trash, he took the last sip from his can then dumped them in the stainless-steel reciprocal, when his phone vibrated in his pocket.

"Hello."

"Mr. Scott, this is Agent Martin." Robert wondered if his nervous gulp could be heard on the phone. "I wanted to touch base with you and set your mind at ease. We have a suspect in custody who has confessed to the murder of Reeva Kaplan."

"What a relief," Robert said as he peeked out the break room door then ducked back inside. "My firm had an email this morning from her saying she would do business with us."

There was a slight pause. "Yes. I see here she emailed someone about business being completed and they could count on moving forward. Must have been—"

"Yes. I can only imagine when it was, Agent Martin. What about those thugs who dragged me out to safety? Who were they?"

"Independent contractors who specialize in problem solving is all I can tell you. They aren't connected to the FBI or any other government agency I know of. Lucky they came along when they did."

"But—"

"And, Mr. Scott, if I were you I'd consider this a one-time get-out-of-jail-free card. Be careful next time who you take to your hotel room."

"I—"

"Have a nice life, Mr. Scott."

The line went dead. Robert couldn't resist pulling the phone out in front of his face, as if by doing so he'd be able to unravel all the cloak-and-dagger mumbo jumbo. No way would he be telling Tessa any of this. Agent Martin was right about one thing; he'd dodged a bullet, literally.

CHAPTER FIFTEEN

Director Benjamin Clark of Enigma considered his people some of the best in the country when it came to problem solving a national security issue. Since President Buck Austin took office, they had been given access to impossible scenarios needing a quick and speedy solution. Special Forces were needed for big ops, and other agencies covered things allowed under the law. Enigma wasn't bound by the law because, technically, they didn't exist. Their funding came from private individuals who desired solutions to insure economic stability in the world. Director Clark didn't have to tiptoe around Congress and plead for support or money.

He caught a glimpse of his reflection in the window overlooking the campus of Sacramento's University of Science and Technology. His short-cropped hair glowed more white than gray these days. Most men with such responsibility developed health issues or their appearance changed markedly, as exhibited by the US presidents when they left office. Benjamin Clark wasn't one of those. If anything, he thrived on the ability to solve conflict and make the world a better place as long as the United States benefited from it. Running his hands down the front of his navy-blue suit then taking a deep breath, he faced Captain Chase Hunter's team.

"You're going to tell Tessa about Robert." Ben didn't like keeping her in the dark even though she might come unhinged when she found out her husband wasn't the saint she told them about.

"Tell me what?" Tessa entered the conference room, balancing a stack of folders and a vanilla latte she'd bought on her way in. She eyed the group sitting at the table and reached up to rub her temples. "No one is making eye contact with me except Sam, so this can't be good."

Ben rolled out his chair and sat down, extending his hand toward an empty chair next to him. "Sit. Chase can fill you in later." He silenced Sam's snide chuckle with one of his angry glares. The woman might be enjoying this turn of events too much. "Where is Mr. Jones, Chase?"

"My guys have him next door."

"Excellent. Let's begin. Tessa, what do you have for us? I trust the children had no lasting effects after your close call the other night."

"They've already moved on. Sean Patrick thinks he wants to go into law enforcement, and Daniel has gone back to snooping on the school principal." Ben's eyebrows went up. "But I totally disconnected him. Promise," she insisted as she raised her hand in some kind of show of surrender. "Heather is a little clingy, but she is a mommy's girl anyway."

"Glad to hear it. What do you have for us?" Ben took the folder she handed him then passed the stack along to the others. He felt a little amused at the pastel coloring of the folders since everything else connected to Enigma bordered on being invisible, including file folders.

"This is some information about the current situation with the mining industry in southern Africa. I focused on Botswana primarily because over the last thirty-five years there has been a wave of complaints about human rights violations and a move away from democracy."

"What is this picture?" Sam pulled out an 8x10 photograph.

"This is the Black Kalahari diamond found in a diamond mine about one hundred kilometers from Gaborone, the capital of Botswana. It is roughly eight hundred karats that was divided and ended up as part of Britain's crown jewels."

"Black diamonds? I thought those were unremarkable compared to the glittering white ones." Sam laid it down and raised her all-knowing eyebrows at Tessa.

"You're confusing black diamonds with the chocolate ones you buy at a mall or your favorite jewelry store. Those really aren't remarkable. The commercial market for black diamonds is a little tricky unless you know what you're looking for."

"Explain," Ben chimed in.

"Diamond merchants have a way of artificially changing white diamonds into chocolate ones, which affects their sparkle and value. Their lack of clarity also might make them a little more affordable. More sparkly, more money. However, they are still beautiful and in demand. I, for one, love chocolate diamonds."

"Of course, you would," Sam mumbled.

Tessa took a deep breath as she shifted her gaze to the director. "It is important to know black diamonds are mined in Botswana and a few other places in world. They are extremely valuable and sought after. Botswana is the world's largest producer of diamonds, and the trade should have transformed it into a middle-income nation where most people benefit from this GNP."

Dr. Samantha Cordova had a Ph.D. in economics and could finally offer her insight. "I suspect someone is skimming off the profits and sending them to offshore accounts instead of investing in the country."

"The country never quite recovered when President Mombasa died suddenly some forty years ago." Tessa pulled out a copy of a news article from her folder then pointed to her teammates. "Some suspected he'd been poisoned, but there was never an autopsy or investigation. The Coalition for a Free Africa Party, or CFAP, consisted of wealthy white businessmen who hired a young military man who'd served as a tank commander in the Mozambique army."

Chase tapped on his folder. "I've heard of him. Mozambique has had one of the largest armies in Africa. I think they booted him out for a tendency to shoot first and ask questions later. He enjoyed his job a little too much, if you get my drift."

Zoric smiled broadly. "You act like this is a bad thing." His sinister laugh got him a disgruntled frown from the director.

"When President Mombasa died, there wasn't enough support

for his vice president to take over, and he also took ill and died several weeks later anyway. The CFAP let their hired guns loose on areas of opposition, suggesting they were behind the deaths. They wanted to make sure they placed someone in power who could help them gain control of their congressional bodies."

"Isn't the United Nations supposed to step in and solve these kinds of issues?" Carter Johnson didn't usually pay much attention to these meetings unless he thought the end result would be more action like he'd seen over the weekend. He was easily bored with the everyday things in life.

"The UN had their hands full with Sierra Leone, North Korea, and Kashmir at the time," Ben interjected. "So, I'm assuming this commander made his sponsors happy?"

"Yes. His new name is President Baboloki, meaning 'savior.' The name insinuates powerful, yet lighthearted. He has also named his son this and often speaks of the day he will follow in his footsteps, which brings us to the present."

"And the CFAP?" Chase's forehead creased.

"They are still in power. No other party exists. They underestimated Baboloki's ability to control the masses and have had to make a great number of concessions to stay in control of the government. For all practical purposes, it is a dictatorship."

"Let's take a break so everyone can go through the materials. Chase, you catch Tessa up to speed." Ben stood and glared down at his agent like he was the next meal of a hungry bald eagle. "All of it," he growled. Chase's nostrils flared, and he also rose, shifting his eyes on Tessa who jumped up from her chair with her usual nervous anticipation. "When you're done, bring in Handsome."

"Yes, sir." He tilted his head toward the door as Tessa joined him. "Let's go. We need to talk."

~~~

"I'm going to kill him!" Tessa fumed as she paced across the floor in her small office.

Chase sat on the edge of her cluttered desk with his arms folded across his chest. He listened to her growl insults about Robert through gritted teeth as she threw her hands in the air. She voiced her outrage and choked on tears pooling in her sky-blue eyes.
~~~

"A slow, painful death is what he deserves."

"Agreed. I'd be happy to do it for you. Just say the word," he said nonchalantly as he inhaled. "Will you be wanting to watch while I do it?" Tessa halted her pacing to land a punch to his gut that only managed to make him burst into laughter. "Settle down."

"Settle down? Are you out of your mind? He's a cheat, a liar, probably a money launderer, and who knows what else?" She placed a hand on her stomach. "I think I'm going to be sick."

Chase reached out and grabbed her hand in his, squeezing a little too tight. "You're not going to be sick. Suck it up." She tried to jerk away from his grip, but he refused to release her.

"How can you defend him?" she moaned, stepping into his personal space. He dropped her hand and moved away.

"Because he was scared out of his mind. He thought he was buying diamonds for you at a discount and didn't think about what the woman might really be up to. I swear I'm not sure how the two of you survive in this world. If he hadn't been so gullible, I'd have offed him there on the spot."

Tessa gasped. "You're despicable."

"I most certainly am, and you love it, so stop pretending to be outraged with me. Focus on your pathetic husband who doesn't have enough sense to come out of the rain."

"That is quite enough, Chase."

He laughed again and straightened to his full six-foot-one height. "I couldn't agree more. What do you intend to do with this news? Do I need to send Zoric to your house to remove all sharp objects? Of course, I can't promise he won't take matters into his own hands."

"If you're trying to intimidate or scare me, it won't work."

"I'm hoping you'll blow off steam here, and when we go back in with the others, you'll be the professional I believe you to be."

"How can I? He cheated on me."

Chase huffed a sigh and rolled his eyes toward the ceiling. "He did no such thing."

"I can't believe you're sticking up for him."

"Neither can I, but the facts say he was only flirting with trouble. Besides"—he moved back to grasp each of her arms to make sure she didn't try and escape— "I want to remind you of what you've done the last couple of years." He watched a rosy glow move up her neck then to her face. "In bed with me—"

"Not what it sounds like."

"No. But what if Robert got wind of it? Then there's D.C., and oh yeah, a certain tribesman who carried you off into the wilds of Afghanistan. I'm sure you made some compromises there." Tessa dropped her gaze to stare at her feet. "Sleeping on my couch. The list is growing longer every day you spend at Enigma. Have you lied to him about the work you do here?"

"No. Not exactly."

"Hmm." Chase couldn't resist moving a blonde curl off her forehead. She didn't shy away anymore from his touch. "There are always secrets. You have so many, it would make his head spin."

"You're enjoying this a little too much." Tessa dared meet his gaze. "Thank you for saving his worthless body."

Another chuckle escaped Chase's throat. "You're welcome. Although he may have been in more danger from Sam than everything else going on."

"Sam?"

"She came unhinged when she realized who he was. I had to restrain her." Chase pushed out his bottom lip. "What is it with you two? This love-hate relationship is driving me crazy."

"Complicated."

"Physics is complicated. You two are disturbing on so many levels. I think you enjoy taunting each other."

"Maybe," she said with a shrug then let her eyes search Chase's face with a little more tenderness than he expected.

Chase moved toward the door to put some distance between them. She would be his undoing. "Whatever is going on with Robert, he may know more than he thinks. Daniel hacked into the firm's computers and left a trail the men followed to you and Robert. They were probably going to make sure he was on board with whatever they had planned. I'm not sure how, but Vern took care of all the computer stuff. Time to make Vern and Daniel friends so we know what is going on."

"No. Enigma and family are not to be connected."

Chase walked to the door and opened it. "You don't have a choice if you want them to stay safe. We won't be invasive. Trust me."

Chapter Sixteen

Handsome Jones entered the conference room like a suspicious Goliath ready to wipe out an invading army. He filled up the doorway after Chase walked in ahead of him. Each person followed his slow appearance into the doorway. None of the Enigma team trusted the man or his past. There had been discussion at the warehouse of how typical it was for the CIA to recruit a loose cannon like Handsome.

When Chase realized the man hadn't entered the room, he appraised him from head to toe. "Take a seat," he ordered then found his own across the table from Tessa who smiled at Handsome like a long-lost friend.

The director rolled out his chair then waved an open palm to the table. "Sit anywhere you like, Mr. Jones. Thanks for coming."

He pushed into the room, circled the table, and flopped down in a chair next to Tessa. It squeaked with his bulk. "Not like I had a choice. Who are you?" he snorted at the director.

"This is Director Clark, Handsome." Tessa jumped in the conversation with a voice laced with honey. Handsome frowned over at her but, like a trouper, she kept smiling. "It's good to see you again so soon."

Once again, she proved a valued asset to the team as Handsome let one corner of his mouth twitch up into a grin. "Kids okay?"

"Yes. Thank you. They've ask about you the last few days."

He nodded as if the information pleased him before shifting his attention to the director with a renewed expression of apathy. "Why am I here? I've done nothing wrong, and yet you keep me like a criminal."

The others fixed smirks designed to intimidate Handsome.

"What are you talking about?" she asked.

Zoric took out his switchblade and popped it open to whittle away at something under his fingernails. "He was our guest at the warehouse."

"The warehouse," Tessa gasped. The place served several purposes. "Why?"

"He needed a place to stay where we could talk without interruption." Chase shrugged as he rested back in his chair and began a casual rocking motion.

Handsome glanced over at Tessa. "He doesn't think screaming from other interrogations counts as interruptions."

Tessa's lips parted in a sudden exhale as she laid a hand on Handsome's forearm. "Are you all right? I'm sorry. If I'd known—"

"Stop babying him, Betty Crocker," Sam sniffed. "He's a big boy. We didn't hurt him. We needed some information."

A chuckle escaped Handsome. "How'd that work for you?"

"We're trying to find out what is going on in Botswana," Chase clarified.

"Why?" Handsome snapped. "And what makes you think I know anything about it? Because I'm African American? Please."

"Don't play the race card with us, Handsome. You've been in and out of southern Africa ten times in the last three years." Chase propped his elbows on the table after pulling his chair forward. "You said as much over the last few days. What is your interest there? Those weren't CIA sanctioned trips, and your bank account doesn't indicate you had the kind of money that would allow travel to exotic locales. You certainly don't have frequent flyer miles. Are you working for President Baboloki?"

"Ahh. Why didn't you ask me these questions when we were *not* having an interrogation?" He took his time to survey each person in the room before letting his attention fall on Tessa. "No. I am not working for Baboloki." He shrugged and squirmed in his chair that seemed too small for his bulk. "I am an orphan, so it pleased me to try and find out where I came from."

Chase's eyebrows went up.

"I can give you my Ancestry.com password. You'll see it has become an obsession; no different than many who go to play there." Handsome smiled.

"When you said your mother named you Handsome, you were lying to me?" Tessa couldn't keep the disappointment out of her voice.

"Yes. I'm sorry. Unlike these other people"—he raised his nose in the air as if sniffing something rancid— "you seem like a nice lady. I won't talk to Captain Hunter, but perhaps we could have dinner tomorrow night, and I can explain."

"Like hell," Chase grumbled.

The director stood in a show of dismissal. "Sounds like a reasonable request, considering your stay at the warehouse may not have been up to our usual hospitality." Although he spoke to Handsome, he leveled a deep scowl toward Chase. "You make the reservations, Captain Hunter, since you seem to have a knack for entertaining these days."

~~~

Robert glanced at his watch and realized he needed to run by the deli to pick up his order for tomorrow night's poker game at the house. The kids would already be in bed by the time the guys showed up. Putting only a couple of dimes in the parking meter would give him plenty of time to run in without fear of getting a ticket. When he rushed out, he saw a familiar face inside the jewelry store across the street. Reeva Kaplan.

His gut knotted as he slipped the deli tray onto the front seat of his Lexus. He then dodged a couple of cars crossing the street. By the time he jerked the door of the jewelry store open, he couldn't see her. Taking another quick glance outside then back inside, a clerk approached him.

"Can I help you?" The man spoke with an accent. Robert wondered if it were British or South African.

"I thought I saw someone I knew a minute ago. A woman." He raised his hand to show height. "About so tall. Shoulder-length
~~~

blonde hair. Attractive."

The clerk shook his head. "I'm sorry. There is no woman here except for our employees. Maybe it was one of them. Greta?" he called to someone behind the curtain. A well-dressed woman with gray hair pushed the curtain aside and stepped out. She offered a smile to him. "Is this the woman, sir?"

"No." Confusion washed over Robert. A woman stared back at him from between the open curtains. *Reeva.* She offered him a condescending gaze then disappeared into the dimness of the back area. "Wait. It's her."

"Who, sir? There is no one else here."

Robert was heading toward the door leading to the back when another man emerged and blocked his path. "We meet again, Mr. Scott."

"You," Robert gasped. FBI Agent Martin from his nightmare in captivity.

"Let's take a walk." The agent pointed him toward the door and gently nudged his elbow.

Once across the street, Robert saw a parking ticket on his windshield and snatched it off. "Great," he snapped.

Agent Martin gently relieved him of the ticket and tucked it into the pocket of his overcoat. "I'll take care of this, Mr. Scott. Go home."

"I saw Reeva Kaplan in there. You said she was dead," he fumed.

The agent nonchalantly took inventory of his surroundings. "It's best if you keep your voice down, Mr. Scott."

Robert jabbed the agent in the chest with his index finger. "You said she was dead."

He recognized his mistake when the agent narrowed his eyes then focused his attention on the finger pressed on his chest.

"Guess I got it wrong." The agent's smile reminded him of a predator ready to pounce on his next meal. He stuffed his hands in the pockets of his overcoat. "Run along and get ready for your poker game and leave all this—whatever 'this' is, to me."

"How did you know I had a poker game? Have you bugged my house? My office?" Outrage overwhelmed his fear and confusion. "Do you have a warrant?"

"A warrant?" Agent Martin took another quick survey glance at his surroundings. "I didn't need a warrant, Mr. Scott. You posted tonight's game on Facebook."

Robert dared sigh in relief as the agent pushed his face closer.

"But if I need one"—he patted Robert's lapel— "I'll get one. The FBI is a law enforcement agency, Mr. Scott. We do things by the book."

Robert fell back against the hood of his car. "And when you can't?"

Agent Martin walked around the car and opened the door. "Then we get someone who doesn't need a book." As Robert slipped into the seat, the agent said, "If you know what I mean."

~~~

"Is something wrong, Tessa? You've been giving me the cold shoulder all evening." Robert really wasn't in the mood for her temperamental time-of-the-month attitude. Running into Agent Martin had nearly pushed him over the edge. "Spill it."

Tessa threw her dish towel in the sink and whirled on him. "Nothing. Nothing is wrong."

He threw his hands up in the air. "You always say that when something is wrong. I've had a long day, rough couple weeks, so, please—please, for once, tell me whatever is bothering you so I can set things up for tomorrow night's poker game."

For a couple of seconds, she disappeared into the laundry room then marched out carrying a white shirt. She tossed it to him and took the pose of a disgruntled pit bull. "Lipstick. On. Your. Collar. And it reeks of cheap perfume."

Lifting the shirt up to his nose to sniff, he tried to think. "I agree. Stinky."

Tessa's jaw dropped as her eyes widened, and she tapped her foot on the floor, reminding him of Thumper from *Bambi*. Letting a light chuckle slip, he moved toward her only to have Tessa take two steps away and hold her hand up.

"I'm flattered you think another woman would want me, Tessa, but, seriously. There is no one but you. There never will be."

"Explain the lipstick."

"I met a new client for dinner while I was at the conference. She was South African. You know how those foreigners are: all kissy
~~~

face and 'darling' this or that. She was clingy and gave me a big ole smooch to boot."

"Was she pretty?"

"Yes. But not as pretty as you." Knots formed again in the pit of his stomach. "She was a bit forward and—now, don't freak out—I let her come to my room to show me some diamonds." For a second, he thought he detected steam coming out of her ears. "I told her I wasn't interested but would be happy to represent her mining company's business in the US. I thought I was going to have to call security to get her to leave."

Tessa cocked her head and snarled. "So how did you get her out?"

"Some friends dropped by and sort of tied things up. She didn't have much to say after the interruption, so we went our separate ways. I know it was dumb to not think about how it looked or what it might lead to. Seriously, Tessa, I'm more embarrassed than you can imagine. Nothing happened." He stepped close enough to run his hands up her arms. "I love you. I'd believe you if something like that happened to you." He tried to kiss her, but she dodged him. "Come on. You are everything to me."

"Okay," she sighed. "Stop being so flirty and charming."

He pulled her into his arms. "Except with you."

CHAPTER SEVENTEEN

The restored Old Town of Sacramento remained one of Tessa's favorite spots to take out-of-town guests for dinner or for a quaint tourist experience. Reminiscent of the Old West, the restored buildings, covered-wagon rides, and singing cowboy who strolled the streets, managed to bring an almost-giddy warmth to her, no matter how many times she visited. Since it stood less than a half mile from her apartment, Tessa often liked to walk here after she finished work or prepared to leave for State Department business.

She'd spent the day doing more research for Enigma, a never-ending job, it seemed. Because she'd dropped her car off at the repair shop, Vernon picked her up in a rental then took her to the apartment to freshen up. The two had a special brother-sister kind of bond, although she felt more motherly at times toward the twenty-something genius. He reminded her of her own son who also showed a great deal of promise in the world of technology. Even though he dressed like a hippy snowboarder, Vernon's ability to break through any firewall gave the NSA and the Pentagon plenty of concerns. His gulping down a glass of milk with a hint of Oreo crumbs on his upper lip only endeared him to Tessa.

A long wolf whistle broke the silence when she entered the open-concept kitchen adjoining her tiny living room. "Mrs. Scott, you are one pretty lady." Vernon blushed as he diverted his eyes back to the empty glass.

Shyness around women kept the young man from any real relationships. For some reason, he felt comfortable around her and dropped an occasional sweet compliment. Everyone knew he held a major crush on Sam, who exploited the kid whenever it suited her. Unless he sat in front of a laptop, when the agent asked him a question, he would stutter or get tongue-tied.

"Guess you are never going to call me Tessa," she said, searching for her small evening bag.

"I'll try." He put the glass in the sink and twirled his keys around his index finger. "Did you confront Robert about San Francisco?"

"Yes. He swears it was all innocent. There was a little bit of twisted truth coming out of his mouth, but I think he didn't want to scare me. I pouted the rest of the night, and he tried to be sweet. The man drives me crazy. I really wanted to tell him I knew the whole story."

"Not a good idea."

"I know. No worries. Hopefully, he'll not get into any more trouble tonight. I told him I have an early class in the morning then a meeting. I also said I'd be picking up my car from the repair shop."

"You really are getting good at this. Ready?"

Chase had ordered Vernon to be her chauffeur for the evening and keep track of her movements. After parking her rental, he walked her to the Gold Rush Saloon and Restaurant where Chase waited.

"Nice of you to choose my favorite restaurant." She smiled up at Chase's serious face, hoping to put him in a better mood. The menu consisted of a variety of steak and potato dishes with names like The John Wayne, Randolph Scott, Jesse James Train Wreck, and even a petite steak called The Belle Star, her favorite. "Will you be joining us?" Since this particular restaurant catered to a suit and tie dress code, she gathered his attire of jeans, boots, and denim jacket meant no.

He ignored her question. "Handsome is in a mood from being detained all day at the warehouse."

"Can you blame him?" Tessa took a peek through the large

plate-glass windows and spotted the man already seated at a table. "The warehouse is not the most accommodating place."

"It's not meant to be a Holiday Inn, Tess."

She wrinkled her nose at him and grinned. "Did you put him to work?"

"No. He binge-watched reruns of Law and Order all afternoon."

"Poor baby," she cooed as she waved to Handsome inside.

"Are you talking about me or him?" Chase grinned.

"I'm guessing you two won't be far away?" She stepped forward as Vernon opened the door for her.

Chase instituted the security scan he always did before entering or exiting a building. "Have a nice evening. You've got two hours."

Entering the Gold Rush, she caught a glimpse of herself in the mirror behind the restored bar. The dim lighting and flickering candlelight hinted she was younger than thirty-seven. The conservative red dress hugged her body, creating a sexier appearance than she'd meant to portray. When she moved toward Handsome, he rose slowly without trying to hide his examination of her form. A wave of caution and embarrassment washed over her as she draped her black jacket over the back of the chair. When she pulled it out, he laid a hand on her arm.

"We're moving," he said, lifting her coat off the chair.

Tessa hesitated, stealing a glance out the window into the darkness, but couldn't see her friends or any indication of what she should do next. All this cloak-and-dagger stuff remained confusing to her country-girl mentality. She followed him.

He stopped at a table near the kitchen door. She slipped into the chair he held for her, a little surprised at his manners. Before he joined her, Handsome ran his fingers across her coat and extended his hand for her purse which he examined for bugs. He gave a nod.

"I didn't wear a wire of any kind, Handsome."

"Our table at the window had several listening devices."

She chuckled, thinking of Chase. "The captain thinks of everything."

"I've already ordered for us."

"Fine." She cocked her head and eyed him with new appreciation. "You are living up to your name tonight, Handsome."

"Is flattery part of your training?" he said coolly.

"I'm sure it should be, but Sam isn't very good at it, so I do what comes naturally."

He smiled. "What do you want to know?' He reared back and folded his hands in his lap as a waiter poured each of them a glass of wine.

Tessa didn't drink alcohol so she took a sip of her water as the waiter disappeared. "What do you know about the Kifaru?"

His eyes widened as he tilted his head to stare at her. "It is Swahili for black rhino."

"I know what the word means. But what is it?"

He chewed on his bottom lip then gulped down his wine, appearing uneasy for the first time since they'd met. "A diamond."

"And the significance?"

"The Kifaru is the second largest black diamond ever found in Botswana. Some say when it is held up to the light, the image of a rhinoceros can be seen. It was discovered by a man of the Twsana tribe many years ago and passed down to his son and then his son."

"I'm assuming it is a polished diamond, then. How were these men able to keep it from the mining company?"

"At the time, there was no mining company. The man who found it achieved great success and even became part of the new government of Botswana. With the help of his son, they were able to unite the people of Botswana and live a peaceful life. The diamond in their possession was said to hold great power and luck."

"What happened to it?" Tessa quieted as the waiter placed a salad in front of her.

Handsome sprinkled too much salt on his romaine. "It was given to a son who returned to their village. He was a bright, charismatic man who became very popular in the tourist industry and with local villagers who often asked his advice. Because he was also an engineer, he became a valued partner in digging wells, establishing a school, securing small loans for women to set up their own micro-businesses."

"That doesn't sound like the place I've been researching. What went wrong?"

"The rich mine owners and investors created a movement to take more control of the government so they could retain more of their profits. They were not happy with the tax code or how revenues were distributed for domestic projects like schools and medical clinics, infrastructure and communication systems. Progress brings the attention of others. They feared the rumors of corruption might bring condemnation and even interference. Such interest might cause them to lose control of what rightly belonged to the people of Botswana."

Tessa considered what he'd said. "I came across a story about a village burned down thirty-seven years ago by some unhappy members of a tribal army patrolling the bush in search of poachers. Apparently, the introduction of two hundred rhinos dwindled down to five in a few short years. This paralleled the time when the authorities went in to make some arrests."

"Yes. The story given to the press suggested as much. A large smuggling ring of illegal rhino horns, even some elephant ivory, was collected as proof and put on display in Gaborone. The Camp Kubu director stumbled across the operation and put out a call to park service law officers earlier. Before help arrived, the camp and its guests were also attacked and slaughtered by the very villagers he employed. Eight tourists died, as did any possibility of future revenue from free-spending adventure seekers."

"And the economic stability of a peaceful people was gone."

"Exactly." His dark eyes were luminous in the dim restaurant, hands closed into fists on the tabletop. "One by one, villages suffered the consequences when tourism dried up from fear of unrest. When the mining companies reopened, and Baboloki in power, things settled down."

"And the Kifaru diamond, how does it matter here?" Tessa handed the waiter her salad plate and accepted the sizzling steak and mixed vegetables. She waited patiently as Handsome cut into his T-bone then nodded at the waiter who departed.

"The Kifaru was believed to have been stolen that day by some of the so-called militia in charge of catching poachers. It has never been recovered."

"I don't understand how the Kifaru diamond could possibly change anything in Botswana." Tessa took another bite of steak before continuing. "As long as there is a dictator in power and others in control of the economic growth, there is little anyone can do. The president does pretty well at keeping things off the radar."

He didn't respond right away. The steak took precedence over deeper discussions. Tessa tried to be patient as she enjoyed her well-done steak. For a few minutes, she drowned in the flavors of a meal prepared by someone who must have been a genius. Chewing slowly, Handsome often gazed at her with amusement, almost taunting her to beg for more information until he dabbed at his mouth with the linen napkin and smiled.

"The Kifaru was said to pass to the one who would bring back dignity to the Botswana people. Freedom would be restored, and the truth would be revealed."

"What truth?"

Handsome stabbed the last bite of his steak and shoved it into his wide mouth, chewing slowly, as if savoring the moment before speaking. "The man called John was the grandson of the one who first found the Kifaru and managed to hide the diamond before the militia could find it. There was a doctor in Camp Kubu who did not die in the attack."

"There is no mention of a survivor. All were brutally murdered." Tessa waved off the dessert menu and hushed as the waiter focused on her guest. He pointed to a cream-filled cake. The server declared it a good choice and asked if they'd like coffee. Tessa decided on decaf, but Handsome declined.

When they were once again alone, she continued. "There were no eye witnesses who survived."

He drained his wineglass again then rubbed his chest. "This has been all worthwhile: dinner with you, Enigma picking up the tab, candlelight, soft music—"

"Handsome, are you saying someone survived the massacre?" she whispered.

"So it would seem." He closed his eyes and for a second, Tessa thought he might doze off after eating so much rich food. "The Kifaru, when returned to the people of Botswana, would give them courage to stand up against the dictator and take back the freedoms they've lost over the years. The outside world would again want to invest in the future of this amazing country."

"A piece of glorified carbon can't lead a country to freedom or success."

"I agree. But tradition"—he shrugged— "or legend says the one who possesses it can. These people carry their magic in their stories passed around cooking fires, hunts, and even mining. They pole their mokoros through the Okavango and wonder how long it will be before the government dams up their beautiful delta and forces them to live in cities where the old ways will be lost. They need to believe someone of honor will give them courage and hope again."

"Unfortunately, such a day may never come unless the Kifaru is found."

Handsome smiled with delight. "I have found it."

~~~

"I don't hear anything, Chase." Vernon tapped his earwig. "You?"

Chase rose from the bistro table after throwing a five-dollar tip down. "Let's check on them."

"Did Tessa know you bugged the table?" Vernon slipped on his windbreaker. The night had become chilly after an earlier warm-up.

They strode across the street at a quick pace. "No. I figured Handsome would expect it so I bugged several other tables he might choose. By the kitchen was my best guess."

"I couldn't hear much because of all the noise."

"And that is why Tessa's pearl earrings are the only thing we really needed." He pushed through the door and stared around the dining area. "Guess they needed some adjustment because I only got about every other word."

"So, where is she?" Vernon moved toward the back where a waiter disappeared through swinging doors to the kitchen. "There." He pointed.

The two Enigma agents inspected the area in every direction. Chase lifted the leather sleeve with the bill. When he opened it, two pearl earrings fell to the white linen tablecloth.

Both men took a nonchalant scan of the dining room then focused on the swinging door as a waiter barged through only to snatch the leather sleeve from Chase's hand.

"Can I help you?"

"The couple who sat here. Where did they go?" Chase tried to keep from sounding irritated as he spoke through gritted teeth. He tilted his chin up and scowled down his narrow nose and his eyes
~~~

became hooded.

The waiter glanced at the signed bill and generous tip then let a smile spread across his thin lips. "Out the back. Handed me a couple more hundreds to show them the way out the back." He waved the leather sleeve. "Didn't expect another tip," he chuckled. "The guy must be loaded. No wonder he had a babe on his arm.

Chase felt the familiar flutter of chest pain he always experienced when Tessa got under his skin. He rubbed his chest in a slow circular motion. "The babe. Did she appear upset?"

"No." He watched Chase slip the earrings into his hip pocket. "Is there a problem?"

Chase tilted his head toward the front door, and Vernon moved to leave. "Show me where they went."

"Got another hundred?" The waiter grinned as his eyebrow arched over one eye.

When he pushed his denim jacket back to reveal his weapon, Chase's glare could have melted a piece of steel. The waiter sobered. "This way."

The waiter hustled through the kitchen, drawing concerned glances as Chase stayed on his heels. Pointing to the exit door, he stepped aside for the agent to push through. Once outside, Chase pulled his weapon and searched the area.

"Boss?" Vernon joined him from the street access. "No sign of them."

"Dead end here. Must have slipped out when we went in the front."

"Why would Tessa go with him?" Vernon followed Chase to the street.

"Good question." Chase's reputation for short answers with little or no real explanation drove many at Enigma to distraction. His team had learned a long time ago to go with the flow. "Maybe they went to get her rental."

They picked up the pace, entering the parking area. Vernon pointed to where the car should have been. "That's where we parked. They've come and gone."

"I should have never left them alone." Chase's phone vibrated on the inside of his jacket pocket. "Talk to me." He recognized Tessa's number.

"I'm fine," she whispered.

"And Handsome?" Both men trotted to their van marked with a marijuana leaf on the side.

"I'm at the airport. Come get me. I want to go to my apartment. I'll wait out front."

"On my way." Chase steered the van back toward the interstate. At least they were in a public place. Maybe he planned to fly out on the first available flight. "Is Handsome with you?"

"Yes. Chase, I'm sorry. I'll explain later."

"I trust you, Tess." He fought off a grin, knowing to admit such a thing was like taking a swig of lighter fluid. "We've got all night." A carnal thought raced through his mind for only a second before he shook if off and added, "Be there soon."

They drove only a few miles out of town when Vernon broke the silence.

"Hmm, Boss? We have a problem. Tessa isn't at the airport. She lied to us."

CHAPTER EIGHTEEN

Chase alerted the authorities at transportation hubs from Sacramento to San Francisco about the possibility of a dangerous black man with a female hostage. He tried to contact FBI Special Agent Martin, hoping his judgment, common sense, and contacts could put an end to this nightmare but came up empty. Martin didn't pick up. Chances of Handsome planning ahead remained high.

Vernon sat in the van, fiddling with one of his computer toys, irking Chase. His youngest agent showed little concern about Tessa. "What the hell are you doing? Playing Clash of Clans again?"

"Nope. Following Mrs. Scott in her rental car." He smiled over at Chase. "You didn't think I wouldn't tag her vehicle, did you? I'm offended." He rotated the computer screen toward his boss. "She's headed back up I-80. Maybe they'll stop at Grass Valley on the way."

"I'm sure if she needed anything, she stopped at the apartment to get it, but I wouldn't bet on it. He'll assume we have her place watched. He's putting as many miles between us as possible. Damn. Tessa attracts trouble like a moth to flame." He pulled out into traffic with a screech of tires.

~~~

"Are you afraid?" The deep voice cut through the silence, startling Tessa so she jumped.

"Yes. I am." She faced the window. "Couldn't this have waited until morning?" She wiped condensation from the glass with a bare hand. "I'm not dressed for the mountains. Please, Handsome, take me home. I've changed my mind. I didn't realize you'd hidden the Kifaru diamond at Tahoe." Tessa could feel her resolve crumbling with each mile. The spotty snow appeared along the highway in patches as the road wound gently upward.

"I will not harm you. Didn't I prove it when you needed me a few days ago?"

"I want to go home," she pleaded. "You know Enigma will come after you. This time, they'll come as…"

"Killers? Because they are all killers. Why are you with them? Is it because Chase is your lover?" Handsome took his eyes off the road to glance over at her.

"We are not lovers. We could be a little too close, but I am married. We do not want to cross any lines of impropriety." Tessa pulled out her seat belt to adjust the tightness. "Or, at least I don't," she murmured.

"If you keep spending so much time with him, there will be trouble. He will ruin your perfect family, bring you heartache and loneliness. A man like Chase Hunter will never settle down. Do you want to—"

"You know this is really none of your business. Take me home this instant. There is an exit up ahead with some services. Let me out there. Keep your diamond."

Handsome took the exit as he slowed down. Puffy, dry snowflakes danced across the window. He pulled into a truck stop then switched off the engine before twisting to face her. "I never meant to frighten you. I like you and your children. They are good kids. You are a good woman and have nothing to fear. I believe what you say about your boss. But I need your help. We go get the diamond tonight and then you can call Enigma to come for you."

"I still don't know how I can help you." Tessa stared out the windshield after adjusting the heat. "My kids need me."

"I was going to give you the Kifaru for safekeeping." He smiled
~~~

as he canceled her attempt at increasing the heat.

"Me! Why me?"

"Because people are trying to find it, and someone has told them I have it. Those men were searching for you the other day because Daniel opened some kind of window. With your husband involved and a digital footprint leading to your home, it wasn't hard to connect the dots. They couldn't know it was a kid who found them. Once they found out who I was, we were all in trouble. One of them recognized me. Thanks to your quick thinking at cutting their tires, it gave me enough time to shut things down and slip away. Then I got the call you were in trouble. You owe me."

"You didn't have to come," she snapped. "No one would have been the wiser."

"You had kids with you. I couldn't let anything happen to innocent kids."

Tessa grinned as she faced him. "Turns out one of them wasn't so innocent." He grabbed her hand when she tried to adjust the heat again. His grip remained firm rather than threatening.

"The Kifaru needs to be returned to its rightful owner so Botswana can be rid of Baboloki. His investors want to dam the Okavango Delta to generate energy. It would destroy some of the last pure water of Africa, not to mention the diverse animal species. People who have never known anything but the delta and Kalahari Desert would be displaced to cities they know nothing of."

"And you'll take it back?" She regretted pulling free of his warm hand almost as soon as she'd done it.

"I am being watched by Baboloki's people who will do anything to keep the diamond from falling into the hands of the rightful heir. Trust me when I say it has great significance to the people of the Kalahari and Okavango." Handsome took a deep breath then released it slowly. "Are you a Christian, Tessa?"

She didn't hesitate. "I am."

"Then let me compare the diamond to your faith. Is it not prophesied Christ will return someday, and you as a Christian anxiously wait for such an arrival so there will be much peace and goodwill?"

She nodded then narrowed her eyes at him, trying to send him a warning.

"Baboloki is the Antichrist of the Tswana people. They wait for the Kifaru to give them courage because the man who possesses it will lead them into the future without drowning their way of life. I must get the diamond to them before it is too late. Time is running out."

"Who is this savior you're talking about?"

"I cannot tell you. It would be dangerous for him and for you."

"I'm already in danger. Besides, why do you care so much, Handsome? What do you get out of it?"

"I have my reasons."

"Not good enough if you want my help."

"The rightful heir is a friend of mind, and he can make a difference. I believe in him."

"The rightful heir? Everyone died, except this doctor you claimed was there, which, by the way, I'm not buying."

"There was a child. He is the rightful heir." He paused as if waiting for more questions. The silence weighed heavy between them. "Like the story of Moses in the bulrushes, someone came along to protect the baby."

Tessa had loved Bible stories from the time she was a little girl in Sunday school. How many times had she watched the movie The Ten Commandments? "Sounds epic."

"I sense sarcasm," he said then pooched out his lips. "He stands ready to do what is needed."

"I will not be a party to destabilizing, what seems, for all practical purposes, a stable country. Why should I help you? I am nobody. I have no particular set of skills that can put your plan into motion. There is also no evidence Baboloki is doing anything illegal. Granted, he is a pompous dictator and is lining his pockets with money that should be spent on the people of Botswana, but this is true for most of Africa. Will the Kifaru fix any of this?"

"You cannot destabilize a chair balancing on three legs. The corrupt government is run by self-serving mining companies. Building a dam on the Okavango will change everything for the people of Botswana, and not in a good way. There is much money to be made, but the Tswana people will lose their way of life. I cannot let this happen."

"Again. Why me?"

"No one would suspect a soccer mom of holding the life of a nation in her hand. It is the most innocent of scenarios. You are also a goodwill ambassador for the president on a number of issues, mostly for children, women's health, education, and nutrition."

"And you know this because?" Tessa tilted her head and eyed him.

"I had a lot of time at the warehouse and access to the Internet. Your bio for the university is glowing. A little off the subject, but how is it the president chose you for this position?"

Tessa fidgeted then released her seat belt. "Right place at the right time. Luck, I guess."

It was a difficult story to believe, and most people didn't know her blood ran through the president's veins. Captain Hunter had almost killed her in the process of rescuing the most powerful man in the world.

"I don't believe in luck."

"How about divine intervention?" she cooed, hoping it would take the edge off the tension rising between them.

An amused smirk tugged at one corner of his generous mouth. "I can believe something more in line with a miracle. And this is why I believe you have been placed in my path."

"Then tell me who will use the Kifaru to unite the Tswana people and form a new government for Botswana."

He fidgeted in his seat and stared out the windshield. The red and blue flashing neon lights of the truck stop reflected onto his dark face. "No. But I will tell you if I am found and killed, then all is lost. Only I can return the Kifaru to its rightful owner. Only I can stop Baboloki from using the resources of the country for his own personal gain."

"Who is after you?"

"A rich mining consortium still does business in small numbers of conflict diamonds. They have their ways of getting around identification numbers for the stones. The stones are exchanged for commodities, which are sold. The money is considered clean. This is still worth millions of dollars."

"Why do I get the feeling you're about to tell me something I don't want to hear concerning my husband?"

Handsome's deep, monotone voice sounded as if he might be

reading a stock report. "Your husband's firm was approached by the consortium. In the past, when they have used law firms across the world, fat cats became fatter."

"Until they were caught?"

"Exactly. The trick was to use one of their inexperienced people or, in Robert's case, he isn't a partner, so if he is caught, then the firm will disavow any knowledge of activities and fire his ass as he is toted off to prison for money laundering, fraud, and international deception in order to commit a crime. It is all set up nice and clean, until it isn't. But the real big deal is some of the money ends up in the hands of Boko Haram and Al-Shabaab. Nasty business. Your husband is already a marked man."

"But Enigma—"

"Not their problem if the FBI is already investigating, and apparently they are. Then there is Reeva Kaplan."

"The woman who my husband met with and who ended up dead?"

"The same. Whoever killed her has enough information to blackmail your husband into helping them. They'll promise him it is all perfectly legal and he might even make some serious money for his kids' college fund."

Tessa took a deep breath and grumbled. "The man is constantly consumed with earning more money. I thought it would be enough when I went back to work."

"Reeva was the soft touch. If she is out of the picture, then someone more persuasive steps in."

"Robert would go to the authorities. He is an honest man."

Handsome waited a few seconds to continue. "But is he greedy?" Another pause. "If he doesn't comply, then they move on to you and the kids as a threat."

A new kind of terror welled up inside her.

"They knew things weren't going as planned and moved in on you the other day. Daniel hacked into the firm's files. He didn't cover his trail because he didn't know he did anything wrong or saw something dangerous. And Reeva was still alive then! You were a fire needing to be extinguished."

"How do I protect my family?"

"By helping me."

"Tell me what to do."

<h1 style="text-align:center">Chapter Nineteen</h1>

The warehouse was Chase's first stop. Vernon wanted to try and get a better location on Tessa since her tracker faded on the car. Weather may have been a factor after a storm moved in at higher altitudes. Although he doubted Handsome had found the tracker, a clump of snow or a rock could have jarred it to cause a disruption. If they'd known Handsome would bolt, other options would have been in place. Fortunately, Vernon located them without much effort on his warehouse tech toys.

Tessa's car stopped about halfway to Truckee. The highway patrol was advising to stay off the roads until morning, but Chase borrowed his former Ranger buddy, Ken Montgomery's truck with tire chains and four-wheel drive. Once he got into the snow, he would pull over and slip on the chains if needed. No doubt Vernon would keep him apprised of road conditions and Tessa's whereabouts. While he gathered up warmer clothing, Ken stowed emergency supplies in the back seat floorboard.

"I also included some firepower, Captain. Don't forget there's a winch if you need it." Even though Ken was a civilian, he kept the military behavior and respect for those in charge. "Let me go with you. We all like Tessa. Handsome is a handful, and an extra pair of fists might come in handy."

"Fists won't take Handsome down. Wouldn't have a bazooka

lying around would you?" Chase tried to sound flippant, drawing a half grin from Ken. "Let the others know what is going on. I don't know why Tessa went with him, but it had to be a good reason."

"She is too damn trusting, and you know it. Maybe he promised things he can't deliver. She's also gullible, Chase." Ken stepped back and handed over the keys. "Tom and I will be here if you need us."

Chase slipped behind the wheel. "Thanks." He stared out the windshield for a few seconds before speaking. "Vernon trick this baby out?"

"No. I don't always want people to know where I'm at."

"You're a good man."

"We both know better," he chuckled. "At least Tessa hasn't found out. I'd like to keep her in the dark."

Chase shifted narrowed eyes at his friend and grinned. "Sometimes I think you have a crush."

Ken laughed out loud. "She saved my life. I owe her. I swear the woman would befriend a rattlesnake."

The engine roared to life. "I guess throwing in with all of us is kind of the same thing." He pulled the door shut and backed out.

The highway appeared deserted as he climbed toward Truckee. It gave him time to think about Handsome. The hulk of a man remained enigmatic. Their paths had crossed on multiple occasions in the past, mostly in Africa. He ran with some shady characters known in the conflict diamond business, although he hadn't appeared to have benefited monetarily from such associations. Did he know Reeva Kaplan who ended up dead in the hotel the team raided? He claimed to be clueless and there were no overt signs he was lying, but then again if he was ex-CIA he knew how to avoid such cues.

The roads got progressively worse until he pulled over at a scenic overlook and got the chains in place around his tires. Even then he continued to ponder why Tessa decided to allow Handsome to take her. There were plenty of people around to avoid leaving with him. Even though the voice transmission came and went, Chase caught enough to know the Kifaru diamond was involved. The last thing he thought he heard was Handsome knew how to get the diamond.

Did he tempt Tessa with this find, or was she afraid he'd go off the radar with the gem? She would feel responsible if he disappeared. When she removed her earrings, she ended his ability to hear details he wished he had. Whose idea was coming up here? Did Handsome figure out where to find the diamond, or was there another reason. After all she'd been through in Afghanistan, he couldn't imagine she'd leave with someone as shady as Handsome Jones. Life lessons are a bitch, and she'd had plenty of those in the two years since they'd met. He surmised, no prayed, Tessa was in good hands and Handsome meant her no harm. But then, Ken's "rattlesnake" comment continued to haunt him.

The phone vibrated, and he opened up on the Bluetooth to be hands-free.

"Boss?" It was Vernon.

"What ya got for me?"

"After about thirty minutes, they are still stationary. The tracker on the car still has a weak signal but hasn't moved. Coordinates indicate a truck stop. You're about twenty minutes away, according to your phone signal. With any luck, you'll intercept them. Do I activate anyone?"

"Good job, Vern. I don't need help right now. Thanks."

Chase clicked off and realized he felt a little easier knowing Tessa was in a public place, although it was a truck stop. On a night like this, there would be a few extra patrons to help Tessa if she needed assistance in getting away from Handsome. He remembered how pretty she looked when she arrived at the restaurant. Most of the time, he saw her in jeans and a sweater this time of year. When she took the time to fuss with her hair and clothes, she reminded him of a shiny new penny. Going into a truck stop dressed like a model would certainly get someone's attention. Maybe not the kind he wanted helping her, but at least she had a way out if needed.

The phone continued to give him directions to the truck stop, and he spotted it immediately when he took the exit off I-80. Parked near a large yellow semi was Tessa's rental. He almost missed it because of the white blended with the snow. After coming alongside, he jumped out and peered inside the car in case they were sleeping. Finding it empty, and the doors locked, he placed another tracker on the inside of the wheel cover before walking into the truck stop.

A short, rotund man with his hands on his hips stood in front of the cashier, cussing like a drunk sailor. Chase moved past him to steal a peek into a gift shop resembling a dry goods store instead of a souvenir stand. He moved to the restaurant where several truckers watched an old Claude Van Damme movie. No sign of either Handsome or Tessa. A prickly feeling teased the back of his neck.

The unhappy guy at the cashier station talked on the phone loud enough for everyone to take notice. The older gentleman behind the counter watched with droopy eyes as if it were as exciting as paint drying.

"What's the problem?" Chase asked as he grabbed a granola bar and threw down a couple of bills.

The cashier shrugged and returned the change. He opened his mouth to answer, but the unhappy customer clicked off his phone and continued to cuss. "I'll tell you the problem; somebody stole my 1976 International Scout. A classic!" He snorted. "Gone. Simply disappeared."

Chase took out a picture of Tessa he kept with him all the time. She wore a blue tee shirt and a pair of shorts. Her nose was a little sunburned, but her infectious smile and brilliant blue eyes caught the essence of her personality. "Have you seen this woman?"

The man tried to snatch it away from Chase as he pulled the photo back. "No need to touch it. Have you seen her?"

"Yeah. Maybe. She and some black guy were in here."

Chase showed the cashier, who also nodded. "They bought a bunch of clothes and snacks. The lady changed clothes before they left."

"I bet they're the ones who stole my Scout!" the man yelled.

"How long ago did they leave?" Chase stuck the picture back in the inside pocket of his coat.

"Maybe an hour." The old man shrugged. "Time flies when you're having fun." Normally, Chase would have found his monotone amusing. He liked old folks and believed they were undervalued in modern society. "Your Scout. Did it have four-wheel drive?"

"Damn right it did. Put my chains on before I came in here, too. Called the Highway Patrol but had to leave a message," he shouted. "By the time they get back to me, those thieves will be in

Reno or some other hellhole. You know 'em?"

"I'll see what I can do, sir. Wait here."

"What the hell else am I gonna do?" he growled.

Chase ran to his truck and contacted Vernon with the latest information. "Are we sunk, Vern?"

"I had Tessa wear the hair tracer we designed for her. She didn't want to wear it but caved to my wit and charm," Vernon bragged. "I'm activating it now. You need to get moving. They are off the main highway. Not sure about the range of the tracer in your weather."

~~~

The International Scout shifted into four-wheel drive after coming to a complete stop in the middle of a deserted two-lane road. Handsome struggled with getting it into place until Tessa showed him what he was doing wrong. To relieve her nervousness, she explained how her dad drove an old International he bought new when he was twenty years old. The story seemed to soothe Handsome's irritation at the inability to be in charge of everything. He remained subdued until the end of her story, and the Scout inched along until he got the feel of the road.

"You talk a lot," Handsome spoke offhandedly, glancing over at his passenger who gripped the edge of the seat.

"Captain Hunter says the same thing." She took a deep breath and adjusted her seat belt which must have been an add-on when restored. Riding in her dad's Scout was an adventure in praying you didn't become a projectile through the windshield.

"Humph. He doesn't say much, does he?"

She shook her head. "He is more of a listener. I'm sorry. I'm nervous. How much farther?"

Handsome yawned. "Not far but I'm beat. Need some sleep. Not sure I can find my way in this weather." He inched down a side road. Tessa twisted in her seat to examine the road behind them then ahead. This couldn't be good. "What's wrong?" he mumbled. "Don't you trust me?"

"You're scaring me. You said we'd be back in a few hours. I didn't sign on for this. I can't be gone all night."

"Don't you recognize where we are?"
~~~

"No." Tessa tried to make out details, but the snow and wind had picked up so much, Handsome could only use the low beams on the headlights. "Where are we?"

"The safe house is up ahead. We'll find another place nearby. Almost there. We can wait until the sun comes up."

Tessa rubbed her gloved hands up and down on her new jeans, followed by zipping up her quilted coat. "No. I don't want to do this." Her voice couldn't hide the tremble.

"Listen. We're both adults."

Tessa covered her face with her hands. What had she done? Going off with this man was another mistake to add to all the others she'd made in the last two years. "I want to call Chase."

Handsome took out the burner phone he'd purchased at the truck stop. When he tossed it to her, Tessa juggled it with the clumsiness of a clown then dropped it onto the floor. The seat belt refused to budge as she reached for it.

"Guess you're going to have to wait." Handsome slowed the Scout to a crawl as he drove past a cabin off to the right down a narrow driveway. "I need to sleep. You have nothing to fear from me. I'm not a monster like your friends at Enigma. If I were going to take advantage of you, I could have done it already. Have you seen anyone on the road? No."

They continued another quarter mile when the road forked to the right then angled up a slope. She wasn't sure how he knew where the road was except the trees appeared to be lining a path. When he clicked on the high beams, she spotted a cabin in a clearing on the side of the road. The opposite side appeared to be free of everything, leading Tessa to imagine it might drop off to Lake Tahoe or some other open space spelling disaster in this weather.

The snow fell wet and heavy at this altitude. The evergreen branches, heavy with snow, reminded her of angels who could no longer extend their wings. Wading through it would be work. Handsome parked the Scout in front of the cabin that more resembled a hunting shack than a vacation or safe house.

He shut off the engine and rested his eyes on her. "Tessa. Please believe me when I say the most important thing to me is getting the diamond. I need you to help me." He opened the door. "There is a snow blower inside."

"How do you know?" Tessa's teeth began to chatter, more from fear than the cold.

"Because I put it there two weeks ago when I bought this place. Stay put until I clear a path for you." He pulled out the keys and smiled over at her. "Wouldn't want you leaving me up here all by my lonesome." The door slammed shut as he lumbered off toward the cabin.

With a release of the seat belt, she bent down and grabbed the phone. She pulled one glove off with her teeth and fumbled with trying to call Chase. All she got was an annoying voice saying, "If you'd like to make a call…" What about Robert and the kids? If he'd tried to check on her, which he normally did when she had to stay over in Sacramento, he would be wondering why she didn't pick up. It was 2:00 am. He'd probably already gone to bed. Then her little ones sprang to mind. Would this hulk of a man continue to show her the same protection and kindness he had them?

The sound of the snow blower exploded through the silence. Tessa flinched before trying to call Chase again with no success. She took a deep breath and held it inside long enough air spluttered across her lips when released. Was plowing a path through the snow really for her comfort or a ploy to put her at ease? Maybe he planned to—

Handsome tapped on her window with his knuckles. "Come or stay in the car. I am going to build a fire and go to bed." When she could only manage to glare at him, he jerked the car door open. "Why did you come with me? You had to know your captain doesn't trust me, yet you came. Tell me."

The cold air smacked her in the face as snow fell into her lap from the roof. "I…I." Tessa stopped herself from stuttering. She had a habit of doing it when frightened. "You helped my children. Protected them. I felt like I could trust you."

"And you can. Get out of the car. You will freeze if you think you can tough it out until morning. Are you worried about me or your reputation?"

"I'm calling Chase. He'll be worried."

Handsome nodded and mumbled, "And he should be. You're not acting like a reasonable person. I'm not going to rape, beat, or murder you. I want you to take the Kifaru to a safe place. That is the only thing I care about. I have to take it home before it is too late. Time is running out for me."

She dusted the snow out of her lap in exaggerated motions. "I don't know about— "

Before she could object or continue the conversation, Handsome reached in and grabbed her by the front of her padded coat. She felt like a rag doll as her boots hit the snow and her knees buckled. With his sudden jerk, Tessa found herself in a standing position. Reaching for his large bear-like paw on her chest, she shoved at him as he pulled her toward the cabin. Several times, her feet tangled, causing her to wobble with the grace of a dancing hippopotamus.

Her flailing fist jabs were a waste of time as he pushed the door open with his foot then shoved her inside. The overstuffed chair stopped her from sprawling onto the floor. He moved past her and pointed to the chair.

"Sit. Be quiet."

Handsome adjusted some logs and crumpled paper in the firebox that appeared to have been prepared ahead of time. He patted himself down then searched the mantel until he snatched something up. Tessa watched him kneel next to the logs and strike a match before holding it next to some scrunched wads of paper. The paper must have been damp, or maybe his breath snuffed it out, but either way, Tessa knew they were in trouble. She was close enough to see only one match remained. No way did she want to snuggle with him to keep warm.

"Stop," she yelled. He jerked his head around. "I can light the fire. You can't take a chance with one match." Her teeth chattered, making her words a little slurred. Rising to his feet, he frowned down at her.

"How? How can you light the fire?"

"With our snacks. I mean your snacks. I would never have bought such unhealthy—"

"How?" he repeated a little more forcefully this time.

"Ahh"—she spotted the sack of fatty treats Handsome brought in when they first arrived—"the bags of corn chips, cheese puffy things—"

"Are you having a brain freeze?" He spoke with such impatience, Tessa thought it best to get them herself.

"They are full of fat. They'll burn like a torch." She ripped open the orange-cheese-laden goodies then the corn chips. "Look in the trash for a paper plate or something else to burn."

"I already did. It's in the fireplace."

"Oh. Right." She moved up alongside him and kneeled. Handsome's legs reminded her of tree trunks. "Come on," she coaxed, stealing a shy glance up at him. "What have we got to lose?"

He bent down on one knee and watched her pile several pinky-size cheese puff snacks on top of the paper under the logs. She then held two together as if they were kissing.

"Okay. Strike the match under the center here where they touch. They'll both become a torch. We'll both take one and light the others in the fireplace. Okay?"

He nodded and struck the match. The fire flash flared up on the end of the orange puff as expected. It took only a few seconds to light the others, which caught the paper and kindling on fire. Handsome carefully placed the remaining contents of the bag throughout the stacked wood, and soon the fire blazed warmth into the small cabin.

"How did you know to use this stuff?"

Tessa rested back on her heels and stared at the flames, letting the hypnotic dance relax her. "I used to teach a health unit to my students. When I showed them how much fat they were putting in their bodies, usually lunches switched from chips to carrot sticks."

A chuckle escaped his mouth. "You're good to have around. Maybe I'll take you to Botswana with me."

Tessa jumped to her feet and would have fallen in the fire if he hadn't reached out and blocked her momentum. "What?"

He rose to his feet so slowly his knees popped. A grin pulled at one corner of his mouth. "I'm only kidding. Do you think I want Enigma messing up my plans because I took their girl next door? The way they came storming up here last weekend showed me you have something they need."

"Oh." Tessa backed toward the upholstered wingback chair with a seat cushion resembling a faded pancake. "You best remember that," she warned pointing a finger at him like it might be a loaded gun.

"Did you make your calls?"

"Yes. Chase is on his way."

A smile spread across his mouth. "Really? I've never been able to get reception up here." She opened her mouth to speak, but he interrupted her. "Or maybe you are a terrible liar."

Tessa realized then the only reason he'd given her the phone was because she wouldn't be able to call out. She watched him remove his coat and toss it onto a cluttered kitchen table. A child's doll fell to the floor. He picked it up and tossed it to her, initiating the doll to mew a soft cry. Then he flopped down on the bed. It squeaked with his bulk as he pulled off his boots then lay back across the covers.

"I am going to sleep. The keys to the truck are in my pants pocket, so unless you want to try and get them, you better get some sleep, too." He yawned. In five minutes, he snored like a hibernating bear.

CHAPTER TWENTY

Chase swerved to dodge a tree falling across the road, propelling him into a snowbank. For once, he appreciated having a winch on the front of his friend's truck. Even so, his door was blocked by a wall of snow, preventing him from escape. The winch wouldn't do him much good unless he could free himself. He realized the passenger side angled up enough to keep it from being encased in snow. After managing to move his muscular frame to the other side of the vehicle, he powered the window down. Once again, he realized he wasn't as nimble and young as he once was when he squeezed through the window to fall back into the snow.

He hooked the winch around another tree and, although it took another half hour, he freed the truck from the snowbank. Moving the tree from across the road proved to be a little more time-consuming, and he had to start over several times to get the right grip. The slippery snow created a whole new set of problems he hadn't anticipated. The cold settled in his fingers and toes, making work clumsy. He climbed back into the truck to warm up.

The clock on the dashboard said 3:30 am. Frustration at this current predicament gave him a moment to bang his fist on the steering wheel. Vernon came onto his Bluetooth.

"Boss? You there? Boss?"

"Yeah. I'm here."

"Lost you in the storm. Your GPS stopped working for a

while.”

Chase explained the problem with the tree across the road and the snowbank. “I can’t get the tree to budge. I’ve tried everything.”

“Give me a minute. Maybe I can help.”

“What about Tess?”

Chase could hear his young agent clicking away on some computer toy. “Yeah. Appears they’ve stopped. I doubt she could call out if they are between mountains or off the beaten path. You are a little off track. I’ll get you back on as soon as the cavalry shows up.” Vernon let a quiet chuckle slip out. “I hacked into the orders of the road crew. If anyone asks you, you’re on your way to get your wife who is in labor.”

At least Vernon hadn’t lost his sense of humor. “You are a dangerous man, Vernon Kemp. I’m having a little bro-love here.”

“I’ll be expecting a generous bonus at Christmas. I’ve reprogrammed your phone GPS and Ken’s truck.”

“He said you hadn’t been allowed near it,” Chase mused seeing a flashing red light in his rearview mirror.

“Oops. What he doesn’t know won’t hurt him. You know what he’ll do to me if he finds out.”

“Your secret is safe with me, but it comes off when I get back. Understood?”

“Sure. Sure, Boss. Whatever you say.”

“Gotta go. I’m being rescued. Thanks.” He glanced down at his map on the truck dashboard. Much to his dismay, he saw he was more than a little off track. A snowplow pulled in front of him and used his bumper blade to push the tree off the road like a matchstick.

The driver stopped and swung out onto the ground. Chase powered his window down.

“Where ya headed? It gets tricky up ahead. I’ve already plowed this stretch once. Wife having a baby?”

“Hoping it’s another false alarm, but can’t be too careful.” Chase gave him some road directions.

“That’s a little out of the way. Guess you couldn’t get through the usual route. I’m about to go off shift, so I’ll plow you a path as far as I can. Not sure I can get back there in this monster.”

“Thanks, buddy. You guys are heroes in my book to be out on a night like this.”

The driver nodded then frowned. "And if I can ask, why were you out?"

"Coming off active duty in the Middle East. Was supposed to be home two days ago. Still be in Sacramento if my CO hadn't pulled a few strings after he saw the weather forecast. Then the wife called to say she wasn't feeling so good. Borrowed my friend's truck."

"Better get started, then." He winked. "Follow me. And thank you for your service."

"Appreciate it," Chase called after him. He wondered how Tessa would react to this story.

~~~

The smell of coffee filled the cabin that was smaller than her thousand-square-foot apartment in Sacramento. At least it had a laundry-bathroom combo, including a shower. She wasn't sure how Handsome would ever manage to use it. The kitchen adjoining the living room had a hot plate and a microwave along with a dorm-room-style refrigerator. An old Hoosier cabinet with chipped red paint stood on one wall. Since there were only a few upper shelves on each side of the window to hold mismatched dishes, the cabinet provided storage for supplies. A chrome kitchen table right out of 1955 acted as a divider for the room and had three chairs with yellow seat cushions.

Tessa worried about electricity being available. At least in the kitchen and bath, there were a couple of outlets, but no overhead lights. The full-size bed, positioned in the one big room, along with a metal patio table, was the extent of a bedroom. Handsome remained asleep and resembled a beached whale on top of the covers. It seemed he hadn't changed his position since he fell across the bed. She hoped the smell of coffee would wake him.

Fortunately, the living room had a faded chintz chaise lounge that had seen better days. After checking for bugs, Tessa decided to try and sleep. She had to admit Handsome could have done bodily harm to her on several occasions. His large, intimidating figure twisted the imagination where she became an episode of *Dateline*, the Friday night crime show she usually watched. Even though her gut told her he really wanted her help, and the Kifaru
~~~

diamond was the key, she decided caution needed to be a part of the plan.

Rather than wait for him to stir, Tessa poured herself the first cup of black coffee. Typically, she added a great deal of cream and sugar. Holding the cup with both hands, a warmth spread through her fingers as a curl of steam lifted to dampen lips chapped from the dry heat of the cabin. A log shifted in the fireplace, expelling a crackle of sparks to dance upward. She'd tried to keep the fire going with the logs stacked in a copper tub. The result meant she didn't get much sleep.

Staring out the window, she watched the morning light stretch across the blanket of snow, which reminded her of a fairy-like land from her daughter's favorite Disney movie, *Frozen*. Only a few flakes floated in the morning air after such a stormy night. The snowdrift stacked up outside the kitchen window, but she'd already checked the front porch, and it remained clear even though the path Handsome had plowed was filled in and was void of tracks they'd made during the night. The car appeared as if it might be in the middle of the road, but considering this place was isolated with no neighbors in sight, she guessed it didn't matter. Her concern remained whether or not they could dig out and return to Sacramento after they retrieved the Kifaru diamond.

A grumble and smacking of lips drew Tessa's attention. She watched Handsome push himself up then yawn as he stretched out his arms. After giving his face a hard rub, he focused sleepy eyes on her and stared for a full ten seconds without speaking.

"Coffee?" she asked, moving away from his penetrating gaze. "Storm is over." She poured another cup of coffee and set it on the table, not wanting to get too close. He stood and stretched again then headed for the bathroom. When she heard the bathroom door open, she moved back to lean against the sink.

"What time is it?" His speech sounded like he had a mouth full of marbles. He stared at the clock over the window. It needed a new battery.

"Seven." She pointed to the coffee cup, which he grabbed. "Snow stopped. I'm ready to go."

Once again, Handsome reminded her of the Michelin Man when he walked so slowly. She stepped aside in a quick retreat when he came to peer out the window. He gulped the coffee then poured a second cup.

"I'm hungry," he announced. "Can you cook?"

"I've got three kids. Of course, I can cook," she snapped.

Handsome twisted his thick lips into a half grin before lumbering away from her. "Does your husband help you much?"

"Let's not talk about my husband. Let's get the Kifaru and leave. My family needs me."

"This is true. The question arises, why you threw in with Enigma with so much at stake."

Tessa wondered the same thing every day, right up until the time her skills were needed as a geographer or the country faced a threat. She tried to convince herself patriotism ruled her heart, but, truthfully, the adrenalin rush had become her drug of choice. Working among dangerous people like Enigma who walked up to lines drawn in the sand then destroyed them, gave her an unnatural thrill she struggled with keeping under control. Then there was Captain Chase Hunter.

"Nothing to say?" Handsome continued. "One of those women who like the bad boys?"

"Again. My personal business is none of yours. Let's do whatever you have planned for me then return me home. You do not want to be here when Chase finds us." She let one hand unconsciously reach for her hair to make sure the fake piece was still in place, hoping a signal could still get out to alert her friends where she'd been taken.

Handsome faced her and let his eyes slide up and down her body. She cringed then bolted past him to pull on her coat. A low chuckle escaped his throat as she zipped up her jacket.

"I am not afraid of your boyfriend, Tessa."

She opened her mouth in protest of the relationship, but thought better of it.

He set his cup down then joined her as he snatched up his coat and pulled it on. "First, we need to get some wood in and dig the car out or we won't be going anywhere."

"Fine." She swung the door open and rushed out, happy to be free of such confined quarters. A stack of wood covered in a blue tarp appeared to be dry when she pulled it back. Since the fire had died down, she gathered the smaller pieces first. From the corner of her eye, she noticed Handsome pulling on his gloves as he paused on each porch step to evaluate the surroundings. In seconds, the snow blower broke the tranquil silence.

Tessa threw another log onto the fire in case they couldn't dig their way out enough to make it to the main road. Having used up all the cheese puff snacks, it seemed prudent to be proactive.

She filled the copper tub then piled another stack in a large iron kettle like her grandmother used to plant flowers. When she joined Handsome, the walkway out to the car was free of snow with walls on each side, three feet high. The snow blower, now without gas, sat idle while he used a snow shovel to dig around the car. Spotting another shovel on the porch, Tessa pitched in to help.

Once they stopped to examine their work, Handsome wiped his forehead. He glanced over at her with a pinched brow. "I'm sorry, Tessa. I didn't expect this storm. You would think growing up in Canada a chunk of my life, I'd know better."

Tessa cocked her head. "Canada?"

He changed the subject. "I will do my best to get you home." He sounded frustrated.

She followed his gaze across the road. Tessa noticed how close Lake Tahoe was to them. Down a small ravine and a few trees, the view beyond was magnificent. She could imagine sitting on the front porch in a rocking chair, sipping her morning coffee in the summertime, drinking in the beauty of this place.

"Handsome, my goodness, this is a breathtaking view." Having lost her fear with such an inspiring landscape, she walked up beside him. "Hard to understand how, after seeing this, people can still not believe in God."

He sighed and nodded. "I feel the same way when I float the Okavango Delta. I bought this place as an investment with what little money I had, thinking I could sell it for a profit to use when I go to Botswana. I won't need much once I'm there."

The sound of her voice seemed suppressed with so much snow. "How will you use the diamond, Handsome? Do you mean to sell it?"

"No. It doesn't belong to me. I want to give it back to the people to remind them even though the black rhinos are gone, freedom and choice are not. I want them to have schools, medicine, and jobs while they keep their way of life on the delta and Kalahari. Flooding these lands will destroy a way a life that can never be restored or duplicated." He spoke like a Baptist preacher telling his flock about Heaven. "To pole through the waters in a mokoro at sunset is like nothing else you've ever experienced. I was born to be there, Tessa."

Tessa somehow believed him. "Who are you really, Handsome Jones?"

"The one who intends to make a difference."

~~~

The snow and wind grew so blinding after getting on his way again, Chase realized he needed to stop or get into more trouble. Vernon kept him apprised of the weather, road conditions, and Tessa's whereabouts. Since he drove a gas hog to get this far, he didn't leave the engine running to stay warm while he waited to move on. Once an hour for about five minutes he turned the heat on for a few minutes. He pulled on more layers of clothing and topped them with the thermal blanket Ken threw in the back seat at the last minute. The sun revealed the road ahead would be slow going, but his four-wheel drive should be able to handle it.

"Vern, update."

"The forecast for the next six hours says good weather, but another front moving in. Got a satellite feed showing a structure, a car out front, and a couple of people moving around. Pretty grainy. The director gave the okay for Carter to send in a drone, but he has to be in Truckee or closer to get a good look. He and Zoric are on their way."

"I need someone to check on Robert and the kids. Keep them occupied. Can you call the Irvins to figure it out?" Martha and Francis Irvin lived next door to the Scotts. Robert didn't realize the couple actually worked for Enigma. Martha helped Tessa with childcare when things got hairy at work or school, and Francis was a good-natured biblical archeologist known for getting his team in and out of Middle Eastern hellholes in times of need.

"Already tried. They are in Ireland this week, visiting Martha's family. Sent Sam. She jumped at the chance."

He couldn't resist a smile. "We both know she is really good at distraction. I'm not sure Tessa is going to like this."

"Text from Carter came in. He is setting up. I got you, too. Two
~~~

miles ahead, on your left, you'll see a road where it's been cleared of trees. Should be a large rock outcropping on the one side where a landslide hit during the rainy season."

"Might be covered with snow now."

"Doubt it. Pretty massive slide. Anyway, you should be able to see past it all the way to Lake Tahoe. If the snow plows haven't been down there, then you'll see an eight-foot-high sign honoring the Washoe tribe."

"Maybe the ancestors will be with me."

"Hope so. There's a steep descent. You could fishtail right off into the lake."

"I'll be careful. Thanks, Vern." Chase used his windshield wipers to remove the snow flying back. One more thing to slow his progress.

The sun rose high enough he felt more confident about picking up more speed. The truck's four-wheel drive traveled easier than expected. He paused at the road to survey the outcropping of rocks then up the mountain before calling Vern back.

"Vern, any avalanche warnings out?"

The click of computer keys mixed with the humming of some Maroon 5 song had Chase puffing out his cheeks in exasperation.

"Not where you're at, but Squaw Valley has posted no skiing until late afternoon so they can trigger slides. What's up?"

"Not sure." He pulled out his binoculars to scan the area ahead. "What does the area around the cabin look like?"

A pause then a whistle. "There are some chutes past the cabin indicating avalanches have occurred there. Debris piles of trees and rock. Those are signs of a run-out zone for an avalanche. Appears to be a dead end, but topo maps say there should be a road. Another clue it's an avalanche zone. Privately owned, so it could be abandoned. I guess Handsome may have found the place if he'd been living up here for a while. He seemed like he knew his way around when he picked up Tessa and the kids a few days ago. Maybe why he chose to take Tessa there. Think she's okay?" Vern switched from goofy kid genius to concerned agent.

Chase ignored the question. "I'm going forward." He hadn't gone more than the length of two football fields when he heard it.

Avalanche.

CHAPTER TWENTY-ONE

"I think we should finish what we came up here for and be on our way." Handsome grabbed her shovel, tossed it in the back of the Scout, and shut the hatch tight. "Might need this again."

Tessa took bigger steps than normal to keep up with him. "Is the Kifaru far from here?"

"It is here. I carelessly knocked it on the floor last night. I noticed you tossed it on the chair this morning."

"What are you talking about? You must have been dreaming." She scrambled up the steps to face him. "Handsome, is this another diversion because I'm not amused and I want to go home?"

He gave a patient smile and pushed past her before opening the door. "Baby doll."

"Don't call me that," she fumed.

"I wasn't," he chuckled as he motioned for her to come inside. "The doll." Walking to the wingback chair, he lifted a doll with a plastic head and soft sculptured arms, its faded red-printed dress frayed around the edges. Gently, he pried the head off and dumped the largest diamond Tessa had ever seen into his hand.

At first, she gasped as her hands flew to cover her mouth in awe. She stepped closer and gazed upon the black diamond he believed would change a nation.

"It's true!" Lifting her eyes to meet Handsome's, she reached out to gently touch his arm. "I'm sorry, Handsome. Forgive my behavior and mistrust." She could feel her mouth smile so big it almost hurt. "It's beautiful."

Handsome dropped it back inside the head of the doll and reattached it. "You must keep this safe for me. I helped you avoid disaster when you needed me, and now I need you. Please, Tessa."

He handed her the doll as she whispered, "To save the people of the Okavango."

"To save a nation from itself."

She clutched the doll to her chest. "It would be my honor, Handsome. Let Enigma help us."

"I don't trust them." He frowned. "But if you do, then I hold you responsible."

"Let's get out of here." She kissed the doll then hugged it again. "We have work to do." Her excitement built with the possibilities to make a difference for the people of the Okavango and Kalahari.

Together, they snuffed out the low-burning fire by banking the coals in the back of the firebox then put the fireplace screen in front. Besides a plastic bag of trash from the snacks, there wasn't anything else to clean up. Handsome walked with a lighter step and even took a moment to lop a snowball at Tessa who returned the gesture after stuffing the doll into a plastic bag in the back seat.

For the first time, he laughed at her antics as they got in the car. He pulled the International Scout forward then around, causing the tires to spin. "I brought up some bags of kitty litter after buying this place in case I ever got stuck." He switched off the engine. "We better take it."

"I'll get it," Tessa volunteered, swinging open the door. "I saw it under the sink this morning. Besides, I want to make sure I unplugged the coffee pot."

Tessa stopped at the porch when she heard a rumbling sound up the mountain, past the cabin. "Handsome," she screamed as she jumped off the porch and waved her arms frantically.

She saw him roll down the window and frown at her in what appeared to be confusion then he, too, saw the mountain chute, left by other avalanches. Tessa could only watch in horror as a river of snow and rocks slammed into the Scout and flipped it several times. Then it righted itself and wobbled toward the embankment.

Nothing could stop the cry of desperation escaping her mouth as she stumbled forward, landing flat on her face. When the crunch of metal suddenly stopped, Tessa scampered to her feet and ran to see the Scout still upright and careening on the edge of another drop-off. The sides were smashed and the back window had flipped up, void of glass. She could see Handsome moving. Even though she tried to step with caution and speed at the same time, she lost her footing several times, contorting like a rag doll a child might drop on the floor.

"I'm coming, Handsome!" she called seeing him try to open the door that was a twisted mess.

"I can't get out," he called through the open window, squeezed together in the middle. "I'll try the other side."

Tessa climbed over an exposed rock the size of the wingback chair in the cabin to get to the other side of the car. A couple of rocks and a tree limb partially blocked the door. She worked to remove them and was able to tug on the door as Handsome managed to get into the passenger side of the car.

"I can't get it by myself. Put your shoulder into it, Handsome," she ordered as she continued to jerk on the door handle, which then came off so suddenly she fell back into the snow.

Handsome rammed his shoulder into the door hard enough it came loose enough for him to pry it the rest of the way open. The car rocked, scooting it forward.

Tessa rolled to a standing position and reached for his hand. Blood trickled down his face in several places. His bottom lip was busted open, and he seemed dazed. "Come on," she demanded as she tightened her grip on his hand and jerked. He fell out of the car and onto her, pushing a gush of air from her lungs.

Handsome rolled off almost immediately, but Tessa lay still, gasping for air. He rolled on his side and laid a hand on her diaphragm. "Take some deep breaths. Do it," he ordered.

She rolled her eyes over at him and tried to nod and breathe at the same time. It worked. Although she didn't feel like moving too fast, Handsome was pushing himself up then grabbing the front of her coat to lift her. Both of them shifted their eyes to the Scout when it creaked, a signal it was moving toward the lake.

"Hey down there," came a familiar voice from twenty feet up the hill. "Are you hurt?"

Tessa fell against Handsome and hugged him. "I told you Chase would find me." She laughed.

"Can you come up? I've got a winch." He grabbed the winch hook then navigated the debris field. "We can secure the car until we figure out what to do next." He took a couple of cautious steps down toward them.

"Oh. The doll," Tessa said to herself more than to Handsome as she pulled open the back seat door.

"Tessa, stop!" Chase cried out as he started to pick up speed to join them. "Handsome, stop her. The car will go over."

Handsome grabbed for her as she slipped into the car. "Tessa. No. I'll get it."

She reached over into the back-cargo area where the airborne plastic bag with the doll landed and lifted it over. "Got it." She raised it in the air.

A sudden shift in rocks beneath the vehicle slammed her into the back of the front seat as it slid toward the icy water. Her screaming echoed off the lake as she watched the men try to reach her. As the Scout tipped forward to sink in the blue waters, Tessa lost sight of them as they scrambled down the embankment.

~~~

Robert glanced at his watch and wondered for the tenth time why Tessa hadn't called him to say she was on her way home. She had a morning class to teach at 7:00 a.m. Who would ever sign up for such a time anyway? And why would his wife agree to do it? This teaching position at the university got in the way of his job at the firm, sometimes. Just because President Austin provided a way for her to get her PhD didn't mean it needed to consume her life.

He had enough to worry about with the FBI watching him, or so he thought. Maybe paranoia had led him to be cautious or too sensitive to change. Either way, she'd said she'd be home by ten, and now it was ten fifteen. The kids' school had the day off because of a teachers' scheduled workshop for the district. He heard the front door alarm chime and sighed with relief. Finally.

"Daddy?" It was Heather standing in the doorway of the bedroom. She watched him adjust his tie then lift his suit coat from the rumpled bed. He thought about straightening the covers,
~~~

knowing how an unmade bed drove Tessa crazy. She sometimes would make the bed before they went to sleep at night if it hadn't been done. He curled his lip in protest. Maybe next time she'd get home on time like she promised.

"What, sweetie?" He smelled coffee. Yep. She was back. "Why didn't you run to Mommy like you usually do when she wasn't home to tuck you in at night?"

Heather shrugged. "Mommy says I shouldn't talk to strangers."

"I know. Good girl." He kissed the top of her head. "Let's go see Mommy."

"Are we going to her school?"

"She came in the front door. Remember?"

"Mommy told me never to talk to strangers."

Robert straightened to his full six-foot height. "Who was at the door?"

"A stranger."

"Hey, Dad," Sean Patrick called from his bedroom. "We got company. Whose car is in the driveway?"

"Stay here, Heather. Daddy is going to go check on something. Sean, stay with your brother and sister for me."

The first thing Robert imagined was either Special Agent Martin had decided to make himself at home by brewing a pot of coffee, or those thugs who'd ushered him to a parking garage then showed up at his house to pick up one of Tessa's stray humans, had come to pay him a visit. Either way, the hair stood up on the back of his neck.

He heard humming as he walked into the kitchen. A woman stood bent at the waist with her butt in the air, resting her elbows on the counter, her slim legs showcased by a short faux-leopard skirt. The first thought entering his head was what a lithe, beautiful creature. She tilted her head toward him and smiled like a goddess. At first, she stared at him, not bothering to change her provocative stance. Later he remembered how she stood to her full height in slow motion. In her spiked leather boots, she was as tall as him. Her long dark tresses fell down to the middle of her back after she pushed it off her shoulders.

"You must be Robert." Her husky tone paralyzed him as she took a step toward him, smiling like a beautiful feline about to devour a loved canary, and he decided he would be okay with that.

"Umm. Yeah. And you are?" He really tried to sound nonchalant as her almond-shaped eyes, hazel green with flecks of yellow, narrowed ever so slightly, taking him in, head to toe. One of her eyebrows lifted.

She extended her hand and he probably took it too eagerly. "I'm Dr. Samantha Cordova, Tessa's friend from the university." Robert thought he felt her squeeze his fingers.

"Whose friend?" he mumbled like a forgetful old man.

"Tessa? Your wife?" She withdrew by drawing her fingers slowly across his palm that he continued to dangle in midair until he realized how ridiculous it must look and snatched it back.

"Oh sure. Of course." His nervous laugh filled the kitchen. "Tessa. I don't remember her mentioning you."

This time Dr. Cordova laughed, and Robert joined in because he thought it felt almost musical.

"I'm not surprised, Robert. She does like keeping secrets, doesn't she?"

"No doubt." He felt like a grinning idiot.

"Anyway, Tessa went to pick up her car and there was some kind of problem. She panicked knowing you needed to get to work and her neighbors were gone. Of course, she called me, since I planned to be in Grass Valley for a book signing at the Bee Hive Bookstore later today."

"You're an author?" He really wanted to sound impressed. "Romance writer?"

"I wish. I'm an economic advisor for a nonprofit group in D.C. Really cut and dried. Boring unless you're into that sort of thing. Tessa and I collaborated on the geography angle." Again, the flirty smile.

Robert nodded. "Actually, I love economics."

"Really?" She blinked her eyes as if surprised and pleased. Suddenly, her attention switched to someone behind him. "And you must be Sean Patrick."

With a half pivot he saw his son staring at Dr. Cordova, his mouth agape. He moved zombie-like up next to his father who used his finger to close Sean's mouth. "Say hello to Dr. Cordova, Mom's friend from the university."

"Wow. You don't look like any teacher I ever had." Sean grinned.

Samantha walked up to him, ran a finger down the side of the boy's face, and smiled. "And you are a very sweet young man to notice. Your mom talks about you all the time. I understand you'd like to go to West Point someday."

"Yes, ma'am," he managed to say.

Daniel joined them, leading Heather by the hand. His reaction to Samantha wasn't much different than his brother and father. Heather showed her displeasure by crossing her arms across her chest then shifting weight to one hip.

"Where's my mommy?" she demanded.

Robert patted his daughter on the cheek in hopes of silencing her. "She'll be here a little later." He tugged her behind him and glanced back at the woman who shifted her eyes too quickly to him. It struck a chord of familiarity. Maybe they'd met before. But surely, he would remember such an exquisite creature. "So, what's the plan, Dr. Cordova?" he asked, putting his hands on his hips, which made him feel like a superhero.

"Call me Sam." She strolled around to the coffee pot and poured Robert a cup of brew then brought it to him. "First, drink up. I brewed it myself. Tessa told me you like it really strong." What was she hinting at? "Then you go to work. I'll stay with the kids."

A cheer rose from the boys, but Heather stomped out.

"You can call Dean Clark to verify I am who I say I am. Oh. Tessa." She clicked her tongue. "We are going to have to get together. Maybe we can meet for lunch—or something, the next time you have time. Tessa says you work in Sacramento."

"I do. I do." Too eager, he thought. He took a sip of the coffee. "This is perfect. Tess gets it a little weak for me. Guess you'll have to come over every morning to make coffee." Both of them laughed, and the boys joined in.

"Aren't you in a hurry to leave? I don't want to make you late," she cooed.

"Nonsense. I don't really have to be there until after lunch. Tessa has a propensity for being late or getting her nose buried in her little geography projects. I wanted to make sure I had plenty of time."

"Smart."

He noticed she seemed to speak through gritted teeth. While he tossed her words around in his head, Robert gulped down the rest of the coffee.

"Are those donuts from Mr. Chubbs?" Sean Patrick said, running to the counter and opening up a box full of a variety of donuts. "They are," he informed his brother Daniel, who quickly joined him to grab his favorite.

"Surprise," she said handing them both a napkin. "There's a crème filled for you, Sean Patrick, with chocolate sprinkles. Your mom said it was your favorite."

"Sure is. Thanks." He bit into the long pastry and made smacking sounds of delight.

"How about you, Robert? Tessa says you like the cake donuts with powdered sugar."

Robert wanted to speak then felt his stomach roll. "I'm not feeling so well."

"Oh. Sorry."

Robert backed out of the kitchen and ran to the downstairs bathroom. Diarrhea? Of all the times to get sick. He flipped on the ceiling fan, but it didn't work. Luckily, he spotted the air freshener only to find it empty. Why hadn't Tessa replaced it? Then he remembered she'd asked him to pick up some when he went to fill the car with gas two weeks ago. He exited the powder room and felt another pain coming on. This time, he ran upstairs and barely reached his bathroom in time. Was he going to throw up, too? He felt like it.

~~~

"So, you work with Mom, Sam?" Sean Patrick grabbed his third donut as Daniel poured them both a glass of milk. Heather had wandered back in and was seduced by the pink donut with sprinkles.

"Yes. She and I are best buddies. I have been in charge of her"—she paused for a few seconds to find the right word—"integration into our tight little group."

Daniel wiped his mouth with the back of his hand as Sam passed him a paper towel. "Mom likes her job. But she doesn't talk much about the people she works with. I thought maybe she didn't have any friends. When she worked in Grass Valley, we heard
~~~

about people all the time."

Sam washed out Robert's coffee cup. She didn't want the kids to accidently take a sip out of it and suffer like their father would for the next few hours. She even found a little cleaner with bleach under the sink to ensure no residue would survive her attempt at revenge in spite of finding Robert Scott a rather attractive man. He wore the Ivy League image perfectly. Maybe another time and place she'd see what convinced Tessa to stay with a man like him instead of taking advantage of Captain Chase Hunter's interest in her. Then there was the tribesman from Northern Afghanistan who clearly could have kept a woman happy in his bed for an eternity. Yet she stayed with this character.

Robert entered the kitchen again, pale and dressed in sweatpants and a tee shirt. His smile was a little less flirty, and he propped a hip against the counter. "Thanks, Sam, for stopping by. Oh, how did you get in this morning?"

"Tessa told me where you hid the spare key." She shifted her eyes to a spot near him. "I laid it there. Are you okay?" She tilted her head.

"Oh. Sure. Forgot about the spare key." He seemed to make an effort to straighten up. "I called work and told them I was taking some comp time since I didn't have any clients today and I can work from home if anything comes up."

"Then, I'll be on my way." She smiled as she moved toward him. "Unless there is anything else I can do for you."

His eyes widened. Stepping in closer, she gave him a friendly kiss on the cheek. "Let's get together real soon, Robert. Bye, kids. Enjoy the donuts," she called, leaving the kitchen.

She closed the front door behind her and chuckled all the way to her car.

CHAPTER TWENTY-TWO

The waters swallowed up the Scout quicker than Chase thought possible. He stripped off his padded jacket and sweatshirt. He decided there wasn't enough time to remove his boots and dove in after Tessa. The water felt like someone hit him with a sledgehammer as he pumped his legs against the floating chunks of ice. He could still hear her call his name when the top of the car disappeared beneath the surface. Although, along the shore, the water probably was only about nine feet deep, with freezing temperatures, his body could only do so much to reach her in time.

Before plunging beneath the surface of the water, he took a gulp of air, held it, expelled, and repeated several times then took one large deep intake of air. He could see her trying to escape through the back window when she spotted him. With puffed-out cheeks, he hoped she could hold on a little longer. When he reached her, he saw her motions become sluggish and her eyes widen. She reached for him and almost smiled then shook her head then pointed for him to leave. A white plastic bag, tied around her arm, floated like wavy seaweed in the deep. A snow shovel had wedged her inside. He grabbed hold of the back of the Scout window frame and swung his feet in to knock the shovel loose.

His lungs burned with a pain he'd never known before when he reached in and grabbed Tessa by the hair and snatched her out. Wrapping his arm around her shoulders, he kicked harder than he thought possible, but it wasn't enough. Even though the surface seemed to be inches away, his strength faded, but then something latched onto him, jerking him upward. Tessa was pried from his grip as he was dragged out of the water then across some pebbles, to shore.

Chase found his footing soon enough and discovered Handsome had saved them. The guy's pant legs were wet up to his thighs. He bent over Tessa's limp body and shook his head. Chase dropped down and began CPR. She responded immediately, vomiting up her share of Lake Tahoe, followed by coughing. Chase rolled her to her back then moved her matted hair from her face.

"We've got—to get—her warm." Chase tried to lift her, but weight of so much wet clothing complicated his ability to rush her to safety.

Handsome lifted her like a limp rag doll into his arms. "Go. You both need to get warm. She is in bad shape. If you need help, grab the winch to pull yourself along." He moved upward without waiting to see if Chase followed. "The cabin should still be warm."

Although his body plummeted toward the death spiral of hypothermia, he forced himself to keep up with Handsome. Tessa wasn't moving, but she'd survived the first danger. He needed to get her warm before it was too late.

Handsome staggered up the steps. Chase reasoned his strength must be waning. He managed to catch up and relieve him of her body, freeing the man to open the door.

Tessa squirmed enough to give Chase hope she wasn't going to die in his arms. He tightened his hold when he felt her feet touch the floor. Her legs wobbled so she fell against him and buried her face against his chest.

Chase caught a glimpse of Handsome lumbering in and quickly removed his wet gloves, boots then pants. "Get out of those clothes," he ordered. "I'll stoke the fire."

Chase nodded and led Tessa through the open bathroom door. Her steps reminded him of a zombie. He leaned her against the stacked washer-dryer combo.

"I'm sorry about this, babe." He yelled out to Handsome who kneeled by the fire, which was once again roaring. "Get us something warm to wrap up in then heat some water."

Chase stripped off his shirt and pants, but left his boxers. He'd wait on those. Handsome handed in a couple of extra-large flannel shirts.

"Brought them up a couple of weeks ago," he volunteered then closed the door.

"Okay, Tess. I'm going to get you out of those wet clothes," he said unzipping her coat. She stared down at his hands without saying anything then up into his face.

"No," she said simply. With some effort, she tried to move away, which enabled him to get her free of the coat.

He manhandled her out of her blue sweater. Silent tears rolled down her cheeks as he maneuvered her down on the closed toilet to remove her boots and socks.

"Stand up so I can get those pants off you," he said in a calm voice so not to alarm her. "I've got to get you warmed up, Tess. I'm not taking advantage…" She shook her head no again so he pulled her up and quickly jerked down her pants. "Sit down so I can get them over your feet."

"No," she whispered.

"Fine." He shoved her down again and finished the job.

"Not cold. I'm sleepy."

He slipped one of the flannel shirts over her head. It fell down almost to her knees. "You can slap me for this later," he said, reaching under the shirt and unsnapped her bra. It wasn't hard to remove since she hadn't inserted her arms into the sleeves. Then off came her panties before he managed to slip her arms into the sleeves.

"No. Stop."

Chase donned the other flannel shirt and then removed his boxers. He jerked open the bathroom door, and grabbed her forearm, and tugged. When she barely moved, Chase swung her up in his arms and headed for the bed.

"Turn down those covers, Handsome."

He did straightaway.

Carrying Tessa to the side of the bed, he laid her down then tucked covers around her shivering body. Hurrying around to the other side, Chase climbed in next to her. He shook as he moved closer to the woman who insisted on complicating his life, hoping together, they wouldn't die of this ridiculous event. All he wanted to do was sleep, but his body ached too much for that to happen at first.

Tessa moved her head toward him and untucked the covers separating them. "Thank you," she whispered then rolled to face him as she pressed her body against his. "I'll save you some day," she breathed as her eyelids fluttered then closed.

Chase kissed her forehead, wrapped his arm around her back, and held on tight. "You already have."

~~~

By the time Chase rousted up from the bed, a late afternoon storm had set in. Handsome sat by the fire in the wingback chair. He wanted to chuckle at the sight of such a big body crammed into a once-refined piece of furniture. Swinging his feet to the floor, he discovered his clothes neatly folded at the foot of the bed. It took only a minute to dress and join him at the fireside.

"What time is it?" Chase asked.

"Three. Feeling better?"

He nodded and glanced around the cabin, taking mental inventory to be prepared for whatever lay ahead. The ingrained habit of being suspicious and cautious had saved his life on more than one occasion. The smell of cooked food distracted him until he decided to see what simmered in the iron Dutch oven on the hot plate.

"Help yourself, Captain Hunter. There's soup I threw together. I got Tessa to drink some hot tea a couple of hours ago. She'd warmed up enough to manage on her own, but I wouldn't let her get out of the bed."

That explained why she'd remained pressed up against his back when he awoke. He didn't remember her stirring or slipping from his embrace. The anger inside him surfaced as he moved back to stand in front of Handsome.

"What the hell were you thinking, bringing her up here against her will? Kidnapping is a serious offense." Chase watched the black man rise from his chair to loom menacingly over him. He stared down at him with a calm that unsettled his resolve.

"Who says I kidnapped her?"
~~~

"She has been to hell and back in the last six months. No way would she follow you up here," Chase snapped, jabbing a finger in an iron-like chest. He watched Handsome stare down at the finger on his chest and slowly removed it. "What lies did you tell her?"

Handsome's bottom lip drooped down, making it appear thicker. His expression remained calm, almost trance-like when he spoke. "Like the rest of your criminal entourage, she is an opportunist. I dangled a carrot in front of her nose, and she couldn't resist."

"What kind of a carrot?" Chase snarled.

"One that will make a difference. Unlike you, this woman believes good may change the future. She wanted to be in the thick of it, willing to gamble with her life." Handsome glanced at a doll lying on the fireplace hearth and stepped away from Chase to pick it up. "This is what she went back into the car to get."

"A doll?" Chase growled in contempt. "Give me a break."

"A doll." He walked over to the bed and laid it on the pillow next to Tessa's face.

"How can a doll change the world?"

Handsome shoved Chase aside like a pesky fly, to walk into the kitchen. He ladled up two bowls of soup and brought them back to the table before sitting down. "If I had wanted you to know, or trusted you, then I might have invited you along." Scooping a large spoon of soup into his mouth, he kicked the chair out for Chase. "But I wanted her alone." He cut his eyes over to Tessa then back to Chase and smirked. "It didn't work out exactly as I planned."

Rage threatened to spill over into the conversation. A brutal fight was brewing. Chase wasn't sure he could win against a man the size and power of Handsome. Chances were the man had wanted him to lose control and used Tessa as the bait.

"Shut your mouth."

Handsome pointed his spoon at Tessa, who had begun to stir. "I don't hurt women and children, especially people like her. You need to remember this. I see how you look at her." He slurped up two more spoonsfuls before continuing. "She is with me, like it or not. In spirit, at least. If you prevent her from helping me I will—"

"What? Punish me?"

Lifting the bowl, he drank the rest of the liquid then wiped his mouth with a crumpled paper towel. "No. I will punish her and her children."

"I should kill you right here and now."

"Yes. You should because I am taking Tessa away from you one way or another. And she will do as I say."

"Over my dead body."

Handsome stood and took his plate to the sink. "That sounds pretty good to me. As to killing me, I removed your weapon, ammo, and anything else I thought you might use to disable me. I know all about your Ranger-Delta Force days."

"Then you know I don't need a gun to eliminate you." Chase glanced over at Tessa as she pushed covers away. He lowered his voice. "She isn't like us at all, Handsome. Tessa is a pie-in-the-sky kind of girl. Whatever garbage you've been filling her head to get her involved in your illegal business stops here."

"What are you talking about? What's wrong," Tessa yawned. "You sound angry, Chase."

He walked over to her and sat on the edge of the bed. The temptation to smooth her hair away from her face gave way to patting her cheek. "Nothing's wrong. Talking about when we can get out of here."

"Oh. My. Gosh." Tessa groaned. "My kids. Robert. I've got to get home."

"Taken care of," he promised. "How do you feel?"

"Like I need a bath."

Before Chase could offer to help her out of bed, Handsome brought over a cotton robe like something a great-grandmother would wear. "Found it hanging in the closet. Washed it, so don't worry."

"Thank you, Handsome." She smiled up at him, revealing her trust and admiration. "I know you carried me up the embankment. Chase and I are so appreciative."

Chase frowned.

"Right?" she asked, jabbing a finger in his side.

"Yeah. Good thing I had ahold of you or he might have left me there to be a floater in the lake."

"Don't be silly. Handsome is one of the good guys." She continued to beam at the large black man towering over them both. Pulling on the robe, she pushed the covers aside. "If you'll excuse me, I have a hot shower to take."

When the bathroom door closed, Handsome chuckled and gave a friendly shove to Chase's shoulder. "Yeah. I'm one of the good guys."

Chapter Twenty-Three

Special Agent Martin grimaced at hearing Reeva Kaplan give his people orders. She'd promised to expose her company's money laundering business for protection, with no charges pressed against her. The night he'd shown up at the San Francisco hotel to clean up Enigma's mess, he'd realized immediately what he'd stepped into. For over a year, his office had worked on this case, only to see it vaporize in the last month. They'd scrambled to find out where all the players might be hiding. Something had tipped them off. They'd simply vanished—no chatter, no leads, no trace they ever existed.

Then he walked into Robert Scott's room to find Reeva bound and gagged. It didn't take him long to call in reinforcements, saying he got a tip from one of her disgruntled customers who had been his informant. Several other agents helped him stage the photo shoot of a violent death then handed her off for interrogation at headquarters. Under other circumstances, like a sporting event, high fives would have been an appropriate gesture. But FBI didn't high-five much of anything these days.

Agent Martin wasn't sure why Robert Scott was involved, but he intended to find out since Reeva was scared out of her wits by the time they hauled her off. Something about a couple of missing diamonds and the likelihood she'd be accused of selling them.

"The man—the Robert fella, he has my diamonds. I sold them to him—or I was going to until those criminals burst in on us. I planned to switch them out for fakes when he was in the bathroom but was interrupted."

"Ahh. Too bad. Guess you're going to have to help us to make sure you don't meet with the real bloody end of your operation."

Although she was sophisticated and easy on the eyes, Agent Martin found her abrasive. The South African accent sounded a little condescending when she answered questions or made requests that were more like demands. His superiors felt confident in the information she provided and planned to move against several law firms, banks, and diamond brokers in the next few weeks. What remained unclear was why she sought out Robert Scott.

From what he could tell, the man really was innocent of any money laundering crime. What he was guilty of was a bad decision concerning letting Reeva Kaplan into his room and buying the diamonds. The story he gave about purchasing them for his wife sounded too good to be true, at first. But after a little digging, he determined Robert remained the good guy, clean and innocent of any crime. Of course, that didn't mean he was innocent of being a womanizer. He wouldn't be the first husband in a city like San Francisco who was seduced by a pretty woman with an accent. The number of temptations in The City by the Bay remained endless.

Agent Martin didn't know Tessa Scott very well, mostly on paper because of her dealings with President Buck Austin. He'd met her a couple of times during her tenure in Washington D.C. when a hurricane nearly sent the country back to the Stone Age in a matter of hours. If she hadn't been there, he wasn't sure what the outcome might have been. Because of her quick actions, the president survived an attack by terrorists, and they avoided going to war with Egypt or, possibly, Israel.

Even though she appeared to be a rather ordinary soccer mom with high expectations for her children, educated, and a regular church goer, she was in fact a dangerous woman. Somehow, she'd been recruited for Enigma—maybe because of D.C. or the president's you-can't-refuse-my-offer invitation. Maybe the band of shady agents at Enigma wanted a new pet project to make them feel better about being hired guns in the name of national security.

He remained confident her enlistment wasn't much different from how he'd been dragged into service. Once you help them or they help you, their name is tattooed on your soul, and the only way out is death. But he understood through the grapevine, Tessa's role in this whole diamond business involved another character named Handsome Jones.

"Never heard of him," Reeva said, wide-eyed and straight-faced. "Who is he?" The sound of innocence didn't fit this woman.

Someone higher-up decided Agent Martin should transport her off to US Marshals waiting in Sacramento. They would put her in protective custody until warrants were served and all involved parties were charged.

"He is a person of interest. Used to be in the diamond business, I understand. Thought you might know him."

"No. I don't believe I do. At least not by that name," she offered as a tidbit.

Agent Martin knew the woman could lie with a straight face, and this might be one of those times. No matter. He was tired. It had been a rough couple of days. Handing her off to the Marshals would give him more time to deal with Robert and find out where those diamonds might be. Diamonds weren't much different from using DNA or fingerprints to track someone down. This might be a higher-tech search, but the Bureau had people for such a job.

He spotted the house where he'd arranged to meet the two Marshals. A white sedan should be parked in the driveway with a bumper sticker reading, *Vote for Obi-Wan-Kenobi. He's our only hope.* All the Star Wars mania drove him crazy. He wasn't sure whose idea it had been to use the bumper sticker, but he found it childish.

"Come on. You'll stay here until tomorrow."

"Then what?"

Agent Martin knocked on the door with one knuckle and noticed she canvassed the neighborhood with concern. "This is a safe place. The Office of US Marshals is sending in a plane for you. Remember? I told you yesterday. What's the problem?" He paused, feeling an uneasiness in his bones. "You didn't call anyone, right?"

"No. No. No, of course, not." She shrugged then rubbed her arms as if the February chill had permeated her London Fog jacket.

Three noes equaled a yes in his book. Stealing a glance at her then the street, he shifted his attention back to the door, which was opened by a US Marshal chewing on something. His snack left a spot of mustard in the corner of his mouth.

"You Cline?" Martin asked. The man nodded and stepped aside to let them enter. "Where's Gauen? Haven't seen the old reprobate since we hit Vegas two years ago. He tell you about our brush with the law?" Martin surveyed the room and noticed a chair flipped over, a few magazines sticking out from under the coffee table, and a large drink from a nearby fast food restaurant on its side with dripping liquid trailing across the top.

"Said you were an asshole." The man grinned.

In the time it took to inhale, Agent Martin pulled his Glock and pointed it at the man. "Interesting, considering I don't know a Cline or Gauen, and there's no way in hell, I'd go to Vegas if I did."

Martin wondered where the real Marshals might be. He glanced over his shoulder to say something to Reeva, but she picked up a decorative fleur-de-lis figurine from the entry table and smashed it into his head. The room faded to black as the gun dropped from his hand and the floor swam up to catch him.

~~~

"Vernon, when is this new storm clearing out? The drone won't do us any good with the wind picking up." Carter Johnson fumed as he stood staring out the window of the safe house Tessa had been instructed to escape to a few days earlier. The drone could send them a clearer picture of what was going on on the ground.

"Give it a few hours. This is a little one, I think. The interstate is still open, although traffic is being discouraged. Skiers are wanting to get on the fresh powder."

"Okay. Soon as the wind dies down, I get this puppy up. We've got a signal from Chase's borrowed truck."

"Good because Mrs. Scott's trace died. Not sure why. Boss should have checked in by now. Something isn't right."

"Zoric and I will locate them, map it then head out to assist." Carter grinned at the stone-faced Zoric as he put Vernon on speaker. "Any more news? How'd Sam do with Robert?"
~~~

"Or how exactly did she do Robert?" the Serbian offered in his thick accent. This question irritated Carter enough to narrow his eyes a little. He shouldn't offend his partner, even if it were true.

Vernon responded. "Wasn't there long. She called in to say he decided to stay home with the kids and wait on Mrs. Scott. Ken will pick up her vehicle and meet her in Grass Valley, provided we get her there in time. Robert has got to wonder about all of this."

"If all else fails, we'll send Sam back," Carter suggested. "By the time she's finished with him, he'll forget he ever got married to our little Grass Valley commando."

~~~

Tessa paced the floor from the small kitchen to the front door, past the two men sitting near the fire. Every couple of minutes, she stopped and peered out a different window to check on the storm, exhaled a deep sigh, hugged her arms then repeated the routine. How would she ever explain this to Robert? What if she ended up spending another night in this cabin? All she wanted was to be with her kids, make a difference in the lives of her students, finish up her PhD, and live happily ever after with the love of her life.

The thought stirred her attention to Chase, who glared at Handsome dozing in the chaise lounge she'd rested on last night. His half-closed eyes, which accented his Native American heritage, gave him the threatening appearance he might be ready to strike the much bigger man. With so much winter white surrounding them, his tan skin seemed darker. Once again Tessa realized there wasn't a soft spot on him. If she hadn't seen him breathing, he would have resembled a statue.

She remembered the way he'd undressed her; careful not to touch her inappropriately, quick to finish the job, speaking in short sentences in a quiet voice laced with enough urgency to keep her from hurting herself.

Then there was the bed and him pulling her into his body, also cold from taking a dive into the lake to save her. He warmed faster than she thought possible. She'd cast caution and embarrassment to the wind as she took advantage of his nearness. Even when she woke to find his hand on her butt, Chase remained a saint. When her body warmed, she could have withdrawn, but she didn't. Since
~~~

they recovered, she'd found it difficult to make eye contact or talk to him. Fortunately, he didn't push the issue. Maybe he felt as uncomfortable as she did about how he'd undressed her.

"Why are you staring at me?" Chase cut his gaze to engulf her from head to toe.

She rubbed her arms then dropped them to her sides. "What?" she gulped. "I wasn't staring."

"Okay." He adjusted his body in the chair. "What are you thinking?"

"I'm not thinking," she said pacing past him.

"Exactly."

She stopped in front of him when she circled back. "Meaning?"

Chase pushed himself up out of the chair to tower over her. She became keenly aware how this stance played to his advantage, but she wasn't going to budge.

"Meaning, what the hell were you thinking coming up here with this character? Have you lost your mind?"

"I resent your tone, Captain Hunter. I did what I've been trained to do. Improvise. He didn't tell me the whole truth about the Kifaru diamond."

"The Kifaru?" he asked incredulously. "Does he have it?" he whispered.

"Yes. When I realized it wasn't in Sacramento, it was too late. I thought you'd be able to follow me. Then I realized we were out of range. I begged him to take me home, Chase. It wasn't like I planned to come up here or have you put your life in jeopardy again. I'm sorry I nearly got you killed. I suck at this agent stuff. I'm resigning as soon as we get back. I put everyone in danger each time I'm given a job to do."

Her face and neck grew hot under his penetrating gaze. Was he remembering how she pressed against him, unashamed and even a little clingy? He now knew more about her than she ever wanted him to know. Pivoting on her heels, Tessa stormed into the kitchen with Chase right behind her. He caught her by the arm and pulled her around.

"What is bothering you? Did Handsome hurt you or—"

"No. Of course not," she snapped, jerking free of his hold. "I want to go home."

"Are you upset because I undressed you? Because I didn't have a choice. You were unable to do anything for yourself.”

Tessa diverted her eyes to stare out the window. “I know,” she whispered then cleared her throat.

Using his finger, he moved her chin back so she’d have to look at him. “We are adults and have been through a lot together. Mostly, we are friends. I wasn’t trying to disrespect you.”

“I know. Really. I know. It’s just…”

“What? Are you offended I got into bed with you?” His brow furrowed over his dark eyes. “I needed to warm up fast, too.” She remained quiet. “Tell me. Did I frisk you or something in my sleep…because it wasn’t intentional?”

Tessa couldn’t resist a chuckle. “You didn’t frisk me.”

His eyebrows went up. “Then I guess it must be when you did your own exploring. I’m not sure what you were looking for, but I could’ve assisted with the right kind of encouragement.”

Tessa gasped then landed a punch to his gut. He laughed. “Shut up,” she demanded. “Now you’re wishful thinking.”

“Hmm. Probably,” he said walking away. “Either way, we were in survival mode. Nothing to be embarrassed about, so stop blushing and giving me the cold shoulder.” He glanced back with a mischievous grin on his wide mouth. “No pun intended.”

Handsome yawned and rolled out of the chaise. “How is the weather?”

“Better.” Tessa boiled some water and brought him a cup of hot tea. “We should be able to leave soon.” She sat on the arm of the chair across from Handsome. “Then we can make plans.”

“Whoa.” Chase held up a hand. “Plans?”

Handsome took a gulp of tea before standing and carrying it to the table. As he walked by Tessa, he pinched her cheek then continued to the front door. “We need more wood. Be right back.” The door opened and closed quickly, letting in a gust of cold air.

“What plans, Tessa?” Chase asked with a voice full of caution.

“I’ll explain later. Shush. Here he comes.”

The door reopened and Handsome entered without any wood.

“What’s the matter, sport? Wood too heavy?” Chase teased sarcastically. “Need some help? I’m sure Tessa can lend a hand.”

Tessa elbowed her boss. “He’s teasing. Shut the door. You’re letting all the heat out.” She shivered.

“About that,” Handsome voiced slowly.

Reeva Kaplan shoved her way in around Handsome and leveled a Glock at Tessa. "Handsome is coming with me."

"Handsome?" Tessa stood, and Chase pushed her behind him.

Chapter Twenty-Four

"How did you find us?" Chase figured his anger showed as his jaws clenched, but he managed to keep his voice even and cool. His question, directed at Reeva, brought a smile to her face.

"Handsome called me."

Chase shifted his attention to the big man staring at him. His bottom lip protruded, and his eyelids drooped a bit. "You took my phone when I slept."

Handsome only nodded.

"You look pretty good, Reeva, for someone who died a few days ago." Chase frowned.

She couldn't hide her surprise. "Have we met?"

"No." Lying to her was not a big deal. "But we have a mutual friend I'd like to have a serious conversation with."

A soft chuckle spluttered across her pale lips, leaving her with an undignified appearance. "Would that be Special Agent Martin?"

"It would. Know where I can find him? He has been keeping secrets from me concerning you."

"And who are you exactly?" Reeva waved her gun at him in such a careless manner Chase reached back to make sure Tessa remained safe.

When he didn't respond, Reeva squinted at Handsome for

answers. He lifted his chin a little higher to stare at Chase before speaking. "Independent contractor the FBI uses to mop up their messes."

"Oh. Good to know." She smiled. "And her?"

"Nobody," Handsome said opening the door to leave. "This is her place. He brought me here since they're sleeping together. Thought no one could find me."

"So, two loose ends."

Handsome reached around her and relieved her of the weapon so fast she staggered at the surprise. "Let's go. I have a plane to catch. The way I see it, you're the loose end." He exited, leaving her standing before them. She backed out and slammed the door.

"What are we going to do?" Tessa ran to the front window. "She's taking Handsome. Stop her."

"He's going on his own accord, or didn't you notice?" He searched for his weapon, but it was gone, along with his phone.

"What I noticed was he's taking your truck with four-wheel drive," she said, pointing out the window. Two gunshots followed. "Oh. My. Gosh. He shot her!"

"We can only hope, but I wouldn't count on it."

Chase felt his pockets for his keys then ran out onto the porch. "Get out of my truck, Handsome." His words no sooner left his mouth than Handsome put the truck in gear then revved the engine. As Chase ran toward the vehicle, Handsome sped up, and would have hit him if Chase hadn't jumped out of the way into a snowbank.

Tessa ran to him and helped him up. "Are you okay?" She dusted snow off his tee shirt. Both were exposed to the elements. "At least we have their car," she said optimistically.

"You mean the one with two flat tires. I'm sure the gunshots were so we wouldn't follow."

"Listen. Hear anything?" The snow muffled the sound of Tessa's voice. Chase tilted his ear toward the hollow sound coming from Reeva's car.

Both approached the car to hear a moan along with pounding in the trunk. It felt oddly out of place in such a serene setting.

"Pop the trunk, Tess." She hurried to do so then ran back to join Chase as he lifted the lid.

"Well, as I live and breathe." Chase smiled triumphantly.

"Looks like Christmas is coming a little early this year." Tessa reached in to help the man with the bloodied face and duct tape across his mouth. His hands and feet were tied behind his back. Chase jerked her away then bent over the man to taunt, "Hello, Special Agent Martin. I guess you didn't get the memo about never pulling a fast one on your Enigma brothers and sisters." He clicked his tongue like a teacher reprimanding his students. "I'm afraid I'm going to have to teach you a lesson."

~~~

Tessa never got used to the way Chase could be charming and sexy one minute then transform into Attila the Hun the next. On those occasions, she found herself stepping back from hero worship to embrace a sense of caution with her admiration. She'd learned early on in working with him, mercy wasn't part of his vocabulary if double-crossed, disobeyed, or jeopardized in a key component to a mission. She'd done all those things at one time or another and paid dearly for the lesson.

Enigma agents were tough, mean, and unforgiving when it came to national security. He'd protected her in those early days because she was innocent of the ways of the world. Her mistakes were from a civilian, not as an agent. She'd come a long way since then. The expectations reminded her, some decisions could put you in the crosshairs of dangerous people, and some of those people worked for Enigma.

"You aren't going to leave him in the trunk!" she complained as Chase took the porch steps two at a time. "He's FBI and has helped us in the past. Chase, stop," she demanded.

He halted on the top step and pivoted to glower at her. "You do know he's the one who interviewed your husband, pretended Reeva was dead, and appears to be playing both sides of the fence."

"Yes." She whirled around and trudged through the snow toward the car. "Which is what we do all the time," she called over her shoulder. "Hear him out, Chase. He'll freeze in the car. He's hurt."

By the time she'd reached the open trunk, Agent Martin shivered violently. Chase disappeared inside the cabin and quickly
~~~

returned, carrying a butcher knife, a murderous scowl on his face.

She placed herself between him and Agent Martin. "What are you going to do?"

"Get out of my way," he growled. When she folded her arms across her chest, he reached out and easily pushed her aside.

Agent Martin's eyes widened as Chase focused on him then raised the knife. In one swift movement, he sliced through the bindings on his wrists and feet.

Tessa released a heavy sigh. He swung the knife behind him so she could take it. Next, he reached down and ripped the tape covering the agent's mouth off so roughly, Tessa wondered if he'd taken skin with the action. A number of colorful adjectives spewed out of the man as he struggled to get out of the trunk. When Chase didn't bother to assist, Tessa stepped up, returning the knife back to him and adding a disgruntled glare.

"Thanks, Tessa." Agent Martin threw a leg out then eased out into the snow.

She suddenly realized how cold she was, having run out without a coat. Chase, on the other hand, stood like a statue, eyeing Agent Martin like it might be a summer day. She put her arm around the agent, who leaned into her. Chase pushed past them, offering no support.

"He's fine. Don't baby him." He headed for the porch.

After Tessa helped Martin up the steps, he moved away from her and walked into the cabin on his own. His extended hand drew a smirk from Chase.

"Shame on you, Chase." Tessa followed Martin inside and pointed to the chair near the fire. "Bring in another log and build this fire up for Agent Martin."

She watched him chew his bottom lip for a second before deciding to get more wood. She cleaned the agent's face, even though he protested the effort.

"I got it." Martin grabbed the wet washcloth from her and finished the job himself, keeping a vigilant watch on Chase.

Chase stoked the fire in a methodical fashion before dragging a metal chair into the living room from the kitchen area. Flipping it around, he straddled it and folded his arms on the back.

"Spill it," Chase demanded then pulled the chair closer. Tessa could feel the testosterone battle begin as tempers flared.

"Pretty please," Martin offered sarcastically.

"Pretty. Please." Chase spoke out of the corner of his mouth with a guttural sound that reminded her of a wolf before it took an innocent animal for a snack. Goose bumps formed on her arms.

"One thing we know for sure is Handsome probably saved our lives a few minutes ago with his lies." Tessa slapped her hands together and smiled hoping the standoff would evaporate into a feeling of goodwill.

Chase shifted his gaze to her, making her shiver. Could a stab wound feel like his impatient attitude? "Considering he told her how to get here, I wouldn't say he did us any favors."

Agent Martin explained how the FBI had been investigating money laundering by some South African mining companies. They dealt in conflict diamonds in troubled areas. Profits skyrocketed in their risky business venture. Keep in mind they didn't care about anyone's political cause. It was all about the money. But the money was dirty so they needed overseas markets to clean it up for them. The biggest abusers came from Botswana.

"Black diamonds are pretty rare, so they hold them back to drive the prices up. The lower grade ones, the white ones like we buy in rings, etc., go various places. Some of them are lab-changed into chocolate diamonds. Big market here in the States. But then there are the others, which are more valuable and fetch a profit. They follow the Kimberly Accord to all appearances, but, as you know, there are ways around it. Only about 80 percent of the mined diamonds filter through to be legit."

"You staged Reeva's death," Chase growled.

"You think I was going to let all my work go down the drain because you walked in on Robert Scott having a tryst?" He immediately glanced at Tessa and ran his hand over the lower part of his face. "Sorry. That came out wrong."

Listening to this might not be good for her marriage. Problems already brewed between her and Robert.

Agent Martin's attention returned to Chase. "Why the hell were you there in the first place? You never said."

"No. I never did."

"I have a right to know. I did what you asked and still kept an eye on Robert. I believe two US Marshals lost their lives today because of Reeva and Handsome."

"You do have a right to know. Although, keep in mind, you screwed up with Enigma. I won't forget it."

Agent Martin twisted his mouth into a frown. "Our benefactors at Enigma saw Reeva Kaplan as an agent of an unhealthy change brewing in Botswana. Currently, it is the only stable country in Southern Africa in spite of a dictator who lines his pockets with money that should be going to improve the lives of his people."

Tessa chimed in to fill in some gaps maybe even Chase didn't know. "These mining companies are running out of diamonds, and before long they'll be left with no other revenue. Plans are in the works for building a dam on the Okavango River. Angola tried this years ago but was shut down by international pressure and their own wars. There is another factor, too."

"I guess Handsome filled your head with more nonsense." Chase sounded skeptical.

"Yes. He knows who can make real change in the country. They are scrambling to find out who has the Kifaru diamond."

"Why?" Agent Martin asked.

"With the diamond, the real leader will step forward, and there isn't anyone who will be able to stop him."

The popping of the fire sounded like sparklers on the fourth of July. Both men remained silent for a few minutes. Tessa guessed they were weighing the information she'd given them.

"Do you know who it is?" Agent Martin asked after pushing up off the chaise.

"He wouldn't tell me, but he knows."

"And the diamond?" Tessa knew Chase scrutinized her when he lifted his eyebrow and glared at her. Sometimes such an expressed withered her resolve to be obstinate. "Where is it? You said earlier he had it. I'm assuming when he mentioned it at dinner last night, you thought you could manage all this."

She nodded rapidly. "Which is why I decided to go with him. I knew if the Kifaru really had that much power, we needed to retrieve it for further examination. At that point we could decide if his story had any merit."

"Great." Agent Martin tried to stretch out his stiffness. "So, he leaves with Reeva and the diamond. She will certainly take it and negotiate herself into a position of power. I bet there are factions forming who would promise her anything to be able to present the diamond to someone who discovers which way the winds of change are blowing."

Tessa crossed her arms and couldn't keep from batting her eyes while nodding in agreement. Alluding to the fact that she now possessed the diamond didn't seem to be relevant at this point. Something inside her wanted to protect Handsome's wishes.

Chase surveyed the room. "Sounds like a wild-goose chase coming up here?" He held her gaze, making her squirm a little.

"We were getting ready to go find it when the avalanche occurred. Honestly, I forgot about it after everything that happened afterward. Didn't seem nearly as important. If you know what I mean?" Tessa swallowed hard then hustled into the kitchen. "I'll make some coffee."

"I'll help you." Chase followed on her heels then lowered his voice as Martin faced the fireplace to warm his hands. "You saw the diamond."

"Weren't you listening to me?" Tessa threw the old coffee grounds away while Chase replaced the paper filter.

"After all this time, Tess, I can tell when you are lying."

"I didn't lie," she mumbled, stealing a glance into the living room. "With you undressing me, climbing into bed and holding me, my mind and heart raced. I'm not proud of those thoughts, but it is what it is."

Chase raised his chin and glared down his nose, narrowing his eyes. An amused grin nearly let his wolfish laughter erupt, but he fought to return to sour faced. "If only you were telling truth," he mused. "I swear to all that is holy, one of these days I'm going to pull you across my knee and spank you for these childish pranks."

"Promises. Promises." She didn't want to give up flirting yet. Maybe he would believe her.

He tilted his head and watched her pour in the water. With a new sensual tone in his voice, he continued. "As a side note about spanking you—"

"All right!" She sighed. "I know you're trying to make me uncomfortable. Congratulations. You win. Yes. I saw the Kifaru."

"As usual, you shut me down when it starts to get interesting." He smiled as he flipped the coffee switch. "Where is it?" When she didn't answer, Chase stepped in front of her, so close there was little hope of escape. "And spanking is back on the table. I'm beginning to think you're looking for an excuse. And thanks for the comment about 'heart racing.' My ego is restored. I was beginning to think I'd lost my touch."

She stared up into his dark eyes and realized for the millionth time she didn't care what he did for a living. "I seriously doubt you have an ego problem considering what the brainy bimbos say about you at the university," she hissed. "Get us out of here. I have it."

"Is that why you went back into the Scout?"

"Yes. I was trying…"

"To do a good thing," he said rolling his eyes to the ceiling. "You always do." Stepping back, he stared at her. "Tessa, you shaved ten years off my life when you went into the water. You'll be the death of me."

For the first time since they'd met, she didn't feel nervous about revealing her feelings. "I can't imagine life without you in it."

CHAPTER TWENTY-FIVE

"**W**hat the hell is that?" Agent Martin moved toward the front window, only to have Chase rush to cut him off.

"I'd say it's a drone." He smiled and waved Tessa forward. "Think there's any paper to write a message? I'm pretty sure Carter sent his toy for us. We can let him know we need help." She returned with a paper towel and a black crayon she'd found earlier while searching the drawers for a coffee filter. Chase gave her the message to write then went outside and held it up over his head. The white drone circled several times and returned before hovering about twelve feet above him. Thirty seconds later, the drone disappeared over the trees.

Tessa stood in the doorway with Martin. "I hear something else. Do you?"

Chase stopped in the front yard and then scrutinized where the avalanche occurred down the road from the cabin. He then spun around to inspect where he'd parked his truck at the entrance. "Get inside!" he yelled as he scampered onto the porch and barreled into the two blocking the doorway.

In seconds, Chase had dragged Tessa into the windowless bathroom, with Agent Martin on their heels. Pushing Tessa into the shower stall, he jumped in after her and used his body to shield hers as he felt Martin squeeze in behind him. The agent had grabbed a couple of crocheted afghans off the chairs on his way in and threw them over the three of them. The rumble grew to a roar as the house shifted and glass shattered outside their protected area. The house rocked a bit then felt as if it dropped slightly. In seconds, quiet returned.

Chase could feel Tessa's arms around his waist. She molded her body to his with her heart pounding and face buried against his chest. He realized his fingers were tangled in her curls and wondered how she could breathe with the pressure he continued to hold her in place. There was a slight tremble in her limbs as he stepped her back enough to gaze down at her face.

"Okay?"

She nodded and met his concern with a timid smile.

"Martin?"

"Yeah. I'm good."

Agent Martin backed out and tried to open the door, which appeared to be jammed. The men put their shoulders to the surface and managed to open it only to find snow, rocks, and pine boughs strewn through the cabin. Snow had poured in through the side windows, and the front porch had collapsed forward when the cabin dropped off its foundation.

"Seems we got the edge of the slide. A few feet closer and we'd be in Lake Tahoe," Chase surmised. He moved about the cabin as Tessa emerged. She frantically searched for something, tossing things in the air or digging through snow. Maybe she's in shock, he thought as he tried to stop her. "Tessa. What are you doing? We've got to get out of this place. The roof may cave in any minute."

"No. The Kifaru. I've got to find it."

The roof sagged with a creaking sound. "What am I looking for?"

"A doll. Please. Find the doll."

"You heard the lady. She wants her doll."

"Are you two crazy?" Agent Martin yelled whirling around despite his protest.

"There." Tessa moved toward the kitchen but felt Chase jerk her back. He raced to grab a doll poking out of a pile of snow. He tossed it to her then snatched a backpack someone had brought in earlier off the lopsided table. He pointed to the door to get Tessa moving.

Agent Martin still carried the afghans and lifted a wet down jacket off one of the chairs that had been flipped on its side. They plowed through the front door and climbed over several fallen tree trunks. Chase boosted Tessa up to Martin before attempting to escape himself. Tessa screamed his name as the cabin roof collapsed, throwing what remained of the porch roof at him and burying him under debris.

Martin yanked some two-by-fours off Chase's leg and pulled him out. He helped Chase limp on his gashed leg to the top of the debris pile where they joined Tessa. Agent Martin helped her into her coat, and the three walked across a rocky snowbank leading uphill toward where the road had once been. They managed to ease themselves down to road level but had to maneuver over twisted tree branches cluttering their progress.

Chase heard an engine. "Listen," he said limping up next to Tessa who immediately placed her arm around him on one side. "Snowplow."

In seconds, a large snowplow moved like a determined mammoth, pushing everything in its path to the side. A flashing yellow light swirled on the top of the cab, and a loud honking followed. The snowplow came up within twenty feet of them and opened the door. The driver stepped out on the running board and waved.

"That you, Chase?"

It was the driver who had assisted him out of the ditch. "Sure is. Guess you're going to rescue me one more time." Chase felt Martin wrap a helpful arm around his other side. "By the way, so you guys know...Tessa, you are my wife and very pregnant. I'll explain later."

They didn't ask questions as they stumbled up to the snowplow. Tessa stuffed the doll under her coat to give her a more pregnant appearance. Knowing they weren't going to freeze to death was worth a little more lying. The passenger door swung open, and Martin climbed up then assisted Chase who reached down for Tessa.

"For a momma-to-be, you're pretty gazelle-like." The driver grinned as she positioned herself in Chase's lap then slipped her arm around his neck. "And who are you?" he asked Martin.

"Park ranger. Heard there might be someone back here and came to check."

"Pretty fancy clothes for a park ranger." The driver backed the truck down the rest of the road.

"Yeah. Borrowed some of this guy's after I got caught in the first slide." Martin didn't seem to have any problem spinning a lie. Maybe he would be okay after all.

"Good thing I came along. Got a call from dispatch. Some of your friends said they sent a drone in earlier to find you and noticed a problem. Since I already knew about where you were, I volunteered. They sent the rest of the directions. Said they'd be waiting for you at a closed gas station about five miles from here. I'll swing you by."

"Much appreciated."

"Better get that leg looked at."

"Thanks. I will." Chase tried to be pleasant even though Tessa stared at him inches away from his face. She rubbed the back of his neck then snuggled in as his arm tightened around her. The temptation to kiss her overwhelmed him so much, he caved and pressed his lips against her temple. "We're going home," he whispered.

<p style="text-align:center">~~~</p>

The front door of Tessa's house sounded like a portal to paradise by the time she reached Grass Valley. Sam had relieved Ken Montgomery of the car and headed back to the warehouse in Sacramento where she'd filled her in on the story she'd fabricated. By the time Sam finished, Tessa was too tired to ask many questions and fully expected her husband to retell about the chance meeting with Dr. Samantha Cordova. Having Sam run interference explained why he hadn't tried to call her all day. Maybe.

"Thanks, Sam. I appreciate you coming up here to check on the kids and deal with Robert," Tessa said climbing into her own car. Sam had bought her a change of clothes: jeans and a sweater plus a denim jacket. The snow boots were too big, but fur lined so she didn't care.

Sam only raised her chin in acknowledgment and climbed into the car with Carter, Zoric, and Martin.

Chase lowered his head into her repaired car and eyed her, as if by doing so he might discover some bruise or scrape that would lead to Robert asking too many questions.

"You've got the doll?" he asked in a dry voice.

Tessa focused out the windshield to avoid staring into his face. "Yes. I'll take good care of it." She sighed and faced Chase. "You know, Handsome could have let Reeva kill us and take the diamond. Obviously, he doesn't trust her with the information. He lied to protect us."

"He lied to protect the Kifaru, Tessa. You mean nothing to him. He's using you. If what you told us on the way back is true, then we need to find out who the real owner of the diamond is. For all we know, Handsome plans to take the diamond and promote himself to dictator of Botswana. We need to find the rightful heir to the Kifaru, if there really is one, which I doubt. But Handsome is pretty proficient at spinning a tale to convince people of noble intentions."

He meant her. They all thought she got into trouble because of some do-gooder mentality. She didn't care. Thinking the best about people sure helped her sleep at night.

"Will the Kifaru be safe with me tonight? I can bring it in tomorrow after the kids go to school."

Chase grinned as his eyes slid over her hair and face. "Sure. We have some local cops who owe us a favor who will be watching over you tonight in case someone makes contact. If Handsome shows up, it would be best if the diamond is in your possession. Just don't go anywhere with him."

"I believe him, you know," she said flatly. "Which is exactly what he wants, and I'm good with you believing his crap. You let him keep imagining you with wings and a halo and we'll do the rest."

"You are so condescending," Tessa fumed, frowning up at him.

Chase grinned the way he did when laughter might spill out from deep in his throat. "You do realize because of you, we may be able to stop chaos from engulfing another African country." He reached in and ruffled her hair like she was a rowdy ten-year-old boy. She jerked away from his touch. He laughed.

"So now you don't want me to touch you," he mused. "A few hours ago—"

"You are not to ever mention undressing me," she warned. "The whole story will be misinterpreted. I'll never live it down."

He pounded lightly on the roof of the car with his fist then added a final word. "Just so you know—I can't imagine life without you, either."

The devilish smile made his high cheekbones hard and tight as he shut the door. He walked away, only to join Sam in the back seat of the waiting car.

~~~

"It's about time," Robert called from the family room. "I was getting worried."

Tessa strolled in and dropped her purse on the breakfast bar separating the two rooms. So much for the portal to paradise. "What's in the bag?" he asked, clicking off the television.

She carried the canvas bag Sam had brought with her clothes. The doll was inside. "Oh." She lifted it up in the air then spun away. "There was a little secondhand shop across from the repair shop. Since I had to wait, I thought I'd check it out."

"We need more junk," he quipped. "I'm fine, by the way," he added.

Tessa tucked the bag into a drawer then filled a cup with water and set it in the microwave. "What?"

"I've been sick as a dog all day."

"All day?" she said pushing the start button.

"Well, half the day. Oh. Your drop-dead gorgeous friend came by with donuts for the kids and let me know you weren't coming home."

Tessa took a deep breath. "Sorry about that. She called to say you decided to stay home. Kids asleep?"

"Yes. Went to bed about an hour ago. Where have you been hiding her? Your friend, I mean. She suggested we all get together sometime."

"I bet," Tessa mumbled.

"What?" Tessa hadn't noticed until Robert stood up he had dressed for bed. "Very sweet woman," he continued.

Tessa arched an eyebrow and purred. "Yes. She certainly is. So, you were sick?"
~~~

"Yeah. Your friend makes coffee to perfection. Unfortunately, after the first cup I didn't feel so good."

Tessa removed her cup from the microwave and dunked a tea bag several times. She suspected what had happened, and this time it actually sounded pretty funny to her. "Did the kids meet her?"

"Yeah. Sean Patrick tripped over his tongue when he saw her."

"Are you sure we aren't talking about you?" Tessa tried to sound jealous, although she could care less.

Robert joined her and set her tea on the counter before hugging her. "She can't hold a candle to you."

She smiled and kissed him on the mouth, a little longer than she had intended. "Right answer."

"Ready for bed?" he said stroking her arms.

Tessa needed something. There remained a lot of pent-up emotion or energy stewing inside her. A guilty conscience also needed to be quieted. What better way to do that than to make her husband happy. He was a good man. She didn't deserve him.

"I'll turn out the lights. See you upstairs in a minute."

When the coast was clear, she took the doll and stared at it for the longest time. Then, carefully, she removed the head and shook it. She ran her finger inside.

The Kifaru diamond was gone.

Chapter Twenty- Six

"**G**one?" Chase stood with his legs apart and folded his arms across his chest. He needed to do something to hide his rising irritation. He listened to her explain again she'd last seen the diamond before the first avalanche. "So, while we tried to stay alive, Handsome removed the diamond.

"I'm sick about this," she admitted. "I trusted him." She walked to her office window overlooking the university campus. "I'm sorry. I made so many mistakes. Again."

Chase dropped his arms to his sides. "I think you're underestimating Handsome. Taking the diamond into Africa would tip off the wrong people if caught. He didn't seem to be on friendly terms with Reeva. He only wanted her connections to get out of the country. I can't imagine he'd trust her enough to take the diamond too far."

"So, now what?"

"We wait until we hear from Handsome. He thinks you are going to help him, no matter what. I don't think we've heard the last from him."

Tessa walked out from behind the desk then sat on the edge and braced her hands on the surface. "Somehow, I feel I let him down."

"Dig deeper and see what is going on. Our benefactors for Enigma aren't happy about what is going on over there," Chase ordered.

"And, honestly, why should we care about this, except from a humanitarian point of view, of course?"

"Money laundering isn't good for America, especially when it might involve a ruthless dictator or terrorists. Africa has Al-Shabab, Al-Qaeda, and the one you hear about in the news, Boko Haram. Those guys are a plane ride away, not to mention anyone can slip across our borders if they really want to. We need to make sure these guys aren't funded with US money in any way." He couldn't help remembering how Handsome warned him if Tessa didn't help him, then her family would pay the price. "I suspect he'll reach out to you. But, this time, don't leave me out of the loop, no matter what he says."

Silence rose between them until it became awkward. She eased off the desk then circled back to sit down, wheeling the chair up close. Stacking colored folders then thumbing through some graded papers, she threw herself into the role of disinterested professor until Chase reached over and laid his hand on hers. She jerked her hand back as if bitten by a spider, but Chase left his palm on her stack of papers.

"What?" she snapped. "Is there when I get a lecture on being rogue, stupid, inexperienced, or too trusting?"

He dropped the other hand on the desk and bent farther over the desk so he could be eye level. There was a chance this move may have triggered memories of Afghanistan, but he thought she was working through all those nightmares. Apologizing wasn't going to change the fear following her around like a shadow.

"Why are you so nervous?" he asked. "I don't blame you for any of this. You're an agent, and you're going to find yourself in situations where you have to make decisions. My only problem with what you did was I don't trust Handsome, and I certainly don't trust him with someone as inexperienced and trusting as you. Fortunately, he really did want your help. But what if it was something else?"

Tessa sighed and diverted her eyes. Was she thinking about Afghanistan or the tribesman who kidnapped her and forced her into a relationship she still found difficult to escape mentally? She remained prim and proper around him except for a few instances where he imposed his will on her, like at the cabin.

"About me undressing you." When she narrowed her blue eyes back at him, he rubbed at the familiar pain in his chest.

She followed his movement then frowned. "What about it?" she bristled. "You did what you had to do. I understand. I just don't want to be kidded about it or be reminded of having your almost-completely naked body smashed up against me to save my life."

He straightened then rolled his shoulders. "Guess I better retract the memo to the team that nothing happened." The effort it took to keep a solemn face when horror leaped to her eyes caused him to pivot and head for the door. "I better go take care of it."

The phone rang. She glanced down at the caller ID and frowned. "I need to take this. Heather wasn't feeling well this morning."

Chase grinned and left her. As he shut the door, he touched his earpiece to plug into her office. He stopped in his tracks when he heard Tessa answer the call.

"Handsome. Yes. I'm fine. Where are you?"

~~~

Robert skipped lunch two days in a row, came in early, and stayed late to reclaim time lost the day he stayed home. By the time he drove to Grass Valley well after dark each night and ate some leftovers from the refrigerator, there wasn't much time to catch up with his family. Something seemed to be eating at his wife.

Did she still suspect him of cheating with that South African woman? What about the FBI? Had they contacted her? What a nightmare. Was Reeva actually still alive? The woman in the jewelry shop could have passed for her twin. And why did Agent Martin show up at the same place? Nothing about this made sense. Several times he'd thought someone was following him on his commute home.

"Rough day?" Tessa sat down on the couch and curled her feet beneath her.

Even in sweat pants and a tee shirt, Tessa managed to pull off relaxed elegance. "Yes. I need to catch up is all. You?"

"Met with the kids' school to put the finishing touches on the
~~~

spring festival. Should be a good moneymaker. I invited some people from the university to offer their services." She shrugged and took a sip of her evening cup of decaf tea. "Something different this time."

Robert rubbed his eyes. He didn't care. The FBI had him in the crosshairs of ruin.

"You and I are going to work the cookie booth. I volunteered to make twenty-five dozen chocolate chip cookies. I'm not the only one, of course…"

Robert stopped listening. Cookies? Why did he have to help? He hated this kind of thing. His mind returned to work as he fixed an interested gaze on Tessa's mouth moving while he solved real problems, like billable hours, new clients, making partner, and, of course, what to do with those diamonds he'd paid Reeva for at the hotel. Were they traceable?

"Sam said to tell you hello." Tessa smiled over the rim of her cup.

His attention diverted to his wife. "Oh. Nice. She one of them helping at the festival?" Maybe this school thing wouldn't be a total bust after all.

"Funny. She wanted to know if you'd be helping, too. Guess you guys hit it off. She hasn't committed yet. I doubt it, though. Sam doesn't really do those kinds of events."

"Maybe she could have a booth to sell her book," Robert offered enthusiastically.

"Hmm. Maybe. An economics book seems pretty dry reading for a spring festival. Probably wouldn't sell much, and she'd have to be willing to donate the profits."

Robert could imagine her standing at a booth all dolled up in a sequined dog collar and leather, selling her book. Then he pictured a line of fathers leading out the door and down the block. "Worth a try."

"I'll see what she says. Oh, have you gotten any packages at work in the last day or so?" Tessa set her cup down in a chipped saucer. I had something sent to your office so Heather wouldn't find it. I got her a handmade doll I found on Etsy for her birthday."

Robert rubbed his eyes then squinted, trying to remember. "Maybe. Left it on my desk. Thought it was office supplies I ordered. You know I don't like you sending things to my office,

Tessa." This had an immediate effect on her. She stuck out her bottom lip and diverted her eyes. "Sorry. I didn't mean to sound so snippy. Been a rough week or so at work and, of course, the conference before that."

Tessa picked up her cup again. "You never told me about the conference. Meet anyone interesting, I mean besides that woman who hit on you?"

"Nope. Boring stuff. Boring people."

Tessa's expression sharpened, and he steeled himself for further interrogation, but she uncurled her legs and went to the kitchen to warm her tea in the microwave. Maybe this would be a good time to come clean with the rest of the truth concerning his little conference nightmare.

"Tessa, we need to talk, honey." Robert loosened his tie then ran his hand through his hair and found an escaped gray strand. Maybe he should buy the stuff he saw advertised on television to make men appear younger.

"I'm all ears," she said standing next to him as he pushed himself out of the recliner. "What's up?"

"When I went to San Francisco… Is someone at the door?"

Tessa headed in to the door and peeked out the curtain. He joined her and pulled her back so he could see. His swallow echoed in his ears as he unbolted the door and swung it open.

"Hello, Robert."

"Special Agent Martin. Kind of late, isn't it?"

Tessa extended her hand, and the agent quickly grabbed it. "I'm Tessa. Special Agent? FBI?"

"Yes, ma'am. We don't really go by Special Agent. Can I come in?"

"Do you have some ID?" she quizzed.

"It's all right, Tessa. I know this man." Robert felt like he was about to be marched to the gallows. "Can you make us some coffee, please?"

~~~

While Agent Martin and Robert were chatting, Tessa brewed coffee and opened up her laptop to check the status of the package supposedly on her husband's desk. If she could track it, then so
~~~

could someone else. It wasn't her idea to send it to the office, and she'd told Handsome as much. She carried a small metal tray into the kitchen with a pot of coffee, cups, and a small plate of cookies. The men sat on the edge of their seats, chatting like old friends.

"Thank you so much, Mrs. Scott. I brought someone with me who is waiting out in the car." Agent Martin raised his eyebrows and held her gaze. "I bet he'd like a cup, too."

"Sure," she said eagerly. "Is this a private conversation or can I sit in?"

"Sorry, honey, it has to do with work." Robert's smile created an almost-wax museum image.

"Rats. Sounded juicy. I'll take the coffee out in a disposable cup."

"Thanks." He nodded.

Tessa pulled on a light jacket before she headed out the door with the coffee. When she got to the car, the window on the driver's side was already down. She passed the drink to the driver.

"Chase." She drummed her fingers on the doorframe. "Don't you have a date with one of your brainy bimbos or something?"

"Don't you have something to share with me?" he asked sarcastically.

She pulled a listening device from her jacket pocket. "Here. This is for you. I know you listened to my conversation yesterday with Handsome and then traced the call. Why didn't you confront me? Was it another test of loyalty?"

At his dark, intense stare, she stopped drumming and gripped the door handle. "You really do need a good spanking, you know?" His words didn't hold the usual playful insinuations.

"When you think you can," she said flippantly. "Anyway, we have a problem. There's a package in Robert's office from Handsome. You need to get it because the UPS people have a tracking number attached, and if I can read it, so can hackers." She handed him a keycard. "This will get you inside the building." Next, she pulled out a regular key. "This is to his office. You'll find another doll and the diamond. I'm afraid if we wait until tomorrow, something will happen to it."

"Thanks. I had Vernon take down building security for us. I'm glad you called earlier to let me know what to expect." He returned the keycard. "We already took care of it, Tess."

"Then why are you here?" Tessa observed how he rubbed his chest then reached out the window and grabbed her arm.

"Martin wanted to rattle your hubby a bit. He'll probably spill his guts to you tonight about the entire night's events. Think you can handle it?"

"I handle you all the time. He's no big deal."

This amused him enough to rub his thumb on her arm. "You certainly do, Tessa Scott. One of these days, I'm going to have to put an end to the practice."

"Meaning?" She pried his fingers off her arm.

"Guess we'll find out."

The passenger door opened, and Agent Martin slid in. "Hey, Tess. Recovered yet?"

"Sure. How're the bruises?"

"Gives me a badass look. I'm kind of enjoying the respect."

Her husband came out onto the porch. "I better go. Robert has that deer-in-the-headlights look. Anything I need to know, Agent Martin?"

"He's about to confess to you. Listen for something I missed or he didn't tell me. You already know the whole story so it shouldn't be hard to catch something new."

"See you guys." She patted the door as Chase started the engine and pulled out of the circular drive. Robert waited on the porch for her as she scampered up the steps. "I think the bottom step is loose. Can you check it this weekend?"

He nodded his head in agreement then slipped his arm around her waist. "Let's go to bed. We can talk there."

CHAPTER TWENTY-SEVEN

"**A**frica!" Robert groaned. "Why? Can't the State Department send someone else? Summer is starting. What about all our plans?"

Tessa passed the potato salad to her oldest son so he could have his third helping. "Don't forget to eat some fruit, Sean Patrick." He nodded as he spooned the yellow mix onto his plate next to the second barbeque pork steak. "We've already gone shopping for clothes, supplies, and shoes. Their physical exams were done a month ago, so the boys can play sports in the fall if they choose. Dentist appointments are tomorrow."

"What about you flying with them to your folks to spend three weeks? They can't go alone. You do this every year. Your mom and dad look forward to them coming. I'm sure your folks won't want to fly both ways to make sure the kids don't end up in Upper Sandusky, Ohio."

"I'm taking them with me on a chartered plane. We'll make a short stop in Nashville, and my folks can meet us there. The kids will love it. The State Department is sending the plane for me and a few others tagging along to assist. So, covered." She took another bite of watermelon.

"And what about teacher-parent conferences? I'm not doing it without you. You know I hate those things. They're worthless."

"Conferences are next Monday, and I don't leave until the following Thursday. I've already talked this over with the kids, and with you a month ago. I told you this might happen."

Robert pushed his empty plate away. He rubbed his stomach in satisfaction before leveling a frown in Tessa's direction, not that it mattered. She had come into her own the last couple of years. She no longer bent to his every whim or complaint. Even though he imagined something horrible had gone down in Afghanistan, she appeared to be weathering the secrets, too, in the last couple of months. Part of him didn't want her going to another dangerous place where he might lose her.

"I'm afraid for you, is all. What about disease?"

"Covered. Got shots for yellow fever, typhoid, diphtheria, tetanus, meningitis, and hepatitis B. I begin my malaria meds next week, and I'll take some antibiotics with me." She smiled across the table at him in such a sweet fashion, he wondered if she might be mocking him. A drip of watermelon juice escaped her fork as she pushed another piece into her mouth. "Yum. This is the best melon."

The kids followed her lead and nodded in agreement.

"Okay, but it isn't a safe place. AIDS, Boko Haram, and wild animals."

Tessa reached for another piece of melon and winked at the children. "You're scaring the kids. Stop it. Do you really think I'd go someplace dangerous and jeopardize our happy home?" She followed up by giving the kids some boring statistics about the Okavango Delta in Botswana where she planned to visit then refocused her attention back to Robert. "Besides. Boko Haram isn't in Botswana. I'm not going to have"—she glanced at the boys who argued over the last pork steak— "you know, have contact to be exposed to AIDS." Her smirk caused Robert to feel a little silly. "And the wild animal part is what I'm looking forward to. There are guides if I even get to go on safari. It's not like I'm going to be dropped off in the bush and told to find my way back. Really, Robert, you are such a worry wart."

Robert sighed. "I want you to be safe. Afghanistan—"

"This isn't Afghanistan. That was a fluke."

"You took an unnecessary chance," he reminded her.

"Lesson learned. I wish you'd not bring it up again." She

pushed the remaining food on her plate around like it might be a new kind of hockey game.

"I don't understand why you have to go."

Tessa stood to clear the table and bragged on Heather when she pitched in to help her. The boys continued to eat as Robert joined her at the sink where rinsing had begun.

"I am doing research for World of the Child Foundation. We have finally gotten an invitation from the President of Zimbabwe to offer advice and programs to educate the people against the spread of AIDS and hopefully reach the children before it is too late. Nutrition and women's programs available to them through the UN and American companies will be offered. We'll do the same thing in Namibia and Botswana, where we will stay most of the time. The door to Botswana has been closed for a long time. The president is trying to show his people he cares for them by doing this. The State Department thinks I'm a very nonthreatening spokesperson."

"Sounds like you're spying on them." Robert took the slippery dish she handed him and nearly dropped it as he tried to shove it into an already-crowded dishwasher.

Tessa motioned for the boys to bring their plates to her. "Don't be ridiculous. Do I look like a spy?"

"Yes. A beautiful one." He planted a kiss on her mouth that still tasted like watermelon.

"Ahh. I love you, too," she said, patting his cheek. He understood, although it had been several months, the fact he'd had another woman in his hotel room still grated on her.

"You're going to make us hurl, Mom," Daniel complained.

"I think it's romantic," Heather chirped happily.

Robert tugged on her pigtail. "What do you know about romantic? You're too little for mushy stuff."

Heather put her hands on her hips and pointed to Sean Patrick. "He has a girlfriend and is always trying to get Daniel to find him romantic ideas on the Internet."

"What?" Tessa and Robert said in unison.

Sean Patrick shrugged. "I'm kind of a stud on campus."

Tessa popped him on the leg with the wet dish towel, laughing at his howl. "You're only eleven. I forbid you being a stud until you're twenty-five."

"Too late, Mom." He dashed out of the room with Daniel on his heels. Heather giggled and chased after them.

"They are growing up fast." Tessa closed the dishwasher. "Are we good or not? If you don't want me to go, I'll try and find someone else. I thought the bonus would be great for the kids' college fund." She dropped the number, drawing a whistle from Robert.

"No wonder my taxes are so high."

Tessa wrapped her arms around Robert and pulled him close. He kept trying to make things right with her. "Up to you."

Robert couldn't help keeping an eye on the bottom line of his family's finances, which was why her salary for the trip swayed him. Their savings since Tessa returned to work made it possible for a few extras like college and a new car for him. "Okay. If you're sure it will be safe."

"There will be security the entire time I'm there. I'm sure the State Department will take good care of me."

"As long as you're here for parents' night at the kids' schools. I hate those things."

"Nothing to worry about," she said, running her hand down his backside.

He knew perfectly well she was stroking him to make sure he was on board and wouldn't change his mind.

"All we have to do is get through the school festival and the loose ends will be tied up."

"I love you, Tessa. You're such a doll."

She smiled sweetly. "Hmm. If you only knew."

~~~

Reflecting back, the last few months had kept Robert stealing glances over his shoulder every time he walked to his car or entered his office building. Paranoia consumed him. The FBI continued to watch him. Why after all this time hadn't Reeva's company contacted them about her whereabouts? To investigate might draw attention to himself, so he let it drop.

When Agent Martin arrived at his house back in the winter, he knew he should confess to Tessa about the real reason the man came for a visit. But he didn't. Time slipped away until it sounded
~~~

like a cover-up on his part. The agent wanted to let him know the woman he'd seen in the jewelry store had been located, and she did indeed have a remarkable resemblance to Reeva, but was in fact a sister to the owner, visiting from Florida. One less thing to worry about. At least the agent had checked it out for him. He hadn't expected to be believed. It still bothered him the agent had appeared, but he'd explained he had been following him to make sure no one else might be. The agent wanted him to keep an eye out for any unusual activity in the firm. Robert agreed out of fear more than wanting to help the FBI.

The work stacking up on his desk kept him busy enough to distract him for a chunk of the day. Volunteering with Tessa at the school Explore Our World Festival for several evenings would keep him grounded, since she did most of the planning and would engage the parents. There always seemed to be an abundance of energy in her. Why wasn't she exhausted after work, school, and kids? He tried hard to be supportive, witty, and interested in her latest project to get the community to support her love of books, the arts, and sciences. She'd even secured several people from the university to come and participate.

One was a Dr. Nicholas Zoric, an art professor whose wall-sized paintings had given him fame the last few years. He wondered how she'd convinced the recluse into giving some art lessons to budding painters in Grass Valley as one of the auction items. Even though the man resembled something from a Dracula movie, the children didn't appear to fear him. Robert's own daughter stared at him in wonder.

A Dr. Chase Hunter talked to parents about the importance of reading and literature and even offered to give them tours of the university. He volunteered to start an after-school program for kids who were interested. Carter Johnson teamed up with him, offering ideas for library programs including science and math. As usual, the mothers giggled, smiled, and nodded their support, and pretended to be kept on the edge of their seats.

"I don't think it has anything to do with what they're saying," Tessa commented with a grin. "Those two are quite the lady's men on campus."

"How do you know?" Robert frowned. "And how did you convince them to come here to this community bash?"

Tessa elbowed him good-naturedly. "I'm not without charm, Robert. Or have you forgotten?"

He hadn't forgotten. As a matter of fact, the last year had transformed his wife for some reason. She'd slimmed down, taken on a mysterious air concerning her work, had even spoken to the president a time or two, and once POTUS had called her. Other things remained the same: sleeping in an old tee shirt and socks, drinking too much coffee, clumsy to a fault, and demanding he spend more time with the kids.

The second night of the festival, he'd noticed the astronaut, Carter Johnson, cut her off as she passed him in the hall and smiled wolfishly down at her as he laid a hand on her forearm. She smiled sweetly, as she often did, and pushed his hand away. The gesture appeared to amuse him, as he heard Carter chuckle then whisper in her ear. Tessa didn't like overbearing men, but she did have a groupie mentality when it came to astronauts. Was there something going on between them?

"How well do you know those guys from the university?" Robert noticed several moms had cornered Dr. Hunter and the astronaut.

"We're in the same pod," Tessa said handing some change back to a father and son who'd bought some of her cookies.

He could feel his forehead pinch in confusion as he bagged up two dozen white-chocolate macadamia bars for an elderly couple.

"I mean, everyone at the university is on a committee for one reason or another. My pod is community outreach and marketing. We meet once a week."

"Pod? You mean like killer whales or something? How come you've never mentioned this before?" Robert sat down in a folding chair, bored with being pleasant.

"Killer whales? I never thought of it like that but..." Tessa cocked her head at him. "I haven't mentioned it before because what I really do is illegal and could have the FBI on me in a heartbeat." Her words came out slow and thick like cold molasses. One eyebrow arched like it did when she teased him. The mere mention of the FBI ran a chill up his spine.

"You're very funny. You shouldn't say things like that," he snarled.

Tessa bent down and kissed his cheek then gazed into his eyes.

"What if it's true? I mean, I would want to know if you got into trouble."

Robert wondered if she heard him gulp. "Never going to happen. I'm one of the good guys. Clean as a whistle."

She straightened, cooing, "Hmm. Famous last words."

"You're going to have to stop watching those kinds of television shows. It's not really like you imagine." He felt irritated at her pie-in-the-sky attitude about national security, crime, terrorists, and the law.

Smiling down at him, Tessa put her hands on her hips. "I'm pretty sure it is exactly as I imagine." She waved to the three men from the university as they entered the gym then motioned for them to join her. "I want to introduce you, Robert. These are people I work with. Try to be friendly."

Taking in a big breath, Robert stood and watched them approach. He noticed right away Dr. Hunter took a moment to speak to several mothers with young children and offered his business card. In spite of his worn tweed jacket and black glasses, the women seemed drawn to him; maybe it was the broad shoulders or dark hair and skin. The idea the man might be using a tanning bed to keep that color slipped in and out of his opinion of him. He moved with the confidence of a military man, not a professor who taught literature to a bunch of spoiled college kids.

"Is your friend gay?" Robert said, nodding to Dr. Hunter.

Tessa spewed out her ice tea then had a coughing fit. Next, she started laughing so loud several other vendors stopped and tried to see what was so funny. "Maybe. Could be why he doesn't stay with one love interest very long. I'll have to ask him."

"You wouldn't?" Robert growled as the men stepped up to their booth.

"How's it going?" Tessa choked a little on her laughter, wiping at a tear escaping the corner of her eye. "I hear you've had a lot of interest in your programs." Then she chuckled again.

"What's got you so amused?" the man called Hunter asked as he cut his gaze to Robert.

"Oh, my hubby is so funny. He says the cutest things sometimes." She swallowed hard. "Let me introduce all of you to my better half."

Names were exchanged and handshakes offered. The Dracula

guy didn't speak, but the astronaut jumped in right away, asking if this one or that one was divorced or married. Tessa answered Carter in the flippant tone that drove Robert nuts when she used it on him. Carter only grinned good-naturedly, and Robert wondered again if the man might be trying to make his wife jealous.

The big guy, Chase Hunter, for some reason gave him an uneasy feeling, like maybe they'd met before. His dark eyes haunted him even after he walked away.

"Definitely gay," Robert said under his breath.

"Why would you say such a thing?" Tessa watched the men walk away.

"The other two were glued to everything you said. Must be your blue eyes. But Hunter... He stared at me."

Tessa reached behind him and patted his buttocks. "You are kinda hot, sweetheart."

Robert touched his index finger to his tongue then to his thigh as he let loose a hissing sound to resemble steam. "You remember this hunk of burning love when the astronaut hits on you."

She laughed and squeezed out from behind the table. "I'm going to take a potty break. Too much tea. Can you handle this alone until I get back?"

"Of course. The crowd is thinning. Cookies are almost gone."

As Tessa moved away, Robert's thoughts turned back to his wife who would hobnob with some head of state of a third world country in Africa he'd hardly ever heard of except for a National Geographic documentary on the Okavango Delta. Why would anyone want to go there? Why would the State Department care about reaching out to them? He guessed if President Austin asked him to run errands for his State Department, he'd jump at the chance, too.

The thought of his wife leaving him again to travel in a foreign country where things could go wrong, like Afghanistan, gave him indigestion. She'd assured him Botswana was much safer, and she'd have security with her this time. The excitement in her voice at seeing Africa convinced him to agree to her leaving. Like always, she took care of loose ends with the kids and told him it would be a good time for him to golf and play cards with his buddies.

Tessa hustled to catch up with the three men from the university and felt a twinge of jealousy until a tall lithe beauty stepped in to block his sight of her.

"Hi, Robert. Remember me?"

"Dr. Cordova," he said a little too excitedly. "I mean Sam. Good to see you," he gushed, forgetting exactly what he wanted to ponder concerning his wife.

She handed him a cup of lemonade. "Brought you this." Her mischievous smile made his body feel a little too warm for a stuffy gym. A number of dads nodded at him in approval, as if admiring his good luck.

"You're an angel, Sam. Thanks."

CHAPTER TWENTY-EIGHT

The director of Enigma, Benjamin Clark watched his most successful team file in with their usual banter until they caught sight of him then quieted and took their seats. Things changed several years ago when Tessa Scott stumbled into their lair. War, terrorism, and disrespect of the country forged the people he chose into unemotional machines who carried out their tasks like steel-coated robots with little or no conscience. Sometimes he worried this might not be a good thing.

He still remembered the day Zoric handcuffed Tessa to a desk in an unfinished outer office. Somehow, she escaped, only to be dragged back by Samantha Cordova. Whatever Tessa said to the woman had Captain Hunter laughing for the first time in years. Her influence, although more wacky than logical, brought a belief, perhaps, some good still existed in a world gone mad.

In spite of the team treating her like a good luck charm, Tessa Scott was a menace with a big smile and an uncanny way of manipulating a hardened soldier like Captain Hunter. There were times he wondered how an unassuming soccer mom, who created such chaos, could endear herself to brutal men. The thought occurred to him, the honorable Tessa Scott, had on several occasions circumvented his own no-nonsense demands. Even knowing this, he felt a kind of warm affection for her. This irritated the reasonable side of him.

After everyone arrived and was seated, Tessa rushed in, late as usual. No one asked why. The reasons ranged from traffic on the commute, the kids, the school called, or his favorite, she stopped to get someone at the university a special treat for a birthday or other important occasion. He waited for her to find a seat.

"Good morning all." The director bore his typical no-nonsense tone. "I wanted to let everyone know the arrangements for the Africa trip. The itinerary is in the folder before you." He waited for them to glance through the papers in case there might be questions. "The next item on our list this morning is Robert Scott's law firm." All eyes went to Tessa, who squirmed in her seat.

He watched her swallow, clear her throat then take a sip of water from the glass before her. Vernon activated the screen behind him. "It seems two of the men in the firm were actually involved in the money laundering. After their technical support notified them there had been a breach"—the director glanced at Tessa and raised an eyebrow in hopes of showing his annoyance— "thanks to Daniel Scott, plans were hatched to put the blame on Robert."

Tessa closed her eyes for a few seconds as if she might be trying to compose herself. "I'm really sorry my son got everyone caught up in all this."

"If he hadn't, we'd still be chasing our tail. In spite of the danger it put you and your family in, we managed to cover a lot more ground. The connection to a possible change in Botswana leadership wasn't on our radar so much as corruption among some of the country's powerhouses."

"What about Reeva Kaplan?" Chase's chair squeaked when he rocked back.

"There are still some unanswered questions about her. We know she didn't board the plane with Handsome in Reno the day he left you high and dry. At first, we suspected he'd killed her. Even though there is some indication she took another flight, authorities cannot say for sure she returned to South Africa. With the help of the FBI, we're considering the strong possibility she may have traveled to Australia. They have the largest diamond reserves, estimated at some two hundred ten million carats."

"But no one has spotted her?" Chase reached for his folder and thumbed through it again.

"Australia is a big place with tough characters. Probably has enough friends in the black-market business to keep her safe until the time she needs to finish her real objective. She's on the hook for her role in the murders of those two US Marshals. The Department of Justice wants her head on a platter."

"What will happen to Robert's law firm?" Tessa asked, wide-eyed.

The director nodded to Vernon who switched to a live mode on the screen. "Warrants are being served even as we speak."

Chaos unfolded in the workplace. Office staff, lawyers, and paralegals stood around nervously whispering to each other. Men and women with FBI-marked jackets explored and investigated each area thoroughly.

"What about Robert, Director Clark?" Tessa clenched her fists.

Agent Martin appeared on screen, leading Robert to the side. Both watched silently for the most part. Occasionally, Agent Martin whispered something to Tessa's husband. He would nod, cross his arms in front of his chest then drop them to his side. He appeared uncomfortable and anxious.

Director Clark took a deep breath and addressed her question. "Robert actually helped the FBI in the end. He managed to locate some damning files, which he copied to a flash drive for Agent Martin. It was enough to get a warrant." Computers were being carried out faster than anyone could protest. Several lawyers were marched out in handcuffs as Robert took a step back. "The night he came to your house to make sure Robert was on board with stealing the information was the last step toward bringing this part of the problem to an end."

"He never said a word." She frowned. "Why wasn't I told?" The director understood her frustration.

Chase twisted his lips in a disgruntled expression. "None of us knew. Even the night I took Agent Martin to your house, he never said a word. I agreed to take him so we could hash out some of my distrust of him. I see he only wanted to gain back the confidence I'd lost in him. When he said he wanted to do a little Intimidation 101, I found it amusing enough to tag along."

Tessa leveled a dangerous glare at her boss. The director expected her to be jamming a finger in the man's chest when the meeting ended.

"He has a job to do, too," the director said in the man's defense. "I'm sure we can use his behavior to our advantage another time."

"Is Robert in trouble?" Tessa followed up.

The director shook his head. "No. He might even get a pat on the back from the FBI. However, I'm not sure of his future at his current law firm or if he should even consider staying with them. This is big news in California. Although most news outlets will have dropped the story by tomorrow night, prospective clients won't forget. The publicity may link Robert to criminal activity he had nothing to do with."

"He's talked about opening his own law office in Nevada City for years."

"Might be a good time to consider those options. Get out while he can." The director waved a hand to Vernon who immediately killed the video feed. "Our next plan of action is to proceed to Africa to find Handsome, return the Kifaru to the rightful owner, and make sure Botswana remains a safe and secure country. Our benefactors do not want any more economic instability in that part of the world."

Director Clark dismissed them and wished them safe travels on their Africa trip.

~~~

The team went their separate ways except for Chase and Tessa. They walked side by side to her office and entered.

"Everything okay with you leaving for Africa?" Chase shut the door then rested against it in a nonchalant fashion. "Robert give you any trouble?"

"He's worried something will happen like it did in Afghanistan."

"How much does he know about what happened there?"

"You mean does he know I was kidnapped and married off to one of their tribesman?" Tessa asked sarcastically.

"Not exactly, but yeah." Chase still felt a great deal of guilt not getting to her sooner. He also felt a severe case of jealousy when he realized she may have fallen in love with the guy who saved her from unspeakable abuse. "I'm not letting you out of my sight this
~~~

time, Tessa." He articulated his words in a slow way so she would know she had nothing to fear. "You aren't going to give me trouble over this, are you?"

She grinned mischievously. "What fun would that be?"

"You and I are going to be spending a lot of time together in the coming days. Don't get on my bad side," he warned, opening the door to leave.

"Again. What fun would that be?"

THE END

ABOUT THE AUTHOR

Tierney James decided to become a full-time writer after working in education for over thirty years. Besides serving as a Solar System Ambassador for NASA's Jet Propulsion Lab, and attending Space Camp for Educators, Tierney served as a Geo-teacher for National Geographic. Her love of travel and cultures took her on adventures throughout Africa, Asia and Europe. From the Great Wall of China to floating the Okavango Delta of Botswana, Tierney weaves her unique experiences into the adventures she loves to write. Living on an Indian reservation and in a mining town continues to fuel the characters in the Enigma and Wind Dancer series.

The love of teaching continues in her marketing and writing workshops along with the creation of educational materials and children's books. Try some of her other books to bring a little adventure to your life. http://www.tierneyjames.com